Linda lives in Opelika, Alabama, with her husband and dog, Roscoe. She has one son and two grandchildren. She retired from Bell South/AT&T after 40 years. Linda grew up loving books. She visited the local library every week with her mother, picking out books to take home and read. She usually came out with a selection from the Nancy Drew Mysteries or the Hardy Boys collection. Mysteries were always her first choice. Ironically her first two published books were poetry. This is her first suspense novel but certainly not her last.

In honour of the United States marshals who work to keep our country safe.

Linda Mangram

SCAMMED: The Marshals of Richmond

AUSTIN MACAULEY PUBLISHERS™

LONDON · CAMBRIDGE · NEW YORK · SHARJAH

Austin Macauley is committed to publishing works of quality and integrity. In this spirit, we are proud to offer this book to our readers; however, the story, the experiences, and the words are the author's alone.

A CIP catalogue record for this title is available from the British Library.

ISBN 9781528950411 (Paperback)
ISBN 9781528990059 (ePub e-book)

www.austinmacauley.com

First Published (2020)
Austin Macauley Publishers Ltd
25 Canada Square
Canary Wharf
London
E14 5LQ

Thank you to my husband, Craig, who patiently listened to each chapter as the book unfolded.

Cast of Characters

Nancy Murphy: Sixty-two-year-old retired dispatcher for the local Hadbury police department. She was a straight arrow who always obeyed the law to the letter. Married to Joe for thirty years. Has she stumbled into something that just might get her killed?

Joe Murphy: Nancy's husband and best friend. He retired when Nancy did in order to enjoy these later years with his beloved wife. He had twenty-five years as the head trainer at 'Work for Health' gym. But will his devotion to Nancy be enough to keep her safe?

Jeff Bloom: This bad boy had a rap sheet a mile long. But is he bad enough to hang with the group he has joined up with now? So far, his crimes have not reached the level of murder, but this may be about to change. Will he live long enough to achieve his ultimate goal?

Clint Montgomery: This career criminal was about as bad as it could get. He was hip deep in everything from drugs to smuggling. His criminal empire had grown from coast to coast, and he would not hesitate to kill to keep his illicit empire safe. Are Joe and Nancy now in his crosshairs?

Pete Rollins: Clint Montgomery's first lieutenant. This career criminal had worked his way up in the organisation the easy way. He simply killed anyone in his way. Montgomery had better watch his back. Pete may have higher aspirations than the first lieutenant. Does he have what it takes to cross his crime boss and live to enjoy the rewards?

Deputy United States Marshal Cliff Harrington: Lead investigator for the Murphy case and telephone scams in general around the Richmond area. He may be a little young for this position but well-trained for the job. Is he up for this task or will his inexperience get him killed?

Deputy United States Marshal Bill Everett: This investigator has the most experience in the department. Has he grown tired of working under his current commander?

Deputy United States Marshal Jake Miller: He has his eyes on the top job in the department and not shy about letting his goal be known. But how far is he willing to go to achieve that goal?

Deputy United States Marshal Andrew Long: IT specialist for the Richmond office. His expertise is legendary in the bureau. Andrew's abilities have generated many job offers outside the bureau. Has he been tempted by the lure of more money?

Deputy United States Marshal Hershel Bing: Supervisor for Criminal Investigations in Richmond. This seasoned Marshal has a no-nonsense management style. He is tough as nails but highly respected. Is he tough enough to keep Joe and Nancy safe?

Beth Thomas: Nancy's friend and nurse at Memorial General. She has worked for twenty-eight years and now chooses to work part-time in lieu of retirement. She and Nancy have been friends since school. Has this friendship now put her in danger?

Mary Alice Baker: Nancy's friend and owner of Bullets Firing Range. After years of an abusive marriage, she finally got the nerve to leave and make a life of her own. She learned about firearms in order to keep safe and found she had a real ability with guns. Would she be called on to use this talent in order to keep her and Nancy alive?

Albert Smith: Joe's friend and owner of 'Work for Health' gym. Joe had worked for Albert as head trainer for twenty-five years. After Joe retired, he and Albert remained close friends. How far was he willing to go for his friend?

Chapter 1

As was her habit, Nancy trotted back to the bedroom with her first cup of coffee.

After retiring last year, this little ritual still seemed like a dream. Working as a dispatcher for thirty years had precluded this little pleasure. Her husband Joe, not one for coffee or staying in bed past dawn, had been outside doing yard work for the past hour. They had both retired last year and had fallen into a comfortable routine. Maybe to a boring routine, but it suited them just fine. Joe and Nancy had a large circle of friends, most of which dated back to high school. As in most small towns, a lot of people got local jobs after graduation and tended to stay close to the familiar.

Just as Nancy raised her cup for the second sip, the house phone rang.

"Dang! Why can't people use my cell this early in the morning?" she grumbled as she climbed out of bed.

The temptation to let it ring was strong, but who knows it might be important this time. Joe and Nancy had discussed many times having the house phone disconnected. They both had cells, and it seemed lately when the house phone rang, it was either a robocall or someone soliciting money for what they claimed a really very worthy cause. For whatever reason, the blasted thing was interrupting a perfectly good cup of coffee.

"Hello," she said, trying to keep the impatience out of her voice.

"Hello, this is Deputy United States Marshal Jeff Bloom. Is this Mrs Nancy Murphy?"

"Yes, this is," Nancy said, wondering what in the world a United States marshal could be calling her for. *I guess he is raising money for the widows of marshals killed in the line of duty*, she thought. Surely, a worthy cause, but retirement money just stretched so far.

"Mrs Murphy, I have a bench warrant for your arrest for failure to appear."

"Hey, hold on. Who are you calling again?" Nancy asked, wishing she had brought her coffee with her. This was obviously a wrong number or a very bad joke. The only dealings she had with the law was twenty years back for going a little too fast on her way to the local mall. She had paid for her ticket and dutifully listened to Joe's lecture.

"Mrs Murphy, do you reside at 4210 Pine Haven Circle?"

"Yes, I do, but you must have me mixed up with someone else."

"No, ma'am, you were issued a summons to appear for jury duty two weeks ago at the federal courthouse in Richmond. When you failed to appear, Judge Thomas issued a bench warrant for your arrest. I'm giving you the opportunity to come in, or I'll be forced to serve you at your home and take you into custody."

"Wait. I haven't received a summons to appear for jury duty or anything else. There's no way I would just ignore something like that. I think this must be a mix up of some kind."

"Mrs Murphy, if you have an email address, I'll send you a copy of the warrant and call you back after you've had a chance to look at it. This being Friday, we need to clear this up today. We are not in the office on the weekend and you run the chance of being picked up by the local authorities before Monday."

Nancy gave the deputy her email address and said she would wait for it to come through and for his return call. As soon as she hung up the receiver, she raced to the closet and grabbed the first thing she could reach. She struggled to get dressed and get to the back door and call Joe in from the backyard. To someone else, this might not have been such a big deal, but with Nancy's obsession to cross all the T's and dot all the I's, it was huge. She was a stickler for details. She always filed their taxes on time and documented each and every deduction in detail. She saved all her receipts and checked them against her credit card statements and bank statements. She would never ignore a summons for jury duty. And yet she had just hung up the phone with a United States deputy marshal who said she had done just that.

"Whoa, Nancy, where's the fire? Slow down, take a breath, and tell me what's wrong." Joe had seen Nancy in good moods, bad moods, happy, sad, and all in between. However, he had never seen her so upset; she put her blouse on the wrong side out. This had to be something really bad, or else his beloved had gone off the deep end. He hoped this was not the case, or he would have to dive in after her. No way was he going to spend his retirement years without her.

"Joe, I think I'm in trouble. I think I'm going to be arrested." Nancy started to relate her phone conversation to Joe, but by this time, she had worked herself up into a panic. No one in her family had ever been to jail, and she did not want to be the first. Of course, there was Uncle James, but no one in the family talked about him, so he didn't count.

"What did you do? Write a check at the grocery store and forget to log it in the bank book? I don't think that would be the end of the world. I think our balance would withstand a little hit like that." Joe had been the head trainer at 'Work for Health' gym for twenty-five years. His pension along with Nancy's had insured them of a secure retirement. He still worked out at the gym and looked far younger than his sixty-three years. Although Nancy's senior by a whole year, she liked to tell people she had married a younger man.

"No, this is serious. I have a warrant out for my arrest." As she hurriedly fixed her blouse, she related her conversation with Deputy Marshal Jeff Bloom. Although she had worked as a dispatcher for the Hadbury Police Department, her duties hadn't included issuing warrants. In fact, she had never even seen one or had any dealings with the judges. She mainly handled calls between the station and the officers in the field.

At this bit of news, Joe sobered somewhat. "Nancy, hold on. Nobody is going to arrest you. Let's call the station and get this straightened out. I'm sure this is a mistake or some of your buddies at the police station are playing a joke on you."

"Joe! You're not listening; this is federal. The call did not come from our local police station. It came from the federal courthouse in Richmond." A little calmer now, Nancy related the entire conversation with Deputy Marshal Bloom.

"All right, let's go see if the email has come through and wait for this Bloom guy to call back. When he does, put him on speakerphone so I can listen. If a summons for jury duty was sent, it didn't reach our mailbox, and this should be easy to clear up."

Joe and Nancy went to what they referred to as their computer room. Originally, a small bedroom; they had converted it into a place for their computer, printer and a variety of filing cabinets. These holding all the records, Nancy insisted they would one day need. Nancy sat at the computer to pull up her email, and Joe had a seat in an old blue rocking chair that had belonged to Nancy's grandmother.

Nancy located the email and printed it out.

"Joe, I have never seen a warrant, but this certainly looks authentic to me," she said as she handed the print out to Joe.

"I've seen one or two, and this one seems to have all the correct information on it. It has a case number, the name of the judge, your correct information, and I know this is the correct address for the federal courthouse in Richmond. I had a guy that worked there in one of my training classes."

As if on cue, the phone rang, and the number the marshal had called from before displayed on the caller ID.

Nancy answered the phone and hit speaker.

"Hello," Nancy said, her voice coming out much more confident than she actually felt.

"This is Deputy Marshal Bloom. Is this Mrs Murphy?"

"Yes, yes, it is, and I have my husband Joe here as well. I put you on speakerphone so he could hear as well."

"That's fine. Did you get my email containing the arrest warrant?"

"I did, and it looks official. What do I need to do to get this taken care of?" Nancy asked as she and Joe looked at each other.

At this point, Joe was frowning. Nancy was the love of his life, and he didn't like seeing the frightened look on her face. Whatever it took, he decided that they would take care of it today and put it behind them. Although knowing Nancy; she would tell all her friends and they would never let her live it down. Nancy had been friends with Beth, Bobbie and Tina since grammar school. In high school, they belonged to the same clubs and as adults the same organizations. Sometimes, Joe suspected they were a secret society all on their own.

"Well, Mrs Murphy, as with any warrant, you will have to post a bond until you can go before the judge and get this taken care of. Judge Thomas's docket is full for today. If we can get this bond taken care of, I may be able to get you on the schedule for Monday. You will have to go and purchase a Green Dot Card and keep me on the line with you in case you get stopped so I can explain to the local office that we are taking care of this. We don't want you to spend the weekend in jail, and this could happen if you get picked up."

"Deputy Bloom, I know all of the local officers, and I doubt any of them would take me to jail."

"They would have no choice. They would otherwise be derelict in their duties. If you have an outstanding warrant and they don't take you in, they would be severely reprimanded."

Nancy could not imagine any of those wonderful officers taking her to jail. She knew all of them from her job as a dispatcher. She even knew some of their families. But she also knew how dedicated they were to do their duty. She didn't want to put them in the position of having to choose duty over friendship.

"All right, Deputy Bloom, tell me what you want me to do."

As Nancy listened to the instructions, Joe went to change out of his work clothes. He wasn't sure about all of this but couldn't put his finger on exactly what was bothering him. The warrant looked legal enough, and what the deputy said about the bond and the court appearance sounded right. So why did this feel all wrong? Since he couldn't figure out why he was uncomfortable, he would do whatever was necessary to get this taken care of. When he was ready to go, he went to find Nancy. "So, what's the plan?"

Nancy looked up, her purse in one hand and the phone in the other. We are going to the Community Now Pharmacy and get one of those Green Dot cards and get this taken care of. Deputy Bloom has assured me I can see the judge Monday, and this will take care of it till then.

"The Community Now Pharmacy? Why would we go there instead of the bank or post office and get a money order?" The alarm bells just got a little louder in Joe's head.

"Deputy Bloom said the marshal's office will only accept Green Dot cards because other forms of payment have proven to be so susceptible to fraud. Although other places have them, he has done the research and found that this is the closest place for us to go. He's trying to make this as simple as possible for us. Are you ready?"

Joe went to get the car out of the garage while Nancy continued to talk to the deputy. As they made the five-mile trip to the pharmacy, Joe continued to go over all these details, trying to figure out what was bothering him. He looked over at Nancy and saw the worried look on her face and knew he would do whatever it took to straighten this out. Besides, he had yard work he needed to get back to, and it looked as if Monday would be taken up sitting in court.

Joe pulled into the parking lot of the pharmacy and cut off the car. "I'll wait here unless you need me to come inside with you."

"No, you stay here. I have Deputy Bloom on the phone with me if I need any help finding the right card," Nancy said as she got out of the car and made her way to the door.

Nancy was gone about fifteen minutes when she returned with what looked like an ordinary credit card.

"Okay, Deputy Bloom, I have the card although I wasn't expecting it to be so much. It's a good thing Joe insists I always carry what he calls mad money or I wouldn't have had enough. We would have had to make a trip to the bank."

At this, the bells in Joe's head were making quite a racket. "Just how much is this bond?" Joe asked a little sharper than he intended.

Nancy hesitated. Joe had been nothing but helpful through all of this, but she knew how carefully he handled their finances. They had a comfortable life, and she never thought too much about how much she spent shopping with her friends.

"It's a $1500 card, but the deputy said it would be returned after the hearing as long as we show up on time."

Joe didn't speak. He wouldn't have been able to hear himself anyway over the clanging of the bells.

"What now, Deputy Bloom?" Nancy asked again as she looked doubtfully at her husband.

"Look on the back of the card and you'll see a place that can be scratched off. Take a coin and scratch until you see a line of numbers and just call them off. Then stay on the line so I can verify with our clerk that they came through with no trouble."

Nancy did as the deputy requested and waited for his confirmation from the clerk that they had been received and recorded. This would finally be over and they could get back to their day. She would worry about Monday and go to court later.

After waiting for about three minutes, Nancy looked at Joe and said, "I think we got cut off. I'll call him back. I want to make sure I'm all in the clear."

As Nancy placed the call, Joe watched her face. When she hung up without saying a word, he knew the worse had happened.

"Nancy, what's wrong?"

"The recording said the number has been disconnected. I've been scammed!"

Chapter 2

Clint stood on a cliff high above the small alcove. He watched the waves hit the shore and thought how lucky he was to have found this place. Lucky for him but not for the former owner. Being one of the most wanted men in the country had its advantages at times. Someone a little lower on the food chain was always trying to curry favour. As was the case when one of his associates ended up in jail while trying to rob a convenience store. How stupid and for what, a couple of hundred dollars and a half dozen packs of cigarettes? But lucky for Clint that he landed in a cell with the old geezer that owned this little piece of real estate. Also lucky for Clint that his associate owed him big time for pulling his butt out of a precarious situation several years back. Pity, neither one of the jailbirds lived long enough to enjoy their freedom. Clint's number one rule: leave no witnesses. His number two rule: leave no bodies or other evidence. Another good thing about this place: no bodies would ever be found here. This was not a place that could just be stumbled upon. The thick tree cover made it impossible to see beyond their tops from the air. The alcove was set back from the water in such a way that passing boats would never know it was there. That alcove was also the only access to this island. For all appearances, this was a deserted island with no access from the sea or air. Perfect for his operation.

Clint watched as his men unloaded the last of the smuggled drugs from the small rowboat. It didn't take a large boat to transfer their shipment of drugs from the deeper water vessels that delivered them to this secluded hideaway. Anything larger than a rowboat wouldn't have been able to navigate the small, winding channel. Just another reason this was the perfect spot for his operation. The larger coastguard vessels would be unable to enter the channel, must less reach his hideout.

Clint turned in time to see Pete, his first lieutenant, making his way down the steep path in his direction. "Any problems with this load?"

"All the packages are tested and accounted for. The payment was made and all our men are back safe. Only one small detail that made me kind of uneasy."

"And that was?"

"You know that new guy you hired about six months ago?"

Clint knew exactly who Pete was talking about. Jeff had been highly recommended by another drug lord. He had run afoul of the law when that operation had been busted and everyone had to go underground. Jeff could be a loose cannon and Clint had Pete keeping an eye on him. Jeff was almost as ruthless as Clint himself. But, unlike Clint, Jeff liked to take shortcuts. His negotiation skills were a little rough, and usually, a well-placed bullet in the back worked just fine. Clint found this trait to be an asset instead of a liability. It fit with his number one rule about witnesses.

"What about him? He hasn't gone rogue, has he?" Clint asked as his attention was drawn back to the unloading process down below.

"He was up to something. He was on his cell the entire time we were waiting for the shipment to arrive. When I asked him who he was on the line with for so long, he told me to mind my own damn business. When he finally hung up, he was bragging about not having lost his touch."

Being second in command, this was hard for Pete to swallow. If Jeff hadn't come so highly recommended, he would have handled the situation then and there. His fear of his boss was all that stopped him. That and the fact he was afraid Jeff wouldn't be that easy to handle. He had witnessed first-hand what could happen when someone tried to take him down. So far, no one had succeeded and no one had lived to complain.

"Tell him to meet me back at my cabin when the unloading is complete. Maybe it's time to have a little chat with our new friend. No matter how he came to us, he needs to understand he is not expendable. We have a chain of command, and if he can't follow it—well, let's just say that can be handled as well." Jeff turned and strode back up the hill to their camp.

Pete walked away with a grin. He hadn't liked Jeff from the start and had just been waiting for him to mess up. He saw him coming up from the shore and intercepted him before he could enter the barracks where all the men except for Clint and Pete stayed.

"Boss wants to see you in his cabin. Now we'll see if your damn business is so important." Pete smirked.

Jeff reversed his direction and headed to see the boss. He wasn't scared of Clint, but he respected his authority. Besides, he knew the type of man he was dealing with. One just like himself; and that could be dangerous. If it came to a confrontation, it wouldn't just be Clint he would have to face but Pete as well. However, he also knew the kind of man Pete was and that he had plans to take over the operation at the first opportunity. Jeff figured he would just wait for that to happen, and then he would only have one to deal with. He intended to run this show very soon. Taking orders wasn't in his future plans, and this was the smoothest operation he had run across. He definitely planned to take it over.

Jeff tapped on the door and, not waiting for a reply, entered. He never saw it coming. Clint's fist smashed into the side of his head and sent Jeff skidding across the room.

Jeff tried to pick himself up just to be met with a hard boot to the side. *This was not going as he had planned,* he thought. He had been trying to win favour with his boss until the time was right for a takeover.

"What the hell was that for?" He ground out from between gritted teeth. He was trying not to show how bad those two blows had affected him. Weakness was not what he wanted Clint to see. He wasn't ready, however, to show him the extent

21

he could go to in order to protect himself or bring the other man down. The time would come, but it wasn't now.

Clint reached down a hand and helped Jeff to his feet. "Just thought you might need a little reminder of your position in this organization. When my first lieutenant asks you a question, you give him an answer. Now how about giving me that answer? Why were you spending so much time on the phone in the middle of an operation?"

Jeff made a mental note to be more watchful around Pete. At least until the time came to deal with him permanently.

"I have this little scam I run on the side. It doesn't take much time and it brings in a little extra dough. You see, I set up this account in a fake name and call and tell people I'm a United States marshal and I have a warrant for their arrest for failure to appear in court. Then I get them to send me money for a bond to keep them out of jail until they can see the judge and straighten it all out. You'd be surprised how many people are dumb enough to fall for that. Most people are easy pickings when it comes to the law. It never hurts to bring in a little extra money."

"What hurts is that you are compromising this operation for your own gain. Use your stupid brain. What if one of those schmucks is not as dumb as you think and gets the right authorities involved and they trace your little scam back to you, and as a result of your stupidity back to me? Do you have any idea what the U.S. marshals could do to us? They have resources and manpower and unlike these local idiots could cause us some grief. If that happens, it's coming back to you and I'll make sure you're the one that takes the fall."

Jeff's desire to end this confrontation right here and right now was almost more than he could resist. Instead, he just sneered, "I'm not that stupid. I use a burner phone and an offshore account. The cards they put the money on has a number that's scratched off to give me access to the cash. When it goes in my account, which takes about two minutes, I disconnect the number and throw the phone away."

"And you don't think with today's technology that some of that could be traced back to you? Get out of here and you'd better hope this little stunt doesn't bring the authorities to our door. One more stunt like this, and the marshals will be the least of your worries."

Pete watched as Jeff left the boss' cabin. He made his way to the door and knocked before sticking his head in.

"Everything all right, boss?"

"Yeah, come on in; I have a job for you. I want you to keep an eye on our friend Jeff. I have a bad feeling he may be up to something. I don't trust him. Let me know if he makes any more calls or does anything else that doesn't look right. He has some connections I wouldn't want to cross, but I'm not going to let him mess up what we have going here. If we have to take him out, we can do it so no one finds out. He will just cease to exist. Except to the little fishes in the bay."

"Why don't you let me take care of him right now? Why wait until he brings trouble to our door. I can do it, so none of his so-called connections will ever know?"

"No. Just watch him. Most of his connections aren't in any position to cause us trouble at this time, and I'm not afraid of the authorities. I have a few connections in that area of my own. However, there may be a few of his old friends still out there we may not know about. They could have eyes and ears planted anywhere. You've heard the saying 'no honour among thieves'. That's true, but a certain amount of loyalty can be bought depending on how high up you are on the food chain. Just watch him for now."

Jeff watched as Pete slipped into Clint's cabin. He could just imagine the conversation inside. He was going to have to give some serious consideration to moving his plan along a little faster than he had planned. He knew at some point he would have to take Pete out of the equation, but rushing that could cause some backlash he wasn't ready to deal with. His associates didn't seem to be in a position to help him out if needed. He still couldn't believe they had let themselves get caught. They knew how this game was played. Either there was a rat in with the rats, or his friends had become careless. Whichever, it had been days since he had contact with them.

Chapter 3

Nancy and Joe sat in the parking lot outside the federal building in Richmond. After realizing she had been scammed, Nancy just wanted to go home and lock herself in their bedroom. She felt like such a fool. How could she have fallen for a scam like that? Was she really that gullible? Yes, she felt she must be. Joe was furious but not at her. He didn't blame her for what had happened. The guy had been good. He admitted he had fallen for it himself. Although a few warning bells had gone off, they hadn't got his attention soon enough.

But Nancy being Nancy, she didn't stay down for long. When she remembered she had added a recording device on her phone as a backup for her bad memory, she knew what she had to do.

"Are you ready to go in, honey? I'm sure the marshals will appreciate you coming forward with the recordings you have."

"I'm ready. If I can help catch this guy so he can't do this to someone else, it'll make me feel a little better. It won't get the money back, but I won't feel as much like a victim. And I do not like feeling like a victim."

Joe and Nancy crossed the busy street to the front of the federal building. It took up almost the entire block and was three stories tall. As they entered the massive front doors, a tall guy in the uniform of a U.S. marshal directed them to empty their pockets on the conveyer belt. Nancy waited as Joe complied, thinking she never knew all the stuff her husband carried around in his pockets.

"Ma'am, that includes your purse too." The marshal couldn't quite hide his smile. The lady was, evidently, so fascinated at all the stuff that came out of her husband's pockets, she forgot to comply.

"Oh, I'm sorry." Nancy turned a bright pink when she realized she had just been standing there. She opened her purse and started to upend the contents onto the conveyor belt.

"Ma'am, you don't have to do that." Just set your purse on the belt and you and your husband step through this gate and wait on the other side.

As Joe and Nancy complied with yet another order, Nancy began to wonder if this had been such a good idea. She wondered if a strip search was next on the agenda. She looked up at Joe and saw he seemed to be unfazed at these unexpected proceedings. Okay, so maybe men didn't take a strip search as serious as she did, but she knew where she was going to draw the line.

"If you both will put these visitor passes on and collect your belonging, I'll show you to the United States Marshals' Investigation Division." The marshal turned and walked away confident they would follow him. It was obvious this was the first time this couple had been through this process. Especially, the lady with the rebellious look starting to bloom on her face.

Nancy picked up her purse and watched as Joe returned everything to his pockets. Later, she thought she would ask him why he carried a pair of needle nose plyers and a ball of twine in his pocket. The knife she understood. Most men carried a pocket knife. The fact that Joe carried two was a little puzzling.

As Joe and Nancy followed the marshal, Nancy couldn't help but admire the beautiful building they were in. In one corner stood the American Flag and in another the State flag. In between were pictures of the president, vice president, attorney general and the governor. The ceilings were high and in one place she could see all the way to the second floor. The marble floors were so clean they gleamed and reflected the light from the large chandelier in the high ceiling. It gave Nancy a sense of pride that this beautiful building represented her government.

The marshal led them through a set of large glass double doors into a waiting area the size of her living room.

"If you'll have a seat, I'll let Marshal Harrington know you're here."

Joe and Nancy took a seat and waited for what would come next. Nancy turned and looked at Joe. "Do you really think the print out of the warrant and the recordings I've brought will help catch this guy? I don't want to reveal how gullible I was unless it will really help. I'm a little embarrassed."

Before Joe could come up with a reply that would reassure his wife, the door on the opposite side of the room opened.

"I'm Deputy United States Marshal Cliff Harrington; you must be Joe and Nancy Murphy. If you'll follow me, we have a room reserved where we can talk. I appreciate y'all making the trip up here. I know this must be a hard thing for you to deal with. Unfortunately, this happens on a fairly regular basis. The fact that you brought us something to help us with this investigation is great. Most people that come in to file a complaint can give us very little to go on."

Marshal Harrington led them into a room dominated by a long table flanked by twelve chairs. Two other marshals already occupied two of them. They both stood when Marshal Harrington, Joe and Nancy entered the room. As nervous as Nancy was, she couldn't help but think that these young men had mothers that had raised them well. They looked too young for this type of job, but their manners were impeccable.

"Joe, Nancy, this is Marshal Bill Everett and Marshal Jake Miller. They will be assisting in this investigation. Guys, this is Joe and Nancy Murphy. As we were discussing before they arrived, they have been caught up in a telephone scam where a guy is claiming to be a United States marshal. Let's all sit down and go over what they have to tell us. I believe they have also brought us some evidence that I think we will find very helpful."

Marshal Harrington took a seat at the end of the table. The other two marshals sat back down in their original seats to his right. Joe and Nancy rounded the table and took the two seats opposite them.

Marshal Harrington waited for everyone to be seated. "First, I would like to tell you, folks, that you're not the only ones to get caught up in this scam. We have had four other people this week to come in and file complaints and more in the previous two weeks. We think this is the same guy in every case."

At this, Nancy relaxed a little. They weren't going to judge her, and she wasn't the only one to fall for this guy's lies.

At the pause, Marshal Everett spoke up. "Mrs Murphy, can you tell us what this guy sounded like? Was he young, old? Did he have any particular accent? Was he black, white, Hispanic?"

Nancy thought for a minute. "Well, he was definitely young and sounded like he came from this part of the country; no accent I picked up on. I'm not sure about black or white. He sounded well-educated. In fact, he sounded just like all of you."

The three marshals around the table looked at each other and grinned. Two of them were black, one was white; all were from the southeast United States and all were well-educated.

Marshal Jake Miller cleared his throat. "Mrs Murphy, that is the same description all the other complainants have given us. This is definitely the same guy. I understand you printed out a copy of the warrant he emailed you. Could you let us take a look at it now?"

Nancy reached in her purse and pulled out the email and handed it over. "I've never seen a warrant, but this one looked real, and it had all the information I would expect to be on one. Joe said it looked real to him too."

At this, Joe squirmed a little in his chair. It was all right for his wife to admit to these marshals that she had been fooled, but he was a guy. He felt he should have been able to see through this crook and protect Nancy. His lovely wife would have said it was just the old macho crap coming out.

Whatever, he was uneasy with the marshals thinking he hadn't been able to protect his wife.

Marshal Miller reached across the table and took the paper from Nancy. All three of the marshals looked at it. Cliff said, "Bill, go get that other one you have in your office. I want to show the Murphys something."

Bill got up and left the office. In two minutes, he was back and handed Cliff a piece of paper. Cliff handed the paper to Joe and Nancy along with the one Nancy had given to them. "What do you see?"

Nancy took the two pages, and she and Joe studied them together. They looked at each other and then back at the three marshals.

"Except for my name, this other one is identical. It even has the same case number and judge on it. Are all the others like this?"

"Yes, ma'am. All the ones that have been brought to us are the same. That just reinforces our belief that every scam has been perpetrated by the same individual. He's good. Don't feel bad for falling for it. You aren't the first, and unless we get this guy soon, you won't be the last."

Cliff took the papers back from Nancy. "You said on the phone you have some of the conversations recorded. Can we listen to them now?"

"I have them recorded on my phone." Nancy fumbled in her purse and came up with the phone and found the recordings and pressed the play button.

All three marshals leaned forward in order to hear better. After about ten minutes, Cliff said, "You have more than one call on here. Are all of these from this guy."

"Yes," Nancy said. "He called the first time, then again after he emailed me the warrant. We got cut off once and I hit redial to get him back on the line. At that point, I thought he was all that was standing between me and jail. I didn't want to lose him. While we were going to get the money cards, we got cut off again and he called me back. That's a total of four calls."

"Bill, would you get Andrew in here?"

"Mrs Murphy, Andrew Long is our IT specialist. Do you mind if he transfers these calls onto his phone? If any information can be gleaned from them, he's the guy that can do it. Andrew is the best, and you might be surprised at what he can pull off these four calls. It's not just what he says, it's the background noises that might give us some clues as to who he is and where he is."

They all sat back and waited for this additional marshal. Nancy was impressed and relieved. She had been afraid they would just dismiss what she had to say. She felt they must have a more urgent business than listening to an old lady who was dumb enough to lose her money to a scam artist.

Nancy looked up when the door opened, and a guy who looked to be a little older than the others entered the room.

"Mr and Mrs Murphy, this is Deputy Marshal Andrew Long. Andrew, this is Joe and Nancy Murphy. Mrs Murphy has brought us some recordings we would like you to transfer from her phone. We need your expertise. We're hoping what this guy says, and any background noises you can pick through might help us catch this guy before he does any more damage."

Deputy Long nodded to Nancy and reached across the table to shake hands with Joe. In his deep voice, he expressed his regret at what they were going through.

"Mrs Murphy, if you'll let me have your phone, I'll see about transferring the calls to mine and take them back to my lab and see what I can learn from them."

Nancy handed over her phone and watched as the calls were transferred.

"Do you think they'll help, Deputy Long?" Nancy asked this new marshal.

"Well, ma'am, you never know. These guys think they are so smart. They forget what can be done with today's technology. Especially, with the training, the bureau puts us through." He looked up at the other marshals, and they all exchanged a smile.

Nancy thought these guys must work well together, and for the first time, she was totally at peace with her decision to come here.

Deputy Long finished and handed Nancy her phone back. "I certainly hope we can catch this guy. We'll do our best."

As he stood to leave, the conference room door opened and one of the largest men Nancy had ever seen came into the room. As if on cue, all the other marshals stood. It was obvious this was the man in charge.

"Folks, I wanted to come in and introduce myself. I am United States Marshal Hershel Bing." He shook hands with both Joe and Nancy.

"I want to assure you these men will do all they can to catch this guy, and I will be here in my office if you need to talk directly to me." He handed Nancy a card with his contact information and looked at each of his marshals in turn and then walked out. You could almost hear the silent sigh from each marshal as he left.

"I take it he's the boss," Nancy said as she studied the other men at the table.

"Yes, he's the boss. He's tough and no-nonsense and about the best we've ever worked under. If he's getting personally involved in this case, this criminal needs to be very nervous. Hershel doesn't usually get involved. He leaves the investigations to us and just keeps up with our reports. If he thinks we need it, he'll offer some suggestions. There must be more to this than we've been told."

As this seemed to announce the end of the meeting, everyone at the table stood up. Marshal Harrington shook hands with both Joe and Nancy and thanked them both for coming in. As they passed through the door, he handed Nancy his card and told her he would be in touch.

Nancy and Joe were silent as they made their way out of the building and back to the car.

"Well, Joe, what do you think? How did it go? Do you think we helped with the information we gave them?"

Joe looked fondly at his wife. She had a habit of asking questions in bunches. "I think the answer to all of that is, it went well. Whether they catch him or not is something we'll just have to wait and see. Now I suggest we put this behind us and let these men do their job. Besides, I'm starving. Let's find somewhere to eat."

Nancy was fine with that. She was tired of worrying about this. It had taken up enough of their lives.

She looked up at her husband and said, "Yes, dear."

Chapter 4

Clint sat in his cabin looking at the log of his latest haul. He had stood on the cliff and watched it being unloaded. While he hadn't counted the bags as they came out of the boat, he had counted and logged them after they made their way up the cliff to the compound. It had looked like more from a distance. While he wouldn't put it past any of his men to steal from him if they thought they could get away with it, he couldn't believe any had the guts to do it right under his nose. He considered setting a trap on the next run. No one in his gang was indispensable.

He stood and walked to the window and looked out just as his phone rang. Fishing it out of his shirt pocket, he looked at the screen to see who was calling. Only a very few people had this number. This one was for business only and never left his possession.

Recognising the number, he thumbed the answer button. "This had better be important." He recognised the number and the voice on the other end.

"Clint, it's me."

"I know who it is, you idiot. No names. Where are you calling from?"

"The Marshal's office. There's something you need to know."

"You're taking a big chance calling from there. How do you know this call isn't being recorded or traced?"

"It's my cell, you remember, the one you gave me for emergencies. I think you'll agree this qualifies."

While having an informant inside the United States Marshal's Office had its advantages, it also had its pitfalls.

"Make it quick."

"An older couple came in to talk to one of the agents this morning. They wanted to report a telephone scam. They had a print out of a warrant that was, of course, false. It had been emailed to them. I don't know how they were lucky enough to get the call on tape, but it was all recorded, and they're willing to testify. The kicker is, in the middle of the discussion, Marshal Bing came into the room and introduced himself to the couple and gave them his contact card. He just doesn't do that. Something's wrong with this whole picture."

Clint was silent for a moment. "What day and time did the couple get the call?"

Clint listened to the rest of the information and disconnected. The timing was the same as his last haul of drugs.

He cursed under his breath. That damn fool Bloom was going to lead trouble directly to his doorstep. He had warned the man. Now it was his mess to clean up. After that, Clint intended to do a little house cleaning of his own. He paced to the door and nabbed the closest man. "Get Bloom in here now!"

Jeff was in the barracks standing at the counter pouring a cup of coffee. Another drug shipment was due tonight, and he had to be on hand. He usually helped unload and haul the drugs up to the compound. Where they went from there was a heavily-guarded secret. He knew Clint kept them locked in a storage facility. He needed to know who was on the receiving end when they left the compound. He had to understand the whole process if he was going to take it over.

Calvin stuck his head in the door. "Clint wants you up at his cabin, and he doesn't sound happy. I wouldn't waste time getting there."

Jeff watched Calvin slam back out the door. He had noticed Calvin unloading the last couple of runs. It looked to him as if he was pilfering a little for his own use. He'd better watch out. Clint wouldn't tolerate any of his men stealing from him. He had seen what could happen when someone tried to double-cross him.

Jeff put his cup on the counter. He wondered what had put Clint in such a foul mood. He had been careful since their last run-in not to bring any more negative attention to himself. Well, only one way to find out.

"You wanted to see me, boss?" Jeff gave a light tap on the door and went on in. He could tell from the look on Clint's face this wasn't going to go well.

Clint sat behind his desk shuffling a stack of papers. "We have a problem. Or I should say you have a problem."

Jeff tried not to look worried but he'd never seen Clint with this look about him. He was a dangerous guy and had killed his share of men without batting an eye. He had no regard for life unless it benefited him. That was why this cold calm demeanour worried Jeff more than if Clint was ranting and raving as it was his usual way when he was upset. And he was upset.

"All right, boss, just tell me what you need me to do." Jeff knew he had to tread lightly until he got a handle on what was going on.

Now Clint's calm demeanour began to crack. His face was now flushed as he got up and rounded the desk. "I had a call from a trusted source in the Richmond Marshals' office a few minutes ago. It seems that harmless little scam you pulled to make a few extra bucks has escalated." He now was in Jeff's face, and what Jeff saw would have terrified a lesser man.

"What do you mean escalated?" Jeff wanted to step back but knew better than to show fear of any kind. It wasn't that he thought he couldn't take Clint, but he knew it was Clint's habit to carry a knife in a sheath at the back of his belt. He had seen Clint gut a man so fast the man didn't even have time to throw up his hands. And as luck would have it, Jeff had walked in unarmed. *I'm slipping*, he thought, *and mistakes like this could cost my life*.

"It seems the old lady decided not to take your little game laying down. She filed a complaint with the marshals. She not only had the fake warrant you sent her, but she also had something no one else could produce. She had the calls recorded, and she's willing to go to court and testify."

Jeff was trying to process this when Clint took another step putting himself squarely in Jeff's face. "Now, I wouldn't worry too much as I don't really care what happens to your sorry ass, but this could bring trouble to my door. Clean it up," Clint said between gritted teeth. "Clean it up, or you won't live to see another sunrise."

"There's no way they could trace that call all the way out here." Jeff was thinking fast. An informant inside the marshal's office. Now that put a new twist on things.

It would have been better if Jeff had just remained silent. Clint reared back and hit Jeff square in the face. Jeff didn't go down but wished he had when Clint followed up with his other fist. Clint was too fast and too close, and the force of the two blows sent Jeff sprawling across the floor.

"You idiot, haven't you ever heard of communication satellites. You know those things way out in space that telephone signals bounce off of. Maybe we don't have cell towers out here, but the signals come from somewhere for you to be able to make your damn calls. Those signals can be traced with damn good accuracy. And what about voice recognition? You have a record which means it's a pretty good bet the marshals or feds or some damn body has your voice on record. You haven't exactly flown under the radar these last few years, and it wouldn't take a genius to put together what happened to you when your late departed friends turned up floating face down. All that being said, when you bring trouble, it doesn't just come to your door, it comes to mine."

Jeff found his feet while rubbing his face. He was going to have a shiner by morning. "Okay, boss, I get your drift. What do you want me to do?"

"You know my policy about no witnesses and no loose ends. When the boat comes in tonight, I want you on it back to the mainland. When you've taken care of this business, you can catch the next boat back. You know where to pick it up."

"You mean you want me to kill that old couple? Do you really think that's necessary? Why don't I just rough them up a little? That should be enough to make them back off. If I kill them, they'll be the bodies to take care of and more of a chance of leaving evidence that could lead back here."

While Jeff had done some pretty bad stuff, he had yet to kill anyone. He had been in this business now for a while and had committed his share of crimes. He was a thief and had worked for pretty bad guys. He had even been the strong-arm for the last gang he was attached too. But as they had all ended up floating in the river, he might not have handled that one so well.

"No witnesses, no loose ends. But you do have a point. Kill the man. Make it look like a robbery. Bring the woman back with you. If anything comes back to us, it wouldn't hurt to have a hostage. If we see we don't need her, you can finish the job by killing her here. This is your mess to clean up, and you'll clean it up in my way. Tonight, after the drugs are unloaded, be on that boat."

"All right, boss, I'll take care of it." Jeff backed toward the door not wanting to turn his back on Clint. Kill one or kill two, if he got caught, he'd still spend the rest of his life in prison. This would take some planning.

Just as he turned the knob, Clint said, "Oh, and I'm sending Pete with you to make sure you finish the job." He watched as Jeff walked across the compound. If he pulled this off like he was instructed to do, maybe Bloom would have a future after all. He still didn't trust him, and that was why he was sending Pete along. He trusted Pete. At least, as much as one crook could trust another.

In the meantime, he had another little matter to take care of. Missing cargo. "I think I'll just pay a little surprise visit to the unloading area tonight."

When Jeff reached the barracks, he poured himself another cup of coffee. He needed to think this through and plan how he could pull this off without either ending up in jail or with a bullet between his eyes. He had no doubt Clint would lay out the plan in detail to Pete. And he was pretty sure, he would tell Pete to kill him if he tried to deviate from Clint's plan. The way he figured it he was right back to where he started from. Him against not only Clint but Pete as well.

While Jeff was in his barracks trying to come up with a plan, Clint was coming up with a plan of his own. He had briefed Pete and had no doubt he would do his part. He would watch Jeff like a hawk if for no other reason than he hated the man and would grab an opportunity to put a bullet in his head. Pete would have done that already if it wasn't for his fear of Clint. He would see this as his chance to do just that if Jeff didn't follow orders.

"So," Clint muttered to himself, "time to take care of another little problem."

Tonight, he didn't want to look like the boss, and he sure as hell wouldn't be standing at the top of the cliff. He wasn't sure who was stealing from him, so he would trust no one. He would handle this little matter all on his own. And if what he suspected was true, he would be one man short after tonight.

It had been dark now for hours. The hauls were always planned for a moonless night. Even though they couldn't be seen from the open water, there was always a chance some stray coastguard could happen by and spot the small boat as it entered the inlet. So far, the coastguards hadn't been a problem. They had no reason to think the island wasn't deserted. Clint had been very careful to keep it that way.

As the men made their way down to the water's edge, Clint fell in step behind them. He was dressed in old clothes with a baseball cap pulled low to hide part of his face. Nobody seemed to notice him. They had a job to do and weren't in the habit of making friends with each other. The unspoken rule seemed to be not to bring any attention to themselves. The fewer who knew anything about them, the safer they were. Most had double-crossed someone in their careers, and who knew, who was sleeping in the cot next to theirs. This played right into Clint's plan.

He stood on the bank with the others and waited. They didn't have to wait long. Clint could see the boat as it made its slow way down the inlet. It came and went from view as it followed the winding flow of water.

As the boat came close to the shore, several of the men waded in to help pull it ashore. Clint moved a little more to the front of the line so he could see as each parcel was unloaded and placed in the cart to be hauled back up the cliff to the compound. This was a sweet operation, and he would be damned if he would let anybody mess it up. And he sure as hell wasn't going to let anyone steal from him.

As he watched, he was beginning to think he might have been wrong. So far, all the parcels that came off the boat had gone into the cart. When all the parcels had been unloaded, he watched as Pete and Jeff boarded the small boat as they had been instructed. He watched as the boat started making its way back out to open water.

Clint faded back into the tall bushes that edged the drop-off location. He let the rest of the men start the journey back up to the top. He hung back out of sight and watched as Calvin brought up the rear. Clint had a pretty good idea now who the thief was. None of them would have taken the chance of being seen stealing from the boss, and the only one out of sight of the others was the guy in the rear. Calvin. Sure enough, about halfway up Calvin eased one of the packages off the back of the cart and dropped it in the bushes. A few yards further, he did the same thing again on the opposite side of the trail. Watching this, Clint had to wonder how the count as the merchandise was unloaded and the count at the top could be the same when some had been left along the way. The one doing the counting was the same at both locations. Pete. He would take care of Calvin now and Pete when he got back.

He waited until they all reached the top. "Calvin," Clint said as he took off his cap, "I think you dropped something along the way."

Calvin turned to look back just as Clint pulled out his gun. He had no time to react. The bullet slammed into Calvin's head and another to his heart. Clint never took any chances. When he killed, he killed for good.

Clint walked over to the body and looked at his other men who had not moved a muscle since this little drama had begun. "This is what happens when you try to steal from the boss." And he turned to retrieve his lost merchandise satisfied his other men got the message.

Chapter 5

United States Marshal Hershel Bing sat in his office with the door closed. He was a large man in his early fifties with dark, curly hair. His complexion was that of freshly-brewed coffee. He had started with the marshals twenty-five years ago. After graduating from the police academy, he hired on with the Richmond Police Department and obtained the rank of detective after only three years. Two years after that, he followed in his father's footsteps and joined the marshals. It was a proud tradition in his family. Not only his father but two of his uncles and one brother had followed the same path. His father, long since retired, had moved to South Carolina to be closer to his only daughter, Samantha. Samantha was a detective in the local police department. She had never joined the marshals and liked to joke that someone had to hold down the other end.

When he was thirty-two, his family had kidded him about being a bachelor. He had no problem with that. He liked his life just fine. If he wanted the whole family thing, he could always visit his sister or one of his brothers and be surrounded by nieces and nephews. Then he would go back home to his quiet life and wonder what all the fuss was about.

And then the unthinkable happened. He met Rebecca. He walked into the courthouse one day and literally walked right into her. She was coming out of one of the courtrooms on the second floor just as he was heading down the hall.

She didn't work at the courthouse but was there to testify at a hearing for a child neglect case. She was a social worker and had removed two children from a seriously-fractured home environment.

He took one look and was instantly smitten. She was his exact opposite. He was six-four, she barely topped five-two. He was big-boned and was a hefty two hundred and fifty pounds of pure muscle. She was tiny and maybe one hundred and ten if she was soaking wet. He was no-nonsense, tough as nails and tended to be suspicious of everybody until they proved themselves. She was soft and gentle and took everybody at face value until they proved different. In other words, they were perfect for each other. A year later, they were married. In twelve years, they had four children: three sons and one daughter. He finally understood what the fuss was about.

But at this moment, his mind wasn't on his wife or children or the rest of his family. His mind was on his job and the unbelievable fact that there was a snitch in the marshal's office. And to make it worse, he couldn't bring in anyone from another office to help because he couldn't be sure how far the corruption went. He looked down at his badge. A five-pointed star inside a circle with 'United States' printed at the top and 'Marshal' at the bottom. The marshals were federal and worked under the Department of Justice. They went all the way back to 1789 when President George Washington appointed a marshal for each of the 13 colonies. They took an oath to faithfully execute the duties of that office. And now someone had betrayed that oath, and in doing so had put lives in danger.

With a tap on the door, Marshal Bill Everett stuck his head in. "Everything all right, boss?" It was unusual to see his commander's door closed. "You're not in trouble with Rebecca, are you?" All his men knew Rebecca could go toe to toe with the boss and hold her own in any disagreement.

"No, I learned a long time ago how to stay out of trouble with her. I just say 'yes dear, okay dear, you're right dear', smile and nod my head. Do you need something, Bill, or are you just checking on my married life?"

"I was just checking. You've been in here with the door closed for a pretty long while. I just thought I'd see if I could help with anything."

"Thanks, but I was just finishing some paperwork and needed a little quiet. I'll be out of the office for a few minutes. If you need me, I'll have my cell."

With this, Hershel stood and strode out the door leaving Bill wondering what had got under his boss's skin. He had worked with Hershel a long time and could tell when something was troubling his friendly boss. Whatever it was, he wished Hershel would share it. There wasn't much Bill wouldn't do for his friend, and he had been on the receiving end of Hershel's understanding on more than one occasion. But he had a strong suspicion: this was related to the office and if it was, it was his place to help his boss with whatever was going on.

Hershel made his way through the bullpen where each of his men worked at a separate cubicle. He looked at each, unable to believe anyone of them would betray their oath to this office. They were good men dedicated to their duty to uphold the federal laws and protect the citizens of this nation. Only one wasn't. And he desperately needed to know which one. A life and maybe more than one depended on his knowledge.

He made his way to the IT department. Andrew Long was in charge of this section, and Hershel knew him to be one of the best. He fielded dozens of requests from outside the bureau for Andrew's expertise. He was lucky to have held on to him for so long. Andrew could make a lot more money elsewhere but so far had shown no desire to leave this job. He hoped it was the dedication to his job and not the extra money he could make on the side being an informant.

Hershel mentally shook his head. He was seeing Indians behind every tree. He had known Andrew for a long time. He had even used his services a time or two while working at the Richmond PD.

Andrew was bent over his computer intently watching the screen as he occasionally pecked in a series of commands. Without looking up, Andrew said, "Hershel, what brings you down to my humble lab? All the exciting stuff happens at your end of the building."

Then all of a sudden, Andrew stopped what he was doing and looked up at Hershel. "You're not in trouble with Rebecca again, are you? Cause if you are, you're not hiding out down here. That little woman can be scary when she gets mad. I had to give testimony last week in a trial where she was the social worker. Seems this crackhead mother sold her baby to get her next fix. When it looked like the judge might be having sympathy for the mother, Rebecca stood up and defended her decision to remove the child from the mother's custody. When she got through, the little guy was remanded to Child Services until the grandmother could be contacted. From all appearances, the grandmother had been trying to get custody of the child since it was born. After court adjourned, Rebecca went up to the judge and they had a few words I couldn't hear. Rebecca left the courtroom looking satisfied, and the judge left looking like he had just been severely reprimanded. No sir, you're not hiding out down here."

Hershel waited for Andrew to finish. Why was it if he happened to look preoccupied everyone assumed that he was in the dog house with Rebecca? He wasn't henpecked and he sure wasn't afraid of her. Although he did go out of his way to stay on her good side. But didn't all husbands do that? And so what if he stayed at the office a little longer and stopped to get flowers on the way home sometimes. He wasn't always in trouble at home; sometimes, he really did have work to catch up on.

"No, Andrew, I'm not in trouble at home. If I was, I would find a better hiding place. Sometimes, I think you guys have more loyalty to Rebecca than you do to me."

Andrew just smiled. All the guys liked to kid their boss about his tiny little spitfire of a wife. "We do, boss. She's prettier and makes a mean cherry pie."

"Just kidding, boss. What can I do for you?" Andrew had noticed Hershel had been a little preoccupied lately, and all the kidding about Rebecca hadn't brought him out of it. His boss certainly had something on his mind, and he was playing it close to the vest.

Hershel couldn't help but smile. Since he and Rebecca had married, she had won the heart of every agent under his command. Her cooking seemed to have that effect on people.

"Andrew, have you had a chance to process those recordings the Murphys brought in?"

"Sure, boss, let me get my report for you. I was just about to shoot you a copy. Let's see. I was able to determine a few relevant details, but I don't know if they will be enough to help you catch this guy."

"First, the calls weren't made from a regular cell phone. The signal didn't ping off a cell tower. It was one of those satellite deals. That's a little unusual in itself. These guys usually use burner phones and dispose of them when they no longer need them and before they can be traced. Second, this guy just didn't sound like a regular scammer. I can't put my finger on it, but something about his voice and the way he phrased things just didn't click for me. Third, I picked up background noise that sounded like he might be on a boat, but that doesn't make sense. In fact, when I put it all together, I have more questions than answers. Something's just wonky."

Hershel had to smile a little at that. "Andrew, your command of the English language never ceases to amaze me. Could you pin down a location?"

"Kind of. The signal kept coming and going and that would work back to the call being made from a boat. And none of that really makes any sense. Like I said, something's just......"

"I know, it's a little wonky. Can you show me a location on the map?"

"Sure, but there's nothing even close to where the signal originated from. Just open water, rough coastline and a few deserted islands." Andrew walked over to a map and pinpointed the location for Hershel.

"How do you know all these islands are deserted?"

"The coastguard checks the coastlines not only by boat but by a flyover. If anything was there, they would pick up on it. That's some pretty rough terrain."

"Okay, thanks, Andrew. Would you make me a copy of those tapes and that map along with the coordinates? I'd like to listen to them again myself. After all, it will give me something to do just in case I need to work a little later tonight."

While Andrew was taking care of his boss's request, Hershel had a few minutes to think. And what he was thinking made cold chills run down his spine. What he had been worrying over since the Murphys had brought in those tapes, was looking a lot more possible. He needed to study the tapes, and he was certain if he found what he thought he would, the Murphys could be in real danger.

"Here you go, boss. Anything else I can do for you?" Andrew hesitated, then added, "You know you can confide in me, Hershel. We've worked together for a long time, and I can tell when you have something on your mind. I don't mean to overstep my bounds, but I'm here to help if you need it."

Hershel felt bad about his earlier suspicions. Andrew had been a good agent and also a friend. This whole deal was making him second-guess himself. Still…he had to maintain his silence for now. Too many lives depended on what he did now. Lives he didn't want on his conscience.

"Thanks, Andrew, I'll let you know."

Hershel took the tapes and map and made his way back toward his office.

He had just entered the bullpen when he was waylaid by Cliff Harrington.

"You got a few minutes for me?" Cliff was the lead investigator of the Murphy case.

"Sure, come on into my office." Cliff was the youngest of his agents and therefore the most inexperienced. Hershel had put him in charge of the Murphy telephone scam because it seemed a safe case for him to rack up a little experience. Most of these cases took a lot of investigation but usually went nowhere. These guys popped up, did their damage and were gone. Usually with someone's hard-earned money.

Cliff waited for Hershel to move around his desk and have a seat. Cliff's mom had taught him to stand for women and his elders. Although he would never have shared that with Hershel.

"Have a seat, Cliff, and tell me what you've got." Hershel leaned back and waited for his junior marshal to assemble his thoughts. He knew Cliff was a little nervous about one on one with the boss.

Cliff cleared his throat. "Well, boss, I've been doing a lot of work on this Murphy scam. I haven't got very far, and what I've found isn't making much sense." Cliff removed the papers from his folder and laid them on Hershel's desk. He then began to outline the details of the case and what he had been able to find. When he'd finished, he looked up at his boss. "Doesn't look like much, and most of it just doesn't make a lot of sense."

Hershel was amazed; his young agent had been able to figure out so much of what he had just figured out himself. He thought about confiding in him. He hadn't been around long enough to have been corrupted. But thinking was as far as he got, Cliff was too new and inexperienced to take this on. Besides, it was just too dangerous for a new agent, and too many lives were at stake.

"Cliff, these kinds of cases go cold fast. That's why these scams are so common. They target the vulnerable, take their money and disappear. You've done well with it. Keep on it a little longer, and if no new leads emerge, put it in the cold case file for now. I have another case waiting for your attention."

Cliff rose and gathered his papers back into his folder. "Thanks, boss, I'll do that." He turned toward the door then stopped and turned back to Hershel.

"Uh, boss, I just want you to know if I can ever help in any way with, you know, with anything you might need help with just say the word." Cliff blushed bright pink. He knew he wasn't saying this right. When he had rehearsed what he wanted to say, it had sounded a lot better. "What I mean is you've seemed a little preoccupied lately, and if I can help, I'm here." With this, he rushed out the door and back to his cube.

Damn, Hershel thought. Was he that transparent that even his youngest agent could read him? He definitely needed to work on his poker face. Evidently, he was slipping. At least, Cliff hadn't mentioned Rebecca.

Hershel picked up the file containing the tapes and map Andrew had given him. He still wasn't sure exactly how to handle this, but one thing he had no doubt about. He had to go see the Murphys. They were in danger.

Chapter 6

Joe stood in their bedroom door and watched Nancy pack. As long as they'd been married, he still couldn't understand why she needed so much stuff when she was only going to be gone a week. Lord, she even had a bag just for shoes, and he had watched her put in four pairs. He could understand two, one for a dress and one for casual, but four?

"Nancy, are you sure you're not leaving me?" Joe asked. "It looks like you're cleaning out your closet."

Nancy looked over her shoulder and smiled at Joe. "Well, I never know what I might need. When Mary Alice and I went last year, I forgot my red heels and had to wear my beige ones with the red suit. I don't want to make that mistake again. I'm sure some of the other ladies were staring at my feet."

"And pretty feet they are too." Joe wasn't going to get into the rest of that statement. He knew when he was in over his head.

Nancy and Mary Alice were going to a conference for The Auxiliary Volunteers of Memorial General. This was a yearly event intended to give additional training for the volunteers and other hospital workers. This was their fifth year to attend, and Joe imagined they spent as much time shopping as they did in the class. Nancy's suitcase always came back bulging at the seams.

Nancy sat down on the foot of the bed. "I need a break. Mary Alice won't be here for another hour. Let's go down and have a glass of iced tea. I can finish up in less than ten minutes."

Joe had never seen Nancy do anything in less than ten minutes. But thirty years of marriage had taught him when to keep his mouth shut.

"That sounds like a great idea," he said as he took her hand and headed out the bedroom door. He liked holding hands with his wife. That's what they did on their first date. Come to think of it, that was what they did on the next five dates as well. The fact that her dad wouldn't let them leave the house probably had a lot to do with it. Her dad said he had to get to know him before he would let him take his daughter off anywhere. Heck, his own dad didn't know him that well.

As they made their way downstairs, Nancy asked, "Are you looking forward to going with Albert to buy some new equipment for the gym?"

Albert was the owner of 'Work for Health' gym. Joe had worked for him for twenty-five years before he retired. Joe was there for the opening, and he and Albert had become close friends over the years. He was glad about his trip to purchase new equipment coincided with Nancy's conference. He hated to be home without her. It was just too lonely.

"I'll be glad to have something to do to pass the time while you're gone. It's too quiet around here without you."

Nancy squeezed his hand. She felt the same way when he was gone. "I'll only be gone for a week. How long do you think it will take to find the new equipment Albert is looking for?"

"No more than three or four days. I think he has scheduled three stops in all.

He learned his lesson the last time we made one of these trips. This time he is having everything shipped back instead of trying to haul it all on his trailer. The last time we had a flat on the trailer and had to unload all that heavy equipment to fix it and then load it all back again. I told him if we had to do that again, he had to put me back on the payroll."

Nancy just laughed at that. "Please, Joe, don't do that. I'd feel like I would have to go back to work too, and I'm having too much fun being retired. Think how nice it's been since we made the decision to retire. We have been able to do what we want. We went on that lovely trip last year to Niagara Falls, and we have planned this year to go to California. I've always wanted to go there. But the nicest thing of all is no stress."

As they drank their tea, they went over everything Joe had to do this afternoon in order for them both to be gone more than a couple of days. Nancy reminded him to stop the paper and have the mail held at the post office and make sure everything was turned off and all the doors were locked.

They finished their tea, and Nancy went back upstairs to finish packing.

Joe washed up the glasses and put them on a towel to dry and then went up to help Nancy bring down her luggage. He didn't want her to try lugging them down the stairs by herself. She was always telling him he treated her like she couldn't do anything on her own. It wasn't that, but as long as he was around, he liked taking care of her. He couldn't imagine his life without her.

They had just placed the bags on the front porch when Mary Alice pulled in the driveway. She hopped out and opened the trunk.

"Hi," she called up to the porch. "All ready to hit the road?"

Nancy waved, and Joe picked up the bags again and loaded them in the trunk of Mary Alice's car.

Joe kissed Nancy bye and helped her in the passenger's seat and watched as they drove away.

Joe walked back in the house to the living room and turned on the television. Then turned it right back off again. He wasn't in the mood to watch TV.

Deciding he would read a little, he went upstairs to retrieve his book from the nightstand in their bedroom. But he put it back down again. He already missed Nancy and just didn't want to stay here in the house without her. *All right*, he thought, *I'll do what always works when I'm at loose ends. I'll go to the gym.*

When he drove into the parking lot of 'Work for Health' gym, he saw Albert locking up.

"What are you doing?" Joe called as he got out of the car. "Has there been a change in plans? I thought you were staying open your regular hours today and closing for the rest of the week for our trip."

"Hey, Joe. You just saved me a telephone call. I talked to one of the distributors on our list, and he is only going to be there a couple of hours in the morning. Since I knew Nancy would be gone by now and you would be walking around lost, I was going to call and see if you were all right with leaving today."

"Couldn't be better for me. Let me run back to the house and pick up my bag."

Albert just shook his head. He figured Joe would be at loose ends and wouldn't want to stay in the house without Nancy. This would work better for both of them.

Jeff and Pete left the boat and walked across the dock. They had already decided to hot-wire a car for their use. If they took one from the parking lot where the seamen left their cars while they were at sea, it wouldn't be missed before Jeff and Pete got back with their cargo. Besides, it wouldn't leave a paper trail. They wanted to get their assignment done and get back to the compound.

They walked around the parking lot until Pete stopped by a new-looking BMW.

"This one will do just fine," he said as he easily popped the lock on the door.

Jeff stopped and looked back at Pete. "I thought the idea was to stay under the radar. Why don't we take that older model Ford over there?"

Pete slammed the door of the BMW and got in Jeff's face. "We're not at the compound now. I'm in charge. Get in or get left."

Pete got behind the wheel and Jeff had no option but to follow. He had a feeling things were going to come to a head between him and Pete before this little trip was done. Clint wasn't here to keep his first lieutenant in line. Well, that was fine with him. Things had been reaching this point ever since he went to work for Clint. Better here than back at the compound where he would have a harder time explaining to his boss why his first lieutenant was dead.

It was only a three-hour drive to Richmond. They would get there about dusk. Catching Joe and Nancy at home should be a piece of cake. They would break in the house, kill Joe, take Nancy and be back on the road in a couple of hours. If they were lucky, they could be back at the dock in time to catch the boat that usually left the dock around midnight. That would be perfect. It would be easier to sneak Nancy on the boat in the dark.

While Pete navigated away from the dock, Jeff programmed in the address Clint had given them into the GPS.

They rode in silence most of the way. Speaking only once when they had to stop and get gas. Pete pumped and Jeff ran in to pay and get some snacks for the rest of the trip. Hopefully, the Murphys' fridge would be well-stocked and they could help themselves after they took care of business. The Murphys certainly wouldn't be needing them.

"Did that sign we just passed say 'Richmond'?" Pete said about an hour after the gas stop. He slowed down to the speed limit. The last thing he wanted was to get stopped by the local law.

"Yea. We're close. Watch out for Pine Haven Circle. According to the GPS, we should be turning within the next few minutes."

They followed the directions given by the GPS until they saw 4210. No lights or cars in the drive.

They drove on by and found a parking place around the corner. After the deed was done, they could knock Nancy out and cut through the woods back to the car.

"Stay here until I come back," Pete said. "I'll make sure they're home before we break-in. No one will question one guy coming to visit friends. Two of us would look suspicious since the neighbours are bound to know we're strangers. I'll come back, and we can move around the block on the backside of the house and either pick the lock on the back door or jimmy a window."

Pete got out and made his way casually down the sidewalk to the corner. He could see no lights on in the house. Maybe

51

they went to bed early. A lot of old people did. He turned the corner and walked to the front of the house. He checked to make sure no one was looking and slipped around the side where he could see in a window into a room that looked to be the kitchen. The room was dark. He made his way a little further along and came to a small deck. He looked to make sure no one could see him and climbed three steps up and tried the door. Locked, and he couldn't see in the window. He left the deck and made his way around the rest of the house. It looked as if no one was home.

As he reached the sidewalk again, he spotted a woman out taking her dog for a walk. He tried to look casual as he approached her and said, "Excuse me, I'm a friend of Joe and Nancy Murphy. I'm from out of town, just passing through and thought I'd stop and say hello to my old friends. They don't look to be home. Do you know when they'll be back?"

The lady stopped and studied Pete for a minute. This was a peaceful neighbourhood, and in fact, the entire town of Richmond had such a low crime rate, people didn't tend to be suspicious, even of strangers.

"Well, I'm sure they'll be sorry they missed you. Nancy has gone to a conference and won't be back for a week. Joe has gone with his old boss from 'Work for Health' gym to pick up some equipment and will be gone for a few days. Tell me your name, and I'll tell them you came by."

"Well, I hate I didn't get to see them. I'll just leave them a note. Thanks for the help."

Pete made his way back to where the car was parked. When he got in, he explained to Jeff what the woman had told him.

"So, what do we do now?" Jeff asked. He didn't like the idea of spending any time in this town.

Pete let his seatback. "We wait. In the morning, we can ask around and get a better idea of when they'll be back."

Jeff thought for a few minutes. "You know, Pete, I don't like hanging around here. The longer we stay, the more likely someone will be able to identify us later."

"You're an idiot, Jeff. We won't be here later."

"Yea, but just think about it. If we wait till they're back in town, we're more likely to get caught. This is a small town, and folks look out for each other. At the first sign of trouble, someone will call the cops."

"Wouldn't it be better if we split up? Take out Joe and grab Nancy while they're out of town where they don't have as many friends looking out for them."

"Only one thing wrong with that little plan. Clint told me not to let you out of my sight and to make sure you got this mess cleaned up." *And besides*, Pete thought, *I don't plan on you being alive when this is finished.*

"Damn, Pete, you don't think I want this taken care of? I admit what I did was stupid, and it's my deal to fix it. But it's crazy to take unnecessary chances or hang around longer than we need to."

When Pete didn't immediately respond, Jeff added, "We'll stick around tomorrow, find out when each is due back. I'll pick an isolated spot on Joe's route back, run him off the road where it will be hard to find his car or his body. That will buy us some time."

"While I take care of that, you can locate the woman. She'll be easier to grab if she's in an unfamiliar location, and people won't realise she's gone as fast as they would here where she's well-known and people are used to seeing her every day."

Jeff paused. He knew Pete didn't trust him. Hell, he didn't trust Pete either, but they needed to get this done and get back to the compound. He needed to keep up with what was happening there. His future plans depended on it.

"We could each take care of our part and meet back at the boat and be out of here by tomorrow."

Pete hesitated for a few more minutes. If Clint found out he had let Jeff out of his sight and hadn't personally watched him take the guy out, he would be in hot water with his boss. However, since he wasn't planning on letting Jeff live to make it back to the compound, Clint wouldn't know he had deviated a little from his plan.

"All right. I guess that makes sense. We'll hang around tomorrow. Find out what we need to know. You make sure you kill this guy, and I'll grab the woman, and we'll meet back at the boat by midnight in two days."

If Jeff had any idea that Pete intended to let him live to return to the island, he didn't any longer. No way would he take a chance on Clint finding out about this little change of plans.

Chapter 7

Nancy and Mary Alice had spent the morning in the class learning how best to deal with family members waiting for their loved one to recover from surgery. In their volunteer work, they dealt with family members as much as they did with patients.

"Now for the fun part," Mary Alice told Nancy, "let's go shopping. I saw a new shoe store on the way in, and I happen to know shoes are your weakness."

It didn't take Mary Alice long to convince her friend. "Now that sounds like a plan," Nancy said as they left the tall two-storey brick building that housed the classes for the volunteers of Memorial General.

This same building was used to train all the personnel from the hospital. The doctors and nurses came here for remedial training, and the EMT's and other emergency workers used it for their training as well. An emergency drill was planned for late this afternoon when all the regular classes were done. As volunteers, Nancy and Mary Alice would be participating. It would be their job to help evacuate patients from the make-believe hospital rooms and help clear out the visitors to a safe location.

They walked the three blocks back to their hotel room. This was such a pretty city; they enjoyed walking whenever they could. Over the years, they had begun to know their way around pretty well and even knew a few of the clerks in the stores they frequented on a regular basis.

As they entered the lobby of the hotel, Nancy asked, "Mary Alice, did you notice that man sitting outside in the park across the street?"

"No. What was he doing?"

"Well, he wasn't really doing anything. He was just sitting there looking at the hotel entrance."

"Maybe he was waiting for someone to arrive or maybe his lunch date was late. It is a little past lunchtime, you know?"

Nancy laughed, "Is that a hint you're ready to eat? I thought you wanted to shop." The man in the park was forgotten.

"We can do both if we hurry. Let's try out that little restaurant a block down the street and then come back and pick up the car and drive to the shoe store."

They hurried up to their room to freshen up and change their shoes. After all, they couldn't wear the same ones to shop as they did in class. It just wouldn't do. Not for two shoe aficionados like Nancy and Mary Alice.

As they exited the hotel, Nancy glanced across the street to see if the strange man was still there. Now, why did she think of him as strange? He wasn't doing anything strange. He was just sitting there. But still, he came across to her as strange. Joe would say her imagination was going wild again. She wondered what Joe was doing. But at the moment, she had bigger things on her mind. Food and shoe shopping.

"Let's pick up the pace, Mary Alice; the shoe store may be having some good sales going on, and we need time to shop."

The restaurant was small, but they had no trouble finding a table. The main lunch rush seemed to be over, but from the look of all the dirty dishes, the food must really be good.

As they waited for their order to be served, Mary Alice said, "Nancy, isn't that the same man from the park?"

Nancy looked over to where her friend was nodding. "It sure looks like it, but he looks a little different without his hat on."

Same hotel, same restaurant, it was seeming a little stranger to Nancy who had developed a more suspicious nature after being scammed several weeks back.

"I guess he decided to wait for his friend here instead of the park," Nancy said. But she knew she would watch when they left to see if he followed.

It didn't take long for their lunch to arrive. They made small talk as good friends do. Then Nancy decided to ask Mary Alice something that had been on her mind for a while. She didn't want to be noisy, but she loved her friend and needed to know if things were okay.

"Mary Alice, I know you don't like to talk about your ex, but he hasn't bothered you lately, has he?"

Mary Alice had endured years of an abusive marriage until one day the beating had been so bad, she had ended up in the hospital. That was a wake-up call. She filed for divorce, took out a restraining order and bought a gun. She had taken lessons and realised she had a real knack for firearms. Knowing she was going to have to make a living, she took what little money she had and opened a firing range. Bullets Firing Range had become an instant success. And as a nod to her past, all battered women entered free of charge.

Mary Alice only hesitated for a moment. At one point, she wasn't able to talk about her abusive ex-husband. Talking brought back flashes from the past. It was only after Nancy introduced her to Beth Thomas that she began to heal and understand what that past had really been about. Control. Beth was a nurse at Memorial General. She also had a major in psychology as well as nursing. The three ladies were now fast friends and depended on each other for support.

"No, not lately. The last time he broke the restraining order, I met him at the door with a gun. He really is a coward, you know. He hasn't been back since then. I don't worry as much anymore, but I heard he had remarried. I don't know her, but that doesn't keep me from worrying about her. When she's had enough, maybe she'll come to the firing range, and I'll give her some free lessons in defence."

Nancy reached over and squeezed Mary Alice's hand. "She'd be lucky to have a friend like you."

Mary Alice returned the squeeze and replied, "You and Beth taught me what being a friend means. Thanks."

"Okay, enough girl talk. Let's get to the important stuff. Shopping." Nancy left a tip to cover both their lunches and got up to leave. She couldn't help looking over at the table where the strange man had been, but he was gone.

They made it to the shoe store with a good hour to shop. Nancy promised herself she would only buy one new pair.

"Oh, look at these," Mary Alice said from across the room. "Wouldn't they look great with the light blue suit you bought last time we went shopping?"

Nancy walked over to examine the shoes her friend was holding. She checked the size. Well, maybe two pairs wouldn't be too many. They would look great with that suit and she certainly wasn't going to put back the pair she had found before Mary Alice called her over.

They spent the next hour going from display to display. When they left the shop, Nancy had four pairs in her shopping bag and Mary Alice had three. Both ladies were satisfied they had left nothing behind that they just couldn't live without.

Nancy looked at her watch. "We'd better hurry if we're going to have time to change before we have to be back for the mock disaster drill."

She never noticed the man standing back in the trees until he lunged at her.

Nancy was caught totally off guard and dropped her shopping bag as she struggled to free herself.

Mary Alice, on the other hand, had lived with violence for too long to be caught off guard. She drew back with her shopping bag and caught the man upside the head causing him to lose his grip on Nancy. But she didn't stop there. She drew back her foot and kicked him in the knee.

By this time, Nancy had recovered enough to jump in. She swung her shopping bag at the man's head just as he reached over to grab his knee. She landed a good solid blow causing the man to stagger backwards.

As he regained his balance for another attack, he noticed they had attracted a fair-sized crowd. Knowing someone had probably already called the police, he turned and ran back into the trees.

Nancy and Mary Alice just stood there for a minute with their shopping bags at the ready in case he decided to come back.

"Mary Alice, I think that was the guy from the park and the restaurant. You know the one I said was strange?"

"I think you're right. He must have thought we were tourists out for a day of shopping and sightseeing. I reckon he thought we must be carrying a bunch of cash and we would be easy pickings."

In spite of the circumstances, they looked at each other and in unison said, "Wrong."

A black and white police car pulled up to the curb. "You ladies all right?" he asked as he climbed out.

"We're fine, officer. I think we ran him off. He went through those trees," Nancy said as she checked her shopping bag to make sure no damage had been done to her new shoes.

The officer took their statements and said he would drive around and see if he could spot anyone with the description they had given him. The fact he would be limping would also be a great help.

He left, driving in that direction, and Nancy and Mary Alice hurried on to their car. They had to hurry now or risk being late.

Pete faded further back into the bushes. His mistake. He hadn't anticipated any resistance. After all, they were just a couple of old ladies. He wouldn't make that mistake again.

As Nancy and Mary Alice got back to the conference centre, the set up for the mock disaster had just begun.

Pete followed at a discreet distance. He already knew where they were going. This little drill they were setting up would work to his advantage. Who would pay any attention to a guy carrying an unconscious woman out of the building when others were being carried out on stretchers?

Nancy and Mary Alice took their places waiting for the action to begin.

"You know, Mary Alice, I tried to call Joe to tell him about our little adventure, but he didn't answer. That's unusual. He picks up on the second ring most of the time. Especially, if we're both out of town."

"Well, I wouldn't worry too much. You can try again when we get back to the hotel. I imagine he and Albert are deep in discussions about what equipment to buy."

Nancy looked at her friend. "I guess you're right. I can try him later. After all, what could happen to him when he and Albert are together? They're both in really great shape. I guess it's all that working out they do."

Nancy watched Mary Alice's face for any expression at the mention of Albert. She had tried to get them together once thinking they would make a great couple. Sadly, that had not worked out so well. Albert was all for the idea. He had been alone for the past four years. His wife had died, and they had no children. However, Mary Alice had been damaged too badly by her marriage to give him a chance.

When the director had everybody in their places, the action began. Ambulances arrived with their stretchers full of 'victims' all bandaged with fake blood all over them.

Hospital personnel were rushing everywhere. It was Nancy and Mary Alice's job to take charge of family members that were arriving in their cars searching for their loved ones.

Nancy was inside taking a family to see their son, who had been badly burnt in a fake explosion. She was making her way back across the room to the front desk to see who needed help next.

Mary Alice was on the other side of the room handing out tags to identify the different families as they came in.

Everyone was too busy to notice a new arrival dressed in a doctor's coat. Pete had no trouble blending in. No one had time to notice an extra guy anyway.

No one that is except Mary Alice. She picked up on him as soon as he came through the door. Maybe she recognised his face or maybe the way he limped.

Whatever, she started making her way over to Nancy when she saw him heading in that direction.

Pete reached Nancy a minute before Mary Alice.

Nancy looked up and was fixing to ask if she could help him when she recognised the cold eyes of the man that had grabbed her in front of the shoe store.

She opened her mouth to scream but no sound came out. She was staring at the small gun he held close to his body. It was hidden so no one could see it except her.

"Let's go," Pete said as he took hold of her arm. "And if you don't want any of these people to get hurt, you won't make a scene."

Nancy was terrified and had just about decided to scream anyway when Mary Alice got to them.

However, Pete was not going to be caught off guard again. He turned and grabbed Mary Alice with one hand and the one with the gun was pointed right at her heart.

"Now if you don't want your friend to end up a real casualty, we'll all walk out the door together. If either one of you tries anything or bring any attention to us, the other one is dead."

The three of them made their way outside without anyone noticing anything strange about two of their volunteers leaving with a stranger dressed as a doctor.

When they got around the corner, Pete opened the back door of a new-looking BMW. "Get in," he said to Nancy.

She saw no way out, so she climbed into the back seat. Besides, he still had Mary Alice and that gun.

Pete locked the door and, having no choice but to take them both, pushed Mary Alice in the front seat. He knew if he left her, she would start screaming her head off, and if he shot her, it would draw too much attention.

Chapter 8

Joe hurried back home thanking his lucky stars he wouldn't have to spend the night at home alone without Nancy. He had to wonder if Albert hadn't decided to close the gym today and start on their trip a day early with that in mind.

He and Albert had been friends for a long time. They had become pretty close over the years Joe had worked for him at the gym. Albert had kidded him many times about his attachment to Nancy. He didn't mind Albert's good-natured kidding. Hell, he was attached to Nancy. She wasn't just his wife, she was his best friend.

They shared everything. Well, almost everything. He didn't share his wife's passion for shoe shopping. When it came to that activity, he was more than glad to leave Nancy in the loving hands of her two best friends.

Mary Alice who owned Bullets Firing Range and Beth Thomas, a nurse at Memorial General Hospital, had been Nancy's closest friends for a long time.

Nancy and Beth had gone to school together. She met Mary Alice when he had encouraged Nancy to take some lessons in gun safety. Mary Alice had moved to town after divorcing an abusive husband and opened Bullets Firing Range.

With the help of Mary Alice, Nancy had become a pretty good shot. She only had one bad habit she had never been able to overcome. As long as she was shooting at a paper target, she hit the bull's eye eight out of ten times. However, he discovered the hard way that when she shot at anything else, she closed her eyes. He found this out when he encouraged her to go on a hunting trip with him the fall after her classes at the firing range.

She had become such a good shot, he figured she would enjoy going with him. That would just be one more thing they could share. It didn't turn out quite that way. The first time she fired at a deer, she closed her eyes and missed by a mile. The second time she took out the right front tire of their car.

After she explained to him that she couldn't stand to see an animal hurt, he left her to her paper targets at the firing range. Oh well, a husband and wife didn't have to share everything.

So, she could enjoy shoe shopping with her two best friends and he could enjoy his hunting trips with Albert.

When he and Nancy were first married, he had been a little jealous of the friendship these three ladies shared. Over the years, he had become thankful for it. If anything ever happened to him, Nancy would never be alone. She had two close friends that would stand with her through anything.

It didn't take Joe long to collect his bag and be ready to head back to the gym. He tried Nancy's cell phone to let her know he and Albert would be leaving a day early. It rang five times and went to voicemail. He thought that a little odd but figured she might be in class and unable to answer. She would get his voicemail and probably call him later.

"Well, that didn't take long," Albert said when Joe drove back up less than thirty minutes after he had left.

"I was already packed and ready to go. All I had to do was pick up my bag and make sure everything was locked up. I tried to call Nancy and let her know about our change of plans but just got her voicemail. I left her a message."

"I can see it now," Albert said with a grin. "She's in jail. She and Mary Alice got into a fight with two other shoe shoppers. They all went to the same sales table at the same time. They were no match for our lovely ladies who, unfortunately, got taken to jail. They were booked for assault with a deadly pair of high heels."

"That's not funny, Albert," Joe tried to say with a straight face. Unfortunately, he couldn't help the grin that spread across his face at the picture Albert painted.

They travelled several miles in silence. The scenery around Richmond changed with the seasons. Joe had often wondered why everyone wouldn't want to live here. But then again, he was glad they didn't. He liked the slower pace of small-town life. He had travelled plenty while in the marines. He had been to France, Germany and Italy before coming back to the states. Stateside, he had been assigned to several different military bases. After six years, he knew military life was not for him. He didn't mind the structure or the rules and regulations, but he wanted to put down roots somewhere. Nancy and Richmond had filled that void for him.

Around 6:00 pm, Albert pulled into a gas station on the outskirts of Williamsburg. "The first place I want to check out is just a few miles down the road," Albert said as he filled the tank. "They won't still be open, so I thought we could get a room for the night and something to eat. Looks like a pretty nice hotel across the road and that truck stop is full. A sure sign of good food."

"Sounds good to me," Joe said as he checked out the place Alert was pointing to. "Those crackers and Vienna's we had down the road are long gone. A nice juicy steak sounds mighty good about now."

Neither Albert nor Joe had noticed the car that had pulled into the back of the station a few minutes after them. A car that looked suspiciously like Joe's.

Jeff parked the car out of sight of the gas pumps. He would pull around and fill up later. He couldn't afford to let Joe or Albert get a good look at the car he was driving.

After Pete had left, Jeff was forced to find another form of transportation. Pete had taken the BMW and left Jeff to figure out how to get another car. Jeff had walked around town for several hours and talked to a few folks to find out what direction Albert and Joe had taken.

When he walked by to check out the gym, he noticed Joe's car parked in the rear. *Perfect*, he thought. No one in town would miss this car, and if he was careful, he could follow Joe and Albert without being seen.

Until he found the car, he had been unsure how to take Joe out with the least amount of unwanted attention. If he hadn't found transportation, he would have had to hide in Joe's house and taken him there. The problem with that was the neighbourhood was close and a gunshot would be heard, bringing the law before he could get far enough away. He had sized Joe up and knew if it came to a face to face confrontation, Joe could hold his own. He figured he could take him but not without a fight that might have caused too much attention.

He had to get this taken care of and get back to the compound. A lot depended on it. A large shipment of drugs was due to arrive there next week. He had to be on hand when that happened. If his information was correct, not only would this be the largest haul so far but one of the top smugglers would be on board. It would be the connection he needed to find out where the drugs were coming from. Without this information, he couldn't put his plan into action.

He watched as Joe and Albert finished pumping gas and pulled across the street to the hotel. He couldn't afford to get a room for the night. He had to stay alert for any opportunity that might present itself.

Albert took the room key from the clerk. "Not a bad place to spend the night," he said to Joe. "Let's go up and leave our bags and check out that truck stop."

"Sounds good to me," Joe replied. "My stomach has started to gnaw its way through my backbone."

They chunked their bags on the bed and took off in search of a juicy steak with all the trimmings.

When they exited the front door of the hotel, neither one noticed Joe's car backed into a parking space at the far end of the parking lot.

Joe and Albert entered the truck stop and found an empty booth. As they waited for service, Joe said to Albert, "You know, we've been friends for a long time and guys just don't meddle in other guys' business."

Albert looked over at his friend. "Why do I hear an unspoken 'but' at the end of that sentence?"

Joe grinned. "You know me too well, my friend. It's just that because you are my friend; I want the best for you. Since Gail died, I sense you're lonely. I know Nancy, against my advice I might add, tried to set you up with Mary Alice. I would never tell Nancy because I try to keep her from matchmaking, but I thought you two would be perfect for each other. You've never mentioned it, so I guess it didn't turn out so well."

Albert looked down at his plate. "That was a mouth full, but I didn't hear a question in all that."

"Don't make me spell it out. You know what I'm asking! What happened?" Joe was beginning to wish he'd kept his mouth shut and remembered the 'guys don't meddle in other guys' business' rule.

"That's just it; nothing happened. I called her and ask her out. She turned me down flat. She wasn't ugly about it, just said one relationship in her lifetime was more than enough for her. I know her story and that she was married to an abuser, but heck, I wasn't asking her to marry me. It was just a date. You know just dinner and a movie. She's lived in our town long enough to know what kind of a person I am. I don't abuse women. Most people like me well enough. I don't drink much, just a beer now and then, and I've never been much of a gambler. It was just a date."

Joe sat back and studied his friend. It was like somebody opened a flood gate. Evidently, Mary Alice's rejection had bothered his buddy more than he would ever have thought.

"Listen, Albert, why don't you give her a little more time? You probably caught her off guard. She's been so busy putting her life back together and establishing her business; I doubt she's even thought about dating."

"I'll think about it. I understand what you're saying. I didn't think about dating either for a long time after Gail passed away. But you know, Joe, a person gets lonely, and it would be nice just to have someone to spend time with."

Joe was saved from having to reply when their waitress placed menus on the table in front of them. They both had the medium rare steak, baked potato and salad.

While Joe and Albert were in the truck stop, Jeff popped the lock on Albert's truck. If he could find an itinerary, he could plan the best place for an attack. This busy hotel and truck stop certainly wasn't one.

He looked over his shoulder to make sure no one was paying attention to him and slid into the front seat. He tried not to disturb anything to cause suspicion that someone had been inside. In the glove box, he found just what he was looking for. It wasn't anything formal, just notations on a scrap of paper, but it was enough. He carefully put it back just like he found it. He took one more look around, slid out and relocked the car. Now all he had to do was to find a map and plot the best place for an attack.

Joe and Albert were back at the truck stop by 7:00 am for breakfast. This time it was a little more crowded. Some truckers were stopping for breakfast after driving most of the night, and others were just getting loaded and ready to head out.

"Well," Albert said when they walked in and found the place packed. "We can stand here and wait for someone to finish or we can drive on down the road and see what else we can find."

Joe looked around and noticed a table for six with only four truckers sitting around it. "Let's ask those guys if we can join them. Truckers are usually friendly, and if they don't have anyone else they're waiting on, I bet they wouldn't mind."

Joe motioned to the waitress that they were headed over to a table already occupied by four brawny guys.

Joe put on his most engaging smile and approached the table. "Hey, guys, if you're not saving these seats, do you mind if my friend and I join you?"

The four guys immediately shifted to make room. "No problem," the biggest of the bunch spoke up. "We're just taking our time. We all have runs that will keep us on the road most of the day. We're just finishing up and waiting for the waitress to fill up our thermoses. Y'all are welcome to join us. Where are you fellows headed?"

Joe and Albert took a seat and spent the next fifteen minutes getting to know these friendly guys that travelled the roads on a regular basis.

By the time their food came, the truckers had their thermoses filled and were ready to head out.

"Y'all be careful out on the road today," Albert said. "There are some crazy drivers out there."

"Back at ya," the last trucker out the door said.

Joe and Albert finished their breakfast, paid at the counter and made their way back to the hotel. After gathering their stuff and checking out, they were back on the road again.

"You know, Albert," Joe said, "Nancy never did call me back last night. I tried again just now, and the call went to voicemail again. I know she's fine, but I can't help but worry."

"I wouldn't worry overmuch, Joe. You know this conference for the hospital volunteers is pretty fast-paced. I'm sure she'll call when she has a break. If she hasn't called by noon, you can try her again. Maybe catch her on their lunch break."

Albert didn't want to add to his friend's worry, but he was a little uncomfortable with the idea of Nancy being out of touch for so long as well. For most people, this wouldn't be so unusual. But Nancy wasn't like most people. She and Joe were always in touch. Albert had a real uneasy feeling; something just wasn't right.

Their first stop of this trip was very productive. Albert purchased three pieces of equipment and had it shipped back to the gym in Richmond.

They had only been back on the road for about fifteen minutes when they reached a long-deserted stretch of highway. The landscape on each side of the road was desolate with sharp drop-offs on each side. Just as they approached a particularly sharp curve, a car pulled out behind them from seemingly nowhere.

"Now that guy's an idiot," Albert said, looking in his rearview mirror. He needs to slow down around this curve. If he lost control, there's nowhere to go but down, and it would be one scary ride."

Joe looked in his side mirror to see what Albert was talking about, but the sun blinded him, and all he could see was a car coming up on them at a fast rate of speed.

"Albert, I think you better pull over. This guy is going to try to pass you, and I don't think there's room."

Albert looked to both sides of the road but there just wasn't room for him to pull his truck off the highway. They made the curve with the other car almost touching their bumper. As they reached straight away on the other side of the curve, the car on their bumper backed off a little. But he was only judging the right angle to hit the back of Albert's truck to make him lose control and go over the side of the embankment.

This is what I was waiting for, Jeff said to himself as he accelerated for the contact that would send Joe and Albert to the bottom of a deep ravine.

Just as he was in position and fixing to step down on the gas, he heard the loud blast of a semi and looked in the rearview mirror to see the big rig bearing down on him.

"Shit, where did that guy come from?" Jeff muttered to himself. The hunter had just become the hunted.

He accelerated and passed Albert as fast as he could get the car to go. As he disappeared around the next curve, Albert pulled over to the side of the road. He didn't have much room, but he was shaking so bad he was afraid he might lose control of the truck.

The semi pulled over behind him, and one of the big, burly truckers that had shared a table with them that morning came around to the driver's side window.

"Man, I thought that fool was going to run you off the road. Drivers like that have no business driving on a road like this. Where are the cops when you need them?"

It took Joe and Albert a minute to respond. It had all happened so fast. What was that guy thinking? They could have been killed and surely would have if not for this trucker.

They both got out to shake hands with the concerned trucker and thank him for his help. This little incident would have turned out much different if not for him.

After taking a few deep breathes and talking about what an idiot the other driver was, they all got back in their vehicles and continued on their way.

The trucker stayed behind them for the next few miles to make sure they were okay. At the next turnoff, he gave a blast of his air horn in farewell and made the turn that would take him to his next location.

"We should be at our next location in about an hour," Albert told Joe. "After we take care of business there, why don't we get a room for the night? I don't think I can go any further today. That really shook me up. We're not in that big of a hurry. We can spend the night and go on to our last stop in the morning."

Joe just nodded his head. He kept thinking how much that car looked like his. Of course, that was impossible. His car was back in Richmond sitting behind Albert's Gym.

Jeff checked his rearview mirror, and when he was sure no one was close enough to see him, he pulled off at the next side road and drove until he was out of sight. He pulled over and cut the motor. His hands were shaking. *What the hell just happened back there*, he thought. One minute the road behind him was deserted, and the next, a huge semi was bearing down on his back bumper.

Now he would have to make the next stop with Joe and Albert and come up with another plan. This should have finished it, and he should be on his way back to the boat to meet up with Pete. Now it would take an extra day. A day he wasn't sure he had.

After buying four more pieces of equipment and being assured they would be shipped back to Richmond the next day, Joe and Albert called it a day. They were both too exhausted and too shook up to go any further.

As they came out of the fitness centre, Joe said, "I saw a nice-looking hotel about three blocks back. What do you say we check in there, leave our stuff and go have a drink?"

"My friend, that sounds like a plan to me. I'm not much of a drinker, but right now I think I could down a double."

Joe slapped his friend on the back, just glad to be alive. "Then let's get back to that hotel, check-in and hope they have a lounge or bar or somewhere we can get that drink. If we get a little tipsy, we won't have far to go to get back to our room."

Neither one of them noticed the car parked down the street. If they had noticed, it would just have looked like an empty car parked on the street. Probably belonging to some of the many shoppers milling about.

They couldn't have seen the guy slumped down out of sight in the front seat. Waiting. Just waiting for his next opportunity to strike again.

After Joe and Albert checked in, they left their stuff in the room and started back down to the lounge they had past when they were catching the elevator up.

Again, they never noticed the guy in the corner of the lobby watching.

"This looks like a nice quiet place," Joe said. "Let's take that booth over in the corner and order that drink."

"Sounds good to me. I'll buy the first round. After all, you almost got killed helping me on this trip to restock the gym with newer equipment. If I had lived, Nancy would have killed me. I might have just done it myself to save her the trouble. Talking about Nancy, did you ever get in touch with her?"

"No, I didn't, but I think I'll step out and try again. If I don't get her this time, I'm going to call Beth at the hospital and have her get in touch with someone working at the conference. They can go check on the girls and get Nancy to call me back. I can't go to sleep another night without knowing she's all right."

Joe stepped out into the lobby, but a large family was at the check-in desk and it was too noisy to hear. He saw a side door that looked as if it led outside. He went through and found himself in a narrow alley. Oh well, at least it was quiet.

Jeff watched as Joe let himself out the side door. He had come in that way so as not to draw any attention to himself so he knew where it went. He hadn't planned it this way, but this was too good an opportunity to let pass.

He cracked the door and saw Joe several feet down the alley with his back turned and his phone in his hand as if he were trying to make a call. He slowly made his way to Joe, taking care not to make any sound that would alert the other man.

When he was close enough, he grabbed Joe around the neck and hung on until Joe went limp. He stepped back and when he didn't see any movement, he checked Joe's pulse and smiled. He took out his phone and snapped a picture as proof he had completed his assignment and faded away into the darkness.

Chapter 9

Hershel prepared to leave his office with the tapes and map he hoped would save the Murphys and keep all the marshals safe. If only he knew who to trust.

Up until now, he would have staked his life on the fact that all the marshals under his command were honest and trustworthy. He now knew this not to be the case.

There was one who had betrayed his oath. One who had betrayed his country. One who had put citizens and marshals alike in danger. Therefore, he could trust no one, and the men he would have staked his life on would have to stay in the dark for now.

Hershel closed and locked his office and made his way over to Marshal Bill Everett's cubicle. Bill was the senior agent under Hershel's command.

"Bill, I'm going to be away from the office for a few days. You're in charge while I'm gone. You may not be able to reach me, but I have no doubt you can handle whatever comes up."

"Is this a little vacation, boss? Because if it is, you certainly deserve one. I don't remember the last time you took a few days for yourself."

As Bill said this, he was thinking, *What's up with you, Hershel? You're never out of contact. Not even on vacation.* He had thought for weeks now that his boss was keeping something from the other men. He just couldn't figure out what and why not share it.

"Well, kind of," Hershel hated to lie to his old friend and agent. "I know I can depend on you to keep things going while I'm gone. You're a good agent, Bill. One of these days you may have to sit in my office and lead these men on a full-time basis. When that time comes, I know the office will be in good hands."

With this, Hershel turned and walked away before Bill could question him further. He could tell Bill hadn't bought his story about a vacation. When all this was over, he would owe Bill an explanation and an apology for the lie.

As Hershel pulled out of the parking lot, he began to think about what he would tell Rebeca. He couldn't tell her the truth either. If she knew he was going into a dangerous situation without backup, she would raise the roof. Worse than that, she would alert his men in an attempt to keep him safe. He couldn't take a chance on that. He knew when this was over, he would be in serious trouble with his wife. When they married, they had each promised the other: no lies and no secrets. He was fixing to break both promises and depend on her loving him enough to forgive him. Eventually.

Hershel pulled into his drive and prepared for the performance of his life. Fooling Rebecca was not going to be easy.

He found his wife in the kitchen. When she was not doing her job as a social worker, she could usually be found in the kitchen. Cooking was her second passion. He just hoped he would still be her first when this was finished.

"What are you making there, hon? It smells great. You're not making something for my men again, are you? You have them all under your spell as it is. Sometimes, I wonder if they're not more loyal to you than to me."

Rebecca turned from her mixing bowl and in usual Rebecca style cut straight to the chase. "What's up. Why are you home this time of day?"

Well, hell, she was suspicious already and he hadn't even told the lie yet. This was going to be even tougher than he thought.

"I found out this morning I'm going to have to be away for a few days. Just a short assignment out of town. That may mean I'll be out of touch as well. I hate to leave you alone, but I know you'll be fine and I'll be back in a few days."

Hershel knew he was rambling but he couldn't help it. He had never lied to her before, and she was standing there looking at him like she wasn't buying a thing he said. He stopped talking before he dug himself into a deeper hole. He knew each lie would have to be answered for later. Better to keep the number to a minimum.

Rebecca picked up her dish towel and wiped her hands. "Uh-huh," she said, watching her husband carefully. "And this assignment that's taking you out of town for a few days, the one that will also keep you out of touch is, where?"

Her husband had her full attention.

"You know it's one of those secret things that the agency requires us to participate in on occasion. You know one of those hush-hush things my job requires sometimes. It's only for a few days, and I'll tell you all about it when I get back." He was rambling again.

"Uh-huh," she said again and turned back to her mixing bowl. He was lying and he wasn't very good at it. She just had to decide how hard to make this for him.

She knew her husband and had sensed something had been bothering him for the past few weeks. She knew it had something to do with work and had thought if she gave him the time, he would share it with her. He always did. Well, she had other ways of finding out what was going on. She also had leverage. Chocolate chip cookies.

"All right, honey. Can I help you pack? Will you be needing your best suit or something more casual?"

This was going worse than he had anticipated. Not only did Rebecca not believe him, but she was up to something. Where were the dozen questions she would normally have asked? Getting by her was harder than getting by all the men under his command. And they were trained in espionage.

Well, he wasn't going to look a gift horse in the mouth. He was going before all hell broke loose. He'd have a lot of explaining to do when he got back. He just couldn't put anyone else in danger.

He leaned over and kissed his wife and hoped she would still be speaking to him when he got back. "Okay, I'll just go pack a few things. I won't need much, just a couple of shirts and some casual pants and some underwear." Yep, he was rambling.

He left the kitchen feeling like a jerk for not telling Rebecca the truth. But if he had, he could have been putting her in danger. That was not an option no matter what. He would just have to live with the consequences.

Hershel left his drive and turned his car toward Hadbury. He had the Murphys' address in his file. He had thought about calling them but had decided against it. If an agent was involved, and he knew one was, they would know how to tap the Murphys' phone. No, this was the only way. Face to face was the safest.

He wondered what would happen when he was forced to confront this agent. Would the guy try to take him out? Would it go that far or would the guy come to his senses? He couldn't depend on that. Too much had been done. Too many laws broken. He had to prepare himself for a fight. A fight with someone he had trusted and called a friend. Well, just like with Rebecca, he would deal with that when the time came. Just like Scarlet O'Hara in *Gone with the Wind*, he would worry about that tomorrow, if he lived to worry about it tomorrow.

Hershel pulled into Hadbury late in the afternoon and found the Murphys' house with no trouble. Hadbury was a small town, and the Murphys' street was lined with upper-middle-class houses. These were good people leading good lives. They didn't deserve to have this ugliness brought to their doorstep. He would do his best to see that didn't happen.

As he pulled into the Murphys' driveway, he noticed there didn't appear to be anyone home. He knew both Joe and Nancy were retired but knew little of their daily routine.

Hershel stood on the porch and rang the doorbell. Even the doorbell had an empty sound. The house was locked up tight. At least, it didn't appear that any violence had taken place here.

He knew that Joe worked out at 'Work for Health' gym and Nancy was a volunteer at Memorial General. He would try the gym first. He wanted to talk to them both at the same time if at all possible. He had to let them know what the situation was and what they needed to be on the lookout for. When they had come into the marshals' office, they had indicated they were willing to testify if they were needed to do so. He had to let them know what danger their willingness to help could have put them in. There were some who had too much to lose to let that happen.

As Hershel made his way back down the front steps, he noticed a lady on the opposite side of the street, walking her dog.

He crossed over and waited for her to get close enough for him to talk to. "Excuse me, ma'am. I wonder if you could tell me when the Murphys will be home or where I might find them? I'm from out of town and just thought I'd make a detour and stop in to say hello."

The lady stopped and took in Hershel's appearance. He looked like a respectable sort, a little more so than the last guy that had asked her the same question a few days back. She never knew Joe and Nancy had so many friends from out of town.

"How did you say you know the Murphys?" she asked. While she didn't have a suspicious nature, it did seem odd that two strangers were asking about the Murphys when they just happened to be out of town.

Hershel thought for a minute. What could he tell this woman to get her to open up to him? He certainly couldn't tell her that he was a United States marshal or that he was trying to warn the Murphys of potential danger.

"Oh, Joe and I go back a ways. We were in the service together. We still keep in touch even though we don't get to see each other much."

"I see," the woman said. "In that case, I'm sorry you've missed them. Nancy is at a week-long conference, and Joe has gone with his friend Albert to buy new gym equipment."

Hershel relaxed a little. If the Murphys were out of town for a while, they should be safe enough until he could make contact with them. No one else could possibly have this information. At least, no one intends on doing them harm.

The helpful neighbour started to carry on with her dog, then stopped and turned back to Hershel. "Why don't you just leave them a note on the door? That's what that other guy did."

Hershel felt a chill go down his spine. "Someone else from out of town was looking for them?"

"Oh, yes. I don't believe he told me his name, but you'll see his note on the door. Just leave yours up there with his."

Hershel had already been to the door. There was no note waiting for the Murphys' return. He would feel better if there had been.

"Thanks. I think I'll drive over to Albert's gym and see if anyone knows when he and Joe might be back. I can leave a note there if they're going to be gone for a few more days. What did you say the name of Albert's gym is?"

"'Work for Health', just a few blocks down that way." She knew she had not given him the name of the gym before, but maybe he just had a bad memory.

Hershel had no trouble finding the gym, but when he pulled into the parking lot, it was deserted. No other cars and no lights on inside. He parked and walked around the building. He hadn't seen a car at the Murphys. He would have expected to find a car or truck here if the two men went together. He thought that a little strange, but maybe Nancy had taken the car and Joe was riding with Albert. That would explain not finding a car here or at the Murphys. That would be a logical explanation, so why did he feel so uneasy.

Hershel left the parking lot and drove around until he found a small diner. He parked and went in. If he acted real causal and just ordered a meal, he might be able to get an idea of where the two men had gone.

When Hershel finished his meal and a fruitful conversation with the waitress, he had a fair idea of where the guys had been heading. He, at least, knew the towns they planned to stop at if not the exact name of the wholesale equipment businesses they would be shopping at. The towns were small. There couldn't be that many places in each that sold gym equipment.

The first place he stopped was in Williamsburg, about eighty miles down the road. He missed Joe and Albert but was able to find out where their next stop would be.

He thought about stopping for the night but decided if he could catch up with the guys at their next stop, he could spend the night there.

As he left Williamsburg, following the route he had been told Joe and Albert would take, the landscape became more desolate and the road narrowed and went into a series of sharp twists and turns. The scenery was beautiful but the drop-offs on each side of the road were treacherous. Hershel thought to himself that if a car went off the road, it might not be found for a long time.

When, at last, he pulled into the next town on his list, he found the equipment place had already closed for the day. He was worried that he had not been able to catch up with them but knew he was going to have to stop for the night. He had been driving all day and was about at the end of his endurance. He would spend the night and get an early start in the morning.

He found a nice hotel not far away and checked in at the front desk. Just on a whim, he asked the clerk if a Joe Murphy had checked in. The guys would have had to stop somewhere for the night.

The clerk checked his records. "No, I'm sorry. We don't have anybody registered by that name."

"How about an Albert—Uh, I'm having a senior moment. I can't even remember my good friend's name. I guess I'm getting old." Hershel had to think fast. He had no idea what Albert's last name was.

"He and Joe are from Hadbury. They might have checked in last night or this afternoon."

The clerk checked his log again. "Yea, there were two guys from Hadbury by those names that checked in a little while ago. They went up to their room, but I think they came right back down. I believe I saw them go into the lounge over there."

Hershel thanked the clerk and headed for the lounge. When he walked in, he had to pause a moment to let his eyes adjust to the dimmer light. He would recognise Joe but had no idea what Albert looked like.

He scanned the room but didn't see Joe or even two guys at a table to themselves. There were three couples at different tables and a guy on each end of the bar. He noticed one guy sitting by himself over at a table in the far corner.

He decided to take a chance. Maybe Joe had gone back to the room or the bathroom or something.

As he approached the table, the guy looked up. Hershel noticed he was in excellent physical condition. Just what he would expect from someone who owned a gym.

"Excuse me," Hershel said, "would you happen to be Albert, Joe Murphy's friend?"

Albert stood up. "You know Joe?" Albert asked. He thought it was a small world if they had come all this way to find one of Joe's friends staying at the same hotel.

He didn't think far enough to wonder how this guy would know they were staying here.

"Sure. We're in town buying gym equipment. Would you like to join us? Joe should be back in a few minutes."

"Thanks," Hershel replied.

The guys made small talk for a few minutes as they waited for their mutual friend. When Joe didn't appear after a few minutes, Hershel asked, "How long has Joe been gone?"

"Well, he went to make a phone call. He's been trying to reach his wife since yesterday. She's at a conference, and Joe hasn't been able to reach her. He was a little worried and stepped out to try again. To tell you the truth, I was getting a little concerned myself. It isn't like Nancy to not stay in touch."

All kinds of alarm bells went off in Hershel's head. He stood up. "Which way did he go to make his call?"

Albert got to his feet too. Something about Hershel's demeanour made him think that this guy wasn't just a casual friend who happened to show up at the same hotel.

"He went toward the lobby but just as he went out, a rather large and noisy family came in," Albert said. "He might have stepped outside to find a quieter place to talk."

Both men crossed the lobby and went out the front door. Hershel scanned the sidewalk in both directions. Joe was nowhere in sight.

"He wouldn't have gone that far," Albert said. "Let's ask the clerk if he saw him go back up to our room."

They made their way back to the front desk. They had to wait as the clerk checked in a couple who seemed to have a million questions. They were trying to find somewhere to eat and couldn't seem to agree on what kind of food they wanted.

When the couple finally left to find their room, they were still arguing about where to go for supper.

Albert stepped forward and asked the clerk if he had seen Joe head back up to their room.

"I did see him about twenty minutes ago, but he wasn't heading up to your room. In fact, I believe he went out that side door. He had his phone in his hand, and I figured he was looking for a quiet place to make a call. I haven't seen him come back in, but I've been pretty busy."

"What's out that door?" Hershel asked. He had a bad feeling and was wishing he had kept his gun with him instead of locking it in the gun safe in the trunk of his car.

"Oh, nothing really, just the alley between the hotel and the gift shop next door. It doesn't really go anywhere. It just connects the streets in front of and back of the hotel."

Hershel and Albert, both turned and made for the side door that led out to the alley. At first, Hershel didn't see anything. The sun had gone down, and the alley was dark. But then he could make out a darker shadow on the ground. He sprinted toward the still form. He recognised Joe before he even got to his body.

He yelled over his shoulder to Albert, "Call an ambulance; it's Joe."

Chapter 10

Clint stood in his warehouse taking stock of the merchandise he still needed to move. Another shipment was due to go out in a few days. He had thought Pete and Jeff would be back by now. He had always depended on Pete to help with this part of the operation. Now that he knew Pete and Calvin had been stealing from him, he would have to make a change in how this end was handled. He had taken care of Calvin, who was now feeding the fishes at the bottom of the ocean. He had plans for Pete to join him as soon as he and Jeff got back to the island.

That brought him to thinking about Jeff. Could he trust him to step into Pete's shoes? He came highly recommended, but he was somewhat of a loose cannon. If he pulled off this latest assignment, Clint would have to rethink his plans for Jeff. Someone would have to take Pete's place.

He watched as two of his guys loaded the cart to be transferred to the next holding location. He only allowed a few of his men to see this part of the process.

From the outside, this building just looked like a warehouse. When he had taken over this island from the previous owner, he had discovered what he would have called a rathole. He just happened on it one day when he was setting up his camp. The opening was just large enough for a man to enter and wound its way down into the depths of the island until it emerged into a large cave. The cave led out to a very small shoreline that was totally covered in bush and small scraggly trees. He had to figure it was an escape route of some kind.

Since the former owner was no longer around to object, Clint had built his warehouse on top of the rathole and enlarged the opening down to the cave at the bottom. He had built a door at the mouth of the rathole so no one could go up or down unless he knew where the latch was located. He had then built a track system that would take the cart filled with his newly-acquired drugs down to the cave. Another door with a hidden latch was built at the bottom.

A boat, not even a small one, could access the small shore outside the cave. To get his drugs off the island, a rubber raft had to be deployed from the shore to a waiting ship that would have to drop anchor in deeper water.

This tunnel system would also make a good escape route if it became necessary. He wasn't planning on that happening, but in this business, you stayed alive by being prepared.

When his men were finished transferring the drugs to the cart and making the transfer to the cave below, he dismissed them so he could be alone to access the hidden latch that would secure the door.

As he left the warehouse, his phone vibrated in his pocket. Another little precaution. He only set it to ring when he was in his office and alone. The men didn't need to know he had this second phone. Only one person called him on this one and then only if he had information that was urgent.

Clint pushed the talk button. "What have you got?"

"Just felt like I should let you know Hershel Bing left the office yesterday without letting anyone know where he was going. Might be nothing, but with the strange way he's been acting around everyone, I thought you should know."

"Thanks. Let me know when he gets back," Clint said and hung up without another word. He thought his informant was getting a little paranoid. He didn't see how Hershel could be a threat to his operation. On the other hand, he couldn't take Hershel Bing too lightly. He knew the man's reputation.

Clint made his way back to his office to wait for a call on his office phone. He liked to be the one calling the shots, but in this case, he would defer for now.

His drug supplier, Diego Garcia, was planning a visit to the island. They had talked for months now about expanding their end of the business. Clint had assured him he could move all the drugs he could supply. So far, they hadn't been able to reach an agreement. He hoped this pending visit would settle the details.

He didn't trust Diego and couldn't afford to let him see too much of his layout. He would show him just what he wanted him to see. Just enough to satisfy the drug lord that Clint could handle the larger shipments. He had no intention of letting him see the secret passage from the warehouse to the cave below.

He hoped Pete and Jeff would be back before Diego arrived. He didn't know how many men Diego would bring with him, but he didn't want to be outmanned. He might even let Pete live until after Diego's visit. But not too much after his visit. He didn't want Calvin to get lonely feeding the fishes all by himself.

He entered his office and poured a cup of coffee to take with him to his desk. He had plenty of paperwork to catch up on while he waited for his phone call.

It took a lot of planning and coordination to keep an operation like this running smoothly. He had distributors in twenty-seven states that stretched from the east coast to the west coast. That meant men, money and a steady supply of drugs to keep the operation moving along at a steady clip. A break down in the chain could cost time and money, and if the authorities managed a bust at any location, he had to be ready to plug the hole with more men in different locations. All this made for a lot of paperwork that he didn't trust anybody else to handle.

He was only about fifteen minutes into the paperwork when his phone rang. He looked at the caller ID and wasn't surprised to see it was blocked. Evidently, he wasn't the only one to take extra precautions.

"Yeah, Clint here," he said after he hit the talk button. For a minute, there was nothing but silence on the other end of the line. He imagined Diego was running a trace to make sure the line was secure. He would have to remember not to take any chances with this dangerous man.

"Hello, *mi amigo*. Are you alone? Is it safe to talk?" Diego didn't trust Clint or his men. So far, their business relationship had been profitable, but Diego knew Clint would turn on him in a minute if it was to his advantage to do so.

"No problem on this end. I'm in the office alone with the door shut. My men know better than to come in without an invitation. Are you secure and alone on your end?"

"Oh, *si*," Diego said as he sneered at the five armed banditos lounging around the cantina he was calling from. Unlike Clint, he kept nothing from his men. He just made sure they were all too afraid of him to try a double-cross. It had only happened once. The example he made of the unlucky man assured no one else would try. He cut the man's hands off, staked him out in the hot sun and poured syrup over him and let the fire ants do their thing. It had never been tried again.

They talked for a while about Diego's upcoming visit. They set the time for two days out at sunset. Just before dark was a good time to access the island. It was still light enough to see how to navigate the small channel, but the lengthening shadows gave sufficient cover. It only took a minute to slip into the inlet and be out of sight. Only those who knew the terrain well would dare try to enter the channel in complete darkness. All the transactions so far between Clint and Diego had been carried out by a third party go-between when the drugs were delivered.

"*Hasta luego*, my friend, I'll see you in a couple of days." Diego disconnected and left Clint to contemplate the upcoming meeting and how to work it to his advantage and stay alive at the same time.

He stood up and walked around his desk to refresh his coffee. Yes, he definitely needed Pete and Jeff to be back by then. He would devise a little plan that would give him some added security if things went south.

He took his coffee and walked outside to where most of his men relaxed at a large wooden table that had been set up under the shade of some large trees. The trees not only provided shade, but they also made excellent cover from the air just in case any reconnaissance planes happen to do a flyover. Not many did. It was pretty much accepted this island was uninhabited.

His men watched as their boss approached. They had walked a wide circle around him after what happened to Calvin. They knew their boss was ruthless, but that was the first time they had seen him pull a gun and shoot one of his own men.

Clint paused for a minute sizing up each of his men. He knew that to a man they would do almost anything for money. Hell, they already had. They were already in this so deep there was no way out. But could he trust them if push came to shove with Diego and his band of cutthroats?

"I have a little job for a few of you who would like to make a little extra money." He named a sum designed to get their attention. He had five men to step forward immediately to accept. He told the others to get lost. The least the others knew the better. He couldn't afford for one of them to sell him out thinking they would get a better deal with Diego. That was the reason for the extra high bonus he named.

He sat down at the table with the five men and outlined what he would need them to do in two days. "I don't plan on any trouble, so this should be easy money. When our guests arrive, I just want you to stay among the trees and follow at a distance. Don't be seen. Just follow them up to the compound and stay out of sight. I don't imagine our business will take more than a couple of hours. Follow them back down as they leave. When they are all on board, follow along the side of the channel until you see them board their ship and head out to sea. Then you can come back and collect your money. Only show yourselves if and when you see trouble starting. If that happens, make sure none of them leaves this island alive."

His men looked at each other. There must be more to it than this. Their boss would never let go of that much extra money for something so easy.

Finally, one, a little braver than the others, stepped forward. "No problem, boss, you can count on us to handle this for you. Just who are these visitors we're going to be babysitting?"

Clint debated how much to disclose to these five men. He knew their allegiance was to the money not to him. He finally decided it would be better to tell them in advance so there would be no surprises.

"Diego Garcia," he said, watching them closely for any sign of nerves. When he was satisfied with what he saw, he turned back toward his office. He took three steps and turned back to his five men.

"Oh yeah, I forgot to add, if you let me down, you will not only not get paid but you won't live to even try to collect." Satisfied he had delivered his message across and turned again and headed back to finalise his plans for the upcoming visit.

His men watched him go, then looked at each other. They were afraid of their boss. He was ruthless. But to a man, they were more afraid of Diego Garcia. They knew where their allegiance would be if a confrontation broke out.

Chapter 11

Nancy and Mary Alice were terrified. They had been kidnapped by a crazy man and had no idea what he wanted.

Mary Alice looked over and took stock of Pete. He looked tough, especially with that gun still in his hand. She could see Nancy out of the corner of her eyes. Her friend looked scared and confused but so far unhurt.

"What do you want with us?" Mary Alice whispered. "If it's money, we don't have any. Our purses are back at the hotel. We don't even have any credit cards with us. If you take us back to the hotel, we'll give you everything we have. We can even go to an ATM and get more. Then you could tie us up and lock us in the bathroom at the hotel. It would be at least a day before anyone would miss us. We were almost finished for the day at the conference centre, and even if we didn't show back up in the morning, we wouldn't be missed for a while. It's not like we have to check-in. By the time someone took the time to look for us, you could be long gone."

Mary Alice stopped and took a breath. She was an expert at negotiating her way out of trouble with a crazy man. She had done it for years with her abusive husband. She had saved herself a beating or two with her sharp mind and fast talk. She had a sinking feeling it wasn't going to work with this guy. He wasn't going to just beat them up; he had a gun.

"Shut up!" Pete yelled at her. "I don't want your money, and I'm certainly not going to take you back to that stupid hotel."

Mary Alice lapsed into silence but caught Nancy's attention from the backseat. Nancy was huddled in the corner. She was unharmed but looked like she was in shock.

Pete drove with one hand and held the gun on Mary Alice with the other. He had to think. He was only supposed to take Nancy and hand her over to Clint.

The only way he could have captured her and got away without being apprehended was to take the other one too.

He glanced in the rearview mirror to make sure Nancy was subdued. He didn't think he would have much trouble with her.

The one in the front was a lot of mouth, but he figured she wouldn't try anything as long as he had a gun pointed at her. Besides, he might need a hostage of his own if things went bad before he got them both on the boat.

There would be plenty of time to dispose of the one with the mouth after they were on board. By then her usefulness would be over and he could strangle her and push her overboard.

Now that he had a plan of sorts, he felt he could relax a little. Which was why he didn't notice Nancy shift over in the seat until she was directly behind him.

His first sense something was wrong was when he was grabbed from behind.

He tried to knock Nancy off, but she hung tight. She was stronger than she looked and evidently not in shock to the point where he could take his eyes off her.

As if that wasn't bad enough, the other woman made a grab for the steering wheel.

Pete slammed on the brakes, reached back and knocked Nancy off and at the same time shoved the gun in Mary Alice's face.

Fortunately, for Pete, they were on a little travelled back road. He was able to steer the car to a stop on the shoulder.

"Get back," Pete growled at Mary Alice. He waited until she had taken her hands off the steering wheel then glanced back to make sure Nancy wasn't fixing to come at him again.

Pete got out and rounded the front of the car, never taking the gun off Mary Alice.

"Get out." He opened the front passenger door and then the rear door.

Both ladies got out and huddled together on the side of the road.

Pete looked up and down the road to make sure no one was coming in either direction. He then went around to the trunk and got some rope he had noticed there earlier.

He pulled Mary Alice to the side of the car and bound her hands and feet and pushed her into the back seat.

He turned back to Nancy. She held out her hands, thinking he would bind her up as well. She wasn't prepared for the backhand slap that sent her reeling into the ditch beside the road.

Mary Alice gasped and tried to go to her friend's aid. The way her hands and feet were bound made it impossible for her to get back out of the car.

"Don't hurt my friend," she yelled, still struggling with the ropes. "Please, don't hurt her. We'll be good. I promise."

Pete ignored her pleas and went to get Nancy out of the ditch. He reached down and pulled her up by her hair.

"If you try anything like that again, I'll kill your friend and make you watch." He shook Nancy and propelled her back to the car. He tied her hands and feet and pushed her in the back seat with Mary Alice.

The ladies looked at each other. Nancy had blood running down the side of her face and her eye was beginning to swell.

Mary Alice pushed her shoulder over to Nancy with an unspoken plea for her friend to wipe her bloody face on her shoulder.

Nancy gave a little smile and did as she was directed. She was touched. There was her friend all tied up in the back seat of a car being driven by a mad man, and she was worried about the blood running down her face.

"Thank you," Nancy whispered. "I'm okay. Did he hurt you? I couldn't see from the ditch where I landed."

Mary Alice shook her head. She was worried. What could this man possibly want with them? She had offered him money and a way to escape and he hadn't been interested in either.

"No, he just tied me up and pushed me back into the car. I imagine you took the hit because you're the one who grabbed him."

Mary Alice had learnt the hard way not to fight back when in the hands of a crazy man. She should know. She had been married to one.

"I can't hear what you two broads are talking about, but you'd better shut up. If I stop this car again, only one of you will live, and at this point, I don't care which one."

Nancy and Mary Alice fell silent and tried to find a more comfortable position, but with the way they were tied, it was virtually impossible. They could only communicate with their eyes, but each knew that the other would be ready to try to escape if the possibility presented itself. What choice did they have? No one even knew they were missing.

Pete drove along for the next hour in silence. He knew he was going to have to stop for gas soon. He didn't think he would have any more trouble with the women, but he wasn't about to underestimate them again.

He would do whatever was necessary to get Nancy back to Clint. That was his assignment, and he didn't intend to fail and have to face Clint empty-handed. The other one, however, was a different story. If she became too much trouble, she was expendable. This deserted, winding road had a lot of places to dump a body.

Night had fallen, and he knew he had to stop soon. His gas gauge was hovering just above empty. A few minutes later, he spotted a gas station around the next bend.

He slowed the car to make the turn into the station. "Listen, you two, I'm going to stop and fill up. If either of you makes a sound or try to draw attention to yourselves, I'll kill one of you and whoever else is at that station. Do you understand me?"

Both ladies nodded, but they were looking out the window to get an idea of what this new situation would present. They couldn't afford to miss the opportunity if one happened along.

Pete guided the car to the pump furthest from the station and any people that might be walking around filling up their own cars. There were only two more cars at the station. One was a family. The guy was filling up the tank while the woman was taking the kids to the bathroom and to get snacks.

The other car held an elderly man waiting for his wife to get back in the car before they pulled back out onto the road.

He waited for the family to all get back in and pull off before he got out to fill his gas tank.

He turned to the backseat before he opened the door. "Not a sound out of either of you. I would hate to leave some do-gooder dead if you try to call attention to yourselves."

Convinced, he had delivered his message across, he got out and filled the gas tank and checked the oil. He didn't want to have to stop again until he reached the boat. If his timing was right, it would still be dark.

That would work to his advantage. Not that he expected any resistance from any of the men on the boat. They weren't exactly knights in shining armour. They were a rough lot and tended to mind their own business. Besides, they all knew he worked for Clint. If their fear of him didn't stop any interference, their fear of his boss would. Once on the boat, he would be home free.

He went in to pay, with one last warning look in the direction of the women.

Mary Alice watched him enter the station. "When he comes back, I'll tell him we have to go to the bathroom. He can't refuse to let us do that. He wouldn't want a mess on his hands. Maybe we can climb out a window or find something to defend ourselves with."

With that plan in mind, they waited for Pete to get back to the car. When he was settled in the driver's seat, Mary Alice said, "We really need to go to the restroom. We haven't been in hours. I don't think we can hold it much longer. Old ladies have old bladders. We won't try anything." She would have crossed her fingers if it had been possible.

For a minute, Pete didn't reply. Then he started the car and pulled around to the side of the station beside the bathrooms. He watched and when he didn't see anyone else pull into the station, he opened the door and untied Nancy.

"Go ahead. I'll be right outside waiting," he said.

Nancy climbed out rubbing her wrists to restore the circulation. "What about my friend? She needs to go too."

Pete just smirked. "She'll get her turn as soon as you get back. Just remember I'll shoot her if you try anything."

With this warning, Nancy turned and entered the bathroom. She half expected him to object when she closed the door.

As soon as she was alone, she took care of business. She really did need to go; she had just been too scared to notice. She washed her hands and wet a paper towel to try to wipe the dried blood from her face.

Joe, where are you, she thought? *I need you. I don't know how Mary Alice and I are going to get out of this. We don't even know what this lunatic wants.*

Why would he abduct a couple of old women? He didn't want money, and he was willing to kill to keep at least one of them.

Knowing Joe couldn't hear her silent thoughts, she looked around for something to use as a weapon. Nothing. Not even an old comb left behind by another who had stopped to use the facilities.

Finally, knowing it would do no good to put it off any longer, she opened the door and stood patiently while Pete retied her hands and feet and pushed her back into the car.

Then it was Mary Alice's turn. He untied her and repeated the same warning he had given to Nancy.

When Mary Alice went in and shut the door, the first thing she did was the search for anything that could be used as a weapon. It would have to be something small. Something she could slip in her pocket and would go unnoticed when Pete tied her back up.

Like with Nancy, she saw nothing that would help, so she used the facilities and washed and dried her hands on a paper towel. Just as she turned to leave, she noticed something on the wall that all ladies' restrooms had. A tampon machine. She searched her pockets for change and found enough to buy four. Slipping them deep into her front pocket, she opened the door and went out. She had no idea what she could do with them, but they were better than nothing.

Within a few minutes, Pete had her retied and back in the car. He was glad to be back on the road. He had stayed longer at that station than he wanted to. The longer it took to get back to the boat, the more chance he could get caught. If he did, he would take the two old ladies out just on principle. At that point, he would have nothing to lose anyway.

As luck would have it, everything went like clockwork for the rest of the journey. The ladies were quiet for the most part. He figured they were worn out and had gone to sleep.

Nancy leant her head over and whispered into her friend's ear, "I didn't find a thing in that bathroom to help us. Did you?"

Mary Alice manoeuvred around so she was talking directly into Nancy's ear as well. "The only thing I found was a tampon machine on the wall. I had enough money to get four. They're in my front pocket."

Nancy looked at her friend. Not understanding why her friend would think something like that could help them.

"Well, it was all I could find," Mary Alice said. "You never know what will come in handy. I don't know how they could help, but if we need them, we have them."

Nancy couldn't destroy her friend's optimism. "You're right. If we need them, we have them."

After this exchange, exhaustion finally took over, and both ladies slipped into a restless sleep. They slept shoulder to shoulder as if the contact could keep them safe.

Sometime after midnight, they felt the car come to a stop. They could smell the open sea but couldn't see a thing in the dark. Was this where this crazy man was taking them? Would they finally find out what he wanted and would he let them live afterwards?

Pete cut the engine and cursed under his breath. He might have known Jeff wouldn't have finished his job and be waiting. He watched as the boat got ready to leave the dock. He wouldn't be on it tonight. He would have to wait for Jeff. If he went back to the compound without him, Clint would

94

know they had split up. His boss had told him not to take his eyes off Jeff, and Clint would probably kill him if he knew he had.

He thought briefly about finishing off Mary Alice but decided against it. He might need her until they were on the boat. After that, he would finish her and Jeff as well. If Jeff wasn't alive to contradict whatever he told Clint, he could get by just fine. Clint would never know about Mary Alice, and he would tell his boss that Jeff had got out of line and he was forced to kill him.

Yes, that would work. With that plan in mind, he settled back to wait.

Chapter 12

Albert yanked his phone from his pocket and made the call. He watched as Hershel bent over Joe's still body. *Good grief,* he thought, *what could have happened to his friend?*

Joe was in excellent condition. He worked out four or five times a week. Maybe he ate a little too much red meat, but heck, what man didn't. A stroke or heart attack was all Albert could think of that would have his friend stretched out in an alley with no apparent sign of life.

Albert rushed over to Hershel's side. "He isn't…?"

"No, he isn't dead, but his pulse is slow, and I can hardly feel it. Are the medics on the way?"

"Yes, they assured me they weren't far and would be here in a matter of minutes. Can you tell what happened? Does it look like a heart attack?"

Albert was shaking. That was his friend Joe laying still in this narrow little alley. What if they couldn't save him? How would he ever be able to face Nancy with this news?

As he thought of Nancy, he knew he had to get in touch with her. He pulled out his phone and tried her number. No answer. He searched until he found the number for Mary Alice. He had saved her number, deciding not to take her rejection as the final word. He had thought to let her get used to the idea of dating again and then call and see if she had changed her mind. No answer.

He wasn't sure what hotel she and Nancy were staying at, but he knew someone who would. He dialled Memorial General and asked to speak with Beth Thomas.

Beth was another close friend of both Nancy and Mary Alice. She was a nurse at Memorial General. She had opted to work part-time in lieu of full retirement. He only hoped this was one of her days on duty.

If anyone would have known how to reach someone at the convention for Memorial General volunteers, Beth would.

As he waited for someone on the other end to page Beth, he watched as the medics arrived.

Hershel was pushed back as the men worked over Joe. He had a worried expression on his face. *Please, God, don't let him be too late*, he silently pleaded. He had been torn in two directions trying to decide what action to take regarding the Murphys. Now that indecision may have cost at least one of them their life.

Where was Nancy? Was she safe or had someone captured her as well?

Hershel stepped back over to Albert and waited until the other man finished his phone conversation.

Albert looked up. "I was trying to reach Joe's wife. She's at a conference for hospital volunteers. Nancy doesn't answer and neither does Mary Alice, the friend that went with her."

"I just got off the phone with a nurse at Memorial General. She's going to get in touch with Nancy and have her call me."

Albert squared off in front of Hershel. He was obviously upset. "Now, tell me again just who you are? Why you were looking for Joe and seemed to know something was wrong when he was delayed returning to the lounge?"

Hershel put his hand on Albert's shoulder, but the other man just shook it off. Something wasn't right, and Albert wanted to know, and know right now!

By this time, the medics had hooked up an IV and placed a collar around Joe's neck and were lifting him onto a stretcher.

"Let's follow the ambulance to the hospital. When we know more about Joe's condition, I'll explain everything. It's a long story and kind of unbelievable. Just know I'm one of the good guys, and I'm here to help."

Albert let Hershel lead him over to where Hershel had left his car. They road to the hospital without speaking again; Albert silently listing all the questions he was going to demand of this guy and Hershel trying to figure out how to explain this whole mess to Joe's friend.

And at the front of Hershel's mind, where was Nancy? Why couldn't they reach her? Had something happened to her as well? He had never felt so alone. If only he had known who in the marshal's office to trust.

As the ambulance pulled into the emergency bay at the hospital, Hershel found a parking spot nearly five rows over. *Busy place*, Hershel thought. I hope that means this is a competent hospital to handle trauma cases. He could still see the bruises around Joe's neck. Joe was lucky to be alive. Either his attacker was in a hurry or wasn't too good at his job.

The pressure it would take to make that kind of bruises should have broken Joe's neck but it hadn't. He had to figure out how that played into the pieces of information he had already put together.

If what he had first thought was correct, then this made no sense. But first things first. They had to make sure Joe was all right. And find Nancy.

By the time Hershel and Albert made it into the emergency room, Joe had been taken to the back.

Albert waited, with Hershel, at the nurses' station until they could get the attention of one of the many nurses rushing in all directions. A two-car crash out on the interstate had brought in multiple victims. Some of which were severely injured.

Albert felt sorry for these folks. He truly hoped all of them would be okay. He hated to hear children crying. It was evident someone's mother was in critical condition. Maybe in the back fighting for her life at that very moment. But right now, his main concern was Joe.

Finally, tired of waiting, Albert reached out and grabbed the arm of the closest nurse. "My friend was just brought in by ambulance. I need to know where he was taken and what his condition is."

"I'm sorry, but as you can see, we have a number of emergencies going on here. I'll be back and find out about your friend as soon as I can." And the harried nurse disappeared down a hall carrying two bags of blood and a stack of fresh towels.

Hershel put his hand on Albert's shoulder. "Come on. Let's take a seat over in that corner where we'll be out of the way. I'm sure they're doing all they can to help Joe. When things slow down again, I'm sure someone will come to tell us how he's doing."

For the second time, Albert wretched away from this stranger. Who was he anyway? Things had seemed to be okay until he showed up. But having no other choice at the moment, he allowed Hershel to lead him over to the seats in the corner.

Hershel took one of the chairs and waited for Albert to take the other. He was trying to decide how much to tell this guy. He knew nothing about him except the fact that he seemed to be close to Joe and he had been really worried about Nancy and the lady she was with.

Instead of sitting down in the chair beside Hershel, Albert picked it up and turned it sideways so he could get in Hershel's face without being too obvious to the others in the emergency room. "Now, tell me who you are?" Albert said between gritted teeth. He took the other man's measure. Sure, the guy had him by at least fifty pounds and was a good three inches taller, but that didn't worry Albert in the least.

Hershel knew he had to defuse the situation fast. He had seen men on the brink of losing control and knew Albert was just about to reach that point.

Besides, if an altercation started, someone might call the police. He didn't want the local authorities involved. They might contact his office to verify his identity. He couldn't take that chance.

He had to trust Albert. He had no choice. "Listen, I know you have a lot of questions and you're worried about your friend, but honestly, I'm here to help."

Before Hershel could get any further, the nurse Albert had stopped before, motioned to them from the hallway she had disappeared down earlier.

They both hurried to join her. "If you'll come with me, I'll take you to your friend." She turned and led them to a room at the end of the hall.

Both men hesitated at the door. Albert's animosity was forgotten. He was afraid to go in. What if Joe hadn't made it? He looked back at Hershel, all of a sudden glad for the other man's presence.

Hershel understood and nodded for Albert to go ahead. He was with him.

As the men pushed through the door, they heard the strangest sound. It wasn't coming from any sort of life support machine. It was coming from Joe.

Joe was sitting up in bed. They had dressed him in a hospital gown, and the IV bag the medics had started was hanging from a pole. A doctor was standing beside the bed trying to take Joe's blood pressure, but Joe was waving him aside and trying to get up.

The doctor was blocking Joe from getting out of bed, and Joe was blocking the doctor from taking his blood pressure. It was a standoff. The only sound was the gurgling coming from Joe's throat and the grunts from the efforts of the doctor.

Joe saw Albert come through the door and immediately the gurgles were directed in his direction.

Albert hurried over. "Hold on, Joe. Let them help you." He turned to the doctor. "Give me a few minutes and let me calm him down."

"Fine." The doctor backed away from the bed and turned to Albert and Hershel. "He's not in any immediate danger. His larynx has been severely damaged as well as his vocal cords. The bruising around his neck is going to be painful for a while, but if he keeps ice packs on it, that part should start to get better in a few days.

It's his voice I'm most worried about. He needs to be totally silent and let his vocal cords rest. They won't heal if he doesn't."

"I've got other patients to check on. See if you can calm him down and get him to be quiet. I'll be back in a few minutes and see about having him transferred to a room. I'm going to admit him for observation for a few days."

At this last statement, Joe sat straight up in bed again and started his gurgling louder than ever.

The doctor shook his head and left the room. The man was, obviously, deranged. Maybe his friends could settle him down.

Albert went over and gently pushed his friend back down on the bed. "Be still, Joe, and let these people help you."

He reached out and touched the horrible bruising that covered Joe's entire neck. "Man, what happened to you? I thought you'd had a stroke or heart attack or something. Who did this to you?"

At this, Joe again started trying to sit up and talk. Why wouldn't anybody listen to him? He had been brutally attacked. The worse part, he hadn't been able to get in touch with Nancy for days. Something was terribly wrong.

Albert could sense his friend's desperation to communicate with them. "Hold on, let me help you sit up, and I'll get you something to write with. The doctor said you need to stay quiet. Stop trying to talk. We'll work this out."

Joe quieted down enough for Albert to help him set up in bed. Albert propped pillows behind Joe and turned to rummage in the bedside table for something Joe could write with.

Hershel stepped forward and offered the pen and notebook he had taken out of his jacket pocket.

This was the first time Joe had noticed Hershel standing at the foot of his bed. His eyes widened as he stared at Hershel. For the first time, he was truly speechless. He recognised Hershel from the marshal's office, but what was he doing here?

Albert reached for the pen and notebook, not noticing his friend's reaction to Hershel.

Joe took the notebook from Albert and wrote something, but instead of handing it back to his friend, he shoved it at Hershel.

Hershel didn't have to take the notebook to see what Joe had written. One large question mark was all that was on the paper. He knew what Joe was asking.

What in the hell was going on?

Before Hershel could try to explain to Joe and Albert the twisted events that had led to them being in this emergency room, the door opened and the doctor came back in.

"Well, Mr Murphy, are you ready to be taken to your room now? When we get you settled, I'll call the police and you can give them your statement. The man that attacked you will likely be long gone, but attacks like this have to be reported to the police."

Hershel couldn't let that happen. But before he could come up with a good reason for the doctor not to involve the police, Joe took the matter out of his hands.

Joe motioned the doctor over and started to furiously write something in the notebook he'd been given.

The doctor stepped over and read as Joe wrote. He frowned. "I know you want to go home, but you need to stay a few days till we can make sure your throat's not going to need further treatment. Besides, you can't leave until you've given your statement to the police."

Joe started franticly writing again. The doctor waited for him to finish.

"We'll notify your wife. Just settle down and let us handle everything. I'm not comfortable with you leaving in your condition."

Again, Joe wrote on his paper and handed it to the doctor as if that was his final word and the doctor could do nothing to change his mind.

The doctor took the notebook and considered for a moment. "I know I can't technically make you stay. If you're determined to go, I can't stop you. Will you, at least, promise me you'll let your own physician check you out as soon as you get home?"

Joe nodded. He'd promise anything to get out of here so he could check on Nancy and find out what in the hell Hershel Bing was doing here.

"Fine. I'll go get your discharge papers ready and notify the police that they need to get someone over here to take your statement."

The doctor turned to leave the room, and Hershel knew he had to speak up now. He couldn't let the doctor make that call.

"No need for that, doc. I'm a United States marshal. I brought Mr Murphy in. He and his friend are in my custody. I'll take over now."

Chapter 13

Joe, Albert and Hershel waited for the doctor to finish his paperwork. No one spoke. Joe had finally given in to the pain and relaxed back on his pillows. Hershel was trying to figure out his next step, and Albert was just plain speechless. When the nurse came in with the wheelchair, Joe got up. He was more than ready to get out of this place and find his wife.

The nurse brought the chair closer to the side of the bed and Joe stood, resigned to the fact that they were going to wheel him out.

It didn't occur to him that he was naked except for the hospital gown. And that same gown was wide open down the back, giving anyone brave enough to look a clear view of his backside.

"Uh, Joe," Albert said. "You might want to put your clothes on before we go, especially your pants."

Joe looked around at his bare bottom. He had tolerated all the delays he was going to stand for.

He reached back to the bedside table and picked up the pen and notebook. He scribbled something, handed it to Albert, took his pile of clothes from the visitor's chair and headed for the bathroom to get dressed.

Albert picked up the notebook, and for the first time since all this had started, he smiled.

"What did he write?" Hershel looked over so he could see the paper.

"It says," Albert read, "I have had enough. Anyone getting in my way can kiss my rusty ass, and I'm leaving this gown open so they'll have a clear place to aim."

Hershel chuckled. "I'll go pull the car around while you wait for your buddy to get dressed."

When Joe was comfortable in the backseat of Hershel's car, Albert got in and buckled up. His mind was working overtime. Had his friend fallen into some kind of trouble he hadn't told him about? He was sure if Joe was in trouble, he would have come to him. He knew if Joe was in trouble, he would come to him!

"Stop this damn car! I don't care if you are a United States marshal. Show me some identification and you sure as hell had better start explaining what this is all about. No way my buddy and I are going anywhere with you until you talk."

Hershel pulled over to the side of the parking lot and stopped the car. He knew the time had come for him to come clean with these guys. They were in too deep now for him to keep them from getting involved. He knew this was going to be dangerous, but he had no choice. He knew Nancy had to be in trouble, and he was going to need help. Like it or not, these two civilians were all he had.

Hershel turned in the seat so he could address both Albert and Joe. He started with the telephone scam Nancy had been caught up in and the Murphys' visit to his office in Richmond. He explained about the informant in his office, which was the reason for him not wanting the doctor to call the local authorities.

"You see if that had happened, the local law would have contacted my office to verify my identification. Not knowing who the informant is, I couldn't take the chance on that happening."

"I was trying to let you know the two of you might have been in danger." Hershel looked back at Joe to see how he was taking this news. The guy had been through a lot, and they still didn't know if Nancy was safe.

He then explained how he had determined a drug ring was operating off the coast. "You see when we traced the path of the telephone signal, it bounced off the satellite to the middle of the ocean where no one should be. I listened to the tapes you guys brought to us, and something just didn't sound right. Some of the words and phrases this guy used caused bells to go off in my mind. He wasn't just a regular scammer. Something else was going on here."

"When I put all that together and figured out that we had an informant in our office, I knew the fact that you and Nancy had agreed to testify would have possibly put you in danger. If this guy was part of the drug ring and the informant had passed this information on to his boss, he couldn't have let you live to do that. It could have endangered his entire operation. You would have been a threat to him, and he would likely try to eliminate you. I had to warn you just in case. Unfortunately, it looks like I was right."

Joe and Albert sat in stunned silence. Hershel gave them time for this stunning turn of events to sink in. He watched as the expressions on their faces turned from blank shock to absolute terror.

"Nancy," Joe croaked. Her name was the first intelligible word he had spoken since his attack. The pain on his face hardened Hershel's resolve to find Nancy and bring these drug smuggling low life's to justice.

"Nancy is supposed to be at a hospital volunteer conference, is that correct?" Hershel asked his two new friends.

"Yes. She and Mary Alice aren't expected back before the end of the week," Albert said.

Joe tried to speak again but the words wouldn't come. He took his notebook, scribbled something and handed it to Hershel.

"Is this the address of the conference?" Hershel studied the paper Joe had handed him.

Joe nodded, then swallowed hard, as if that would help him get the words out.

"Find her."

The fear in his eyes broke Hershel's heart. If this was Rebecca, he would fight heaven and earth to find her. He had no doubt Nancy was either already dead or had been taken for some unknown reason. He hoped it was the latter.

Hershel nodded, started the car and pulled out of the parking lot. He had to come up with a plan. Getting to the conference centre was the first step, but then what? If Nancy and Mary Alice weren't there, he had only a general location out in the middle of the ocean and no idea how to pin it down or get there. And that meant that the ladies had been taken there for some reason. The only alternative was they had already been killed. He prayed that was not the case.

Hershel swung by the hotel so the guys could check out and retrieve their belongings. Albert had collected some ice from the ice machine in the hall outside their room and made some ice packs for Joe's throat. Thirty minutes later, they were on the road. Albert followed behind Hershel and Joe in his truck.

It didn't take long to reach their destination. They pulled up in front of the conference centre and found a parking space. The three men entered the building and stopped the first person they came across.

Albert took the lead. "Excuse me. Can you tell me what room the conference for the volunteers from Memorial General is being held in?"

"Sure. Just go down that hall. It's the second door on the left." He looked at his watch. "They should be about ready for a break. If you want to wait, there's a small lounge just outside the room where most of them will go."

Albert thanked the man and they headed in the direction he had indicated. Just as they reached the door to the conference room, it opened and a flood of people poured out into the lounge.

Joe scoured the crowd for any sign of Nancy or Mary Alice. They weren't among the crowd now gathered around the coke and coffee machines.

Albert checked the conference room to see if anyone was left inside. A lone man was standing at a desk in the front of the room. He obviously was the one conducting the lecture.

"Come on, guys," he said to Joe and Hershel, "this guy can tell us where the girls are."

They all three made it to the front of the room. By silent agreement, they let Albert take the lead. Joe would have never been able to make himself understood, and they didn't have time for him to write everything out. Hershel was a stranger, and it would have been harder for him to explain why he was asking about Nancy and Mary Alice.

"I'm sorry to interrupt you, but we're looking for two ladies attending your conference, Nancy Murphy and Mary Alice Baker."

The guy looked up as Albert spoke. "Yes, they're attending, but they didn't show up this morning. They didn't let me know they weren't going to be here either. I must say I was a little upset about that. We're on a pretty tight schedule, and I don't have time to play catch up with them."

Albert didn't like the guy's attitude, but now wasn't the time for an attitude adjustment. He'd file that away for later.

Joe had been writing in his notebook while Albert had been talking. He figured when this was over, and he and Nancy were back at home, they could read all his scribblings together and she would get a kick out of them. He had to keep thinking this way. The alternative just wasn't acceptable.

He touched Albert's shoulder and handed him the notebook. Albert thanked the guy and took the notebook to see what his friend had written.

As they filed back out of the room, Albert said, "Joe says the girls are staying at the hotel just down the block. Let's go check it out."

The three men walked the short distance and entered the hotel lobby. When they explained who they were looking for, the desk clerk agreed to let them in the room to check on the girls.

What they found just reinforced what they already knew. Nancy and Mary Alice were in trouble. The room looked like they had just left for their class and intended to be back when it was over. Only they weren't back, and they hadn't been to the class at all today. That meant they had to be missing since yesterday.

"Standing here isn't doing any good," Hershel said. "Let's gather up their things and head back to Hadbury on the slight chance they might have gone back there for some reason.

Maybe an emergency had come up and they had to leave in a hurry."

All three men knew this was probably not the case, but neither wanted to voice what they were all thinking.

Hershel got back in his car and Albert into his truck. Joe didn't have a key to Mary Alice's car, but he knew how to get it started without one.

The trip back to Hadbury was made mostly in silence. Hershel was trying to come up with a plan of action but wasn't getting very far. He just didn't know what direction to go in or where to start searching. Albert was thinking about Mary Alice and the missed opportunities for a chance at a relationship that might have developed into something much more. Joe was just wondering how he would live if they didn't find Nancy.

They pulled into the parking lot at the gym just before dark. Albert pulled all the way around back where he usually parked and where Joe had left his car.

The backlot was empty. Joe's car was gone. He turned back as the other two men parked and got out. "Your car's gone, Joe," he said. Two missing women, an attack on his best friend, a stranger claiming to be a United States marshal, and now a missing car. He wanted to hit someone but he couldn't hit his friend, and the other guy was too big and might arrest him.

Joe and Albert just stared at each other, but Hershel came forward and laid a hand on each man's shoulder.

"Think a minute, guys. If someone needed a car, they would be looking for one that wouldn't be missed for a while. The guy who attacked Joe couldn't be the same one who abducted the ladies. There has to be two of them, and they needed a second ride. They, obviously, left Joe for dead. And since there was no sign of violence at the hotel room, I'd say, they took the girls for some reason. Maybe as hostages in case Joe's murder left them trying to flee this area and they were afraid of being apprehended. It makes sense. That means Nancy and Mary Alice are probably all right for now, but we need to find them, and soon."

Joe ran back to Mary Alice's car to retrieve his notebook. He scribbled something as he got back to the other two. He held up the paper. GPS. My car has a GPS, and I know how to track it. Let's get to my house, and I'll show you.

All three got back into Hershel's car, but he didn't head back to Joe's house. He was taking Joe to the hospital first to be checked out. The doctor had been worried about Joe leaving the hospital. He must have had a good reason. It was bad enough taking two civilians into a dangerous situation without one of them already needing medical attention.

When he explained this to Joe and Albert, he didn't get an argument from either man. He figured they were too thankful to have a plan and a chance of getting the girls back unharmed. Hershel hoped it would turn out that way.

Hershel entered the drive to Memorial General and pulled around to the emergency room entrance. They explained to the front desk clerk that Joe had been under the care of another doctor and had been released but instructed to stop in here and be checked out when he got back home. They were shown to a room to wait for the doctor.

After waiting for about thirty minutes, Hershel walked to the door and was nearly bowled over by an angry, petit dynamo in a nurse's uniform.

Before any of them could speak, she held up her hands for silence. She pointed at Joe. "Where's Nancy?" Joe just shook his head; he couldn't write that fast. She then pointed at Albert. "Where's Mary Alice?" Albert figured Joe had got by with it, so he just shook his head too. Finally, the dynamo turned on Hershel. "And who the hell are you?"

She slapped her hands down on the exam table and pointed at Joe. "Sit."

Joe sat, and Albert introduced Beth to Hershel who gave an abbreviated account of the events that had occurred over the last few days.

As she examined Joe's neck and ran a series of tests, she narrowed her eyes at Hershel. "Well, Mr United States Marshal, what do you intend to do to get my friends back?"

Hershel explained how they planned to track Joe's car through its GPS. He wasn't sure where that would lead them, but he wasn't going to tell her that. She reminded him of someone but couldn't quite put his finger on who.

All of a sudden, he went still. Oh lord, it couldn't be. Not two in this world. Change out her straight auburn hair with black curls, change out her white porcelain skin with a dark dusky completion and you would have Rebecca! And he had just spilt his guts to her. This must be some kind of punishment for the lies he had told his wife.

Beth finished with Joe and started tidying up the room for the next unfortunate soul who would need it.

"You know I'm going with you, don't you?" Beth dropped this bombshell like she was asking if they wanted to go to lunch. "Now before you say a word, think about it. You're going after criminals who just might be a tad desperate. You already have one injured man, and you have no idea what shape the girls might be in. Besides that, what if someone else gets hurt, like Albert or even you, Hershel? You need someone with medical experience. I'm not a doctor, but I'm the next best thing. I hold up well under pressure. After all, look where I work. Twenty-eight years of pressure, and I'm still standing."

She put the last of the supplies away and turned to face the three large speechless men in front of her.

Hershel was the first to capitulate. He knew her kind. Hell, he was married to one exactly like her. Except, of course, for the hair and complexion. Besides, what she said made sense. They didn't know what they were going to run into when and if they found the girls. Her medical knowledge might mean the difference between them all getting back alive.

"All right," Hershel said, "but you have to be ready to go when we get back. We're going to Joe's house and pick up the equipment we need to track Joe's car.

We'll gather up everything I think we might need and be back in a couple of hours. Be ready. We don't have much time."

With that, he turned and walked out of the emergency room and back to his car. The other two men were not far behind.

When they reached the car, Albert said, "What just happened back there? How could you give in so easy? I would have thought you would have put up a fight about her going."

"I learned a long time ago that discretion is the better part of valour. Learning that lesson has many times enabled me to live to fight another day." Hershel was dead serious.

"They teach you that at the academy?" Albert said.

"No, Albert, my wife taught me that."

With those words of wisdom, he got in and started the car.

Chapter 14

Jeff slowly backed away from Joe's body and eased down the dark alley to where he had left Joe's car parked.

He hated what he had been forced to do. Smuggling drugs and working for scum like Clint Montgomery was bad enough, but leaving Joe in that alley was different. Even to Jeff's criminal mind, it was just wrong.

Well, nothing could be done about it now; it was done. He knew Clint would have killed him if he had gone back to the compound without completing this assignment. That's the reason he had taken the picture of Joe's body.

He and Pete had separated when they had reached Hadbury and found that Joe and Nancy Murphy had each left town for different locations. Joe had gone with his friend to buy gym equipment and Nancy had gone with a friend to some kind of conference.

Clint had told them to kill Joe and take Nancy hostage and bring her back to the compound. Clint didn't trust Jeff and had told Pete to watch him.

Jeff had been surprised when Pete had agreed to split up and each taking one of the targets. If Cliff found out that Pete had let Jeff out of his sight, Pete would be in big trouble.

That was another good reason for the picture. He could prove he had taken care of his assignment, and Pete couldn't dispute it. Pete hadn't been there, but he couldn't tell his boss that.

He knew Pete hated him and would kill him if he got the chance. He figured Pete would try something while they were away from the island and away from their boss's watchful eyes. Even though Pete was Clint's first lieutenant, he was still afraid of him.

If the opportunity to take Jeff out had not presented itself before they returned to the island, Pete would have made it seem as if Jeff had botched his assignment. Another reason for the picture.

Jeff had a long drive back to the boat. If things had gone smoother for Pete than they had for him, Pete would already be there. He wondered what Pete would do with Nancy. He couldn't kill her because Clint wanted her brought back alive. But Pete had a mean streak. Short of killing her, Pete might do anything. Especially, if the woman gave him any trouble. He could always justify a few bruises, especially, if some of them didn't show.

Jeff thought about stopping somewhere for the night but quickly rejected the idea. He hadn't worried about driving Joe's stolen car before and Joe certainly wasn't in any condition to report it now. But there was still the guy Joe had been travelling with. As soon as he was back in Hadbury, he would notice the missing car and report it.

He also had another pressing reason to get back. He knew Clint had set up a meeting with his drug supplier and he wanted to be on hand for that. He didn't know who this guy was but he needed to. He needed more information than he had now to set his plan in action.

Jeff knew he would pass through a small town in the next couple of miles. He could gas up there and get a bite to eat. Most small towns had a truck stop, and that would work fine for him. Truck stops had a lot of strangers coming and going, so one more wouldn't stand out.

This must be my lucky day, Jeff thought to himself. He could see the sign and lights for the truck stop up ahead, and he didn't even have to go all the way into town to find it.

He could gas up, get something to eat and then bypass the town altogether. That would be even better. Unless Joe's friend got hung up with the law, it wouldn't take him long to handle the details of getting Joe back home and be back in Hadbury. He had no way of knowing how much more time he would have before the car would be reported stolen.

Jeff pulled up to the pumps and started filling the tank. He watched as the different trucks came and went. He wondered what it would have been like if his life had taken a different direction. If he hadn't ended up working for a man like Clint and all the others that had come before him. If he had not done all the things he had either chose or was forced to do in his life.

Would he be like these truckers, free to come and go and travel the roads without worry of being arrested? Would he have a wife and kids? He liked kids. Heck, he was still a young man. It wasn't too late to have a wife and kids. Only it was. He was in too deep with the wrong kind of people. People who didn't value having a wife and kids except as a market for their drugs.

He thought of having a son. A son getting hooked on drugs and ending up in some alley dead of an overdose. It made him sick. He couldn't think of that. He had a job to do.

Besides, he gave up his chance for a family life a long time ago. He couldn't go back now. He had a job to do.

Jeff mentally shook himself. Where had these thoughts come from? He finished filling the tank and went inside to pay.

When that was taken care of, he slid into a booth and picked up a menu.

"Do you need a few minutes or have you decided?"

Jeff looked up to see a young waitress with her pad ready to take his order. She had put a glass of water and some silverware. He had not even realised she was there until she spoke. Back at the compound, that kind of inattention would get him killed.

"Thanks. I think I'll have the hamburger steak and all the trimmings. Do you have any fresh coffee made? I could sure use a cup?"

The waitress smiled. "I just put on a pot. I'll put your order in and check on the coffee." And she was gone.

She was nice, he thought. He wondered if she was married, had kids? He hoped she had a good life and never got involved with a man like him. He would be poison for any decent woman. He was sure this nice lady deserved better.

Jeff finished his meal, left a nice tip and was back on the road in under an hour. He wanted to reach the boat before midnight. That's when it would sail, and he didn't want to spend the night waiting for the next one. Or waiting for Pete to make his move. A move Jeff was sure was coming.

Jeff couldn't afford to draw attention to himself by speeding. He glanced at his watch and checked his speed. It was only ten o'clock. He still had time. He switched on the radio. Maybe he could catch the news and find out if Joe's body had been found.

Joe's friend had been inside in the lounge. At some point, he would have gone looking for Joe. He probably would have searched the hotel and out the front where his truck was parked before he would have gone out into the alley. All that buying him more time.

He listened to the radio, but when the news came on, there was no mention of a body being found. Not even an unidentified one. Sometimes, the authorities didn't release the name of the victim until the family was notified. In this case, it wouldn't be released for a long time. They would have to locate his wife first and that didn't seem likely.

He turned off the radio and drove on in silence. He needed to think. His first plan had gone south when his former associates had been eliminated. He had been on his own after that until he was able to hook up with Clint. He knew that could go bad at any time. He needed a backup plan. But for now, he would have to play it by ear.

At a quarter after eleven, Jeff drove into the parking lot at the dock. He could smell the open water and see the dock reflected in the dim lights. This particular dock wasn't well-lighted. A lot of illegal activity took place here. Perfect for the comings and goings of men like Clint and his bunch of smugglers. The men who sailed from this dock would look the other way for the right price.

If Jeff chose here to try to eliminate him, his body would never be found, and Pete could tell Clint whatever story he wanted to about why Jeff had not returned with him.

He pulled into a parking spot in the darkest corner of the lot. He hadn't seen Pete or the BMW they had stolen when they had got off the boat four days ago.

He took out his gun just in case of an ambush. The shadows were thick in this part of the lot, and it was hard to tell if anyone was hiding amongst the thick growth of trees and scrubby bushes. He stopped to listen. All he could hear were the waves hitting the dock.

As he made his way closer to the dock, he noticed a small building off to the side. He eased up to the only window he could see through.

There was Pete, hovering over not one but two women. He seemed to be threatening them with his gun. His back was to the window, so Jeff was able to watch for a few minutes without being observed.

Pete yanked one of the women up and had the gun pressed against her head. He seemed to be trying to pull her toward a small side door.

Jeff didn't understand what was going on, but he had seen enough. He silently crept around to the door and was standing there when Pete opened it with the frightened woman.

"What the hell are you doing?" Jeff said as he knocked the gun from Pete's hand. "Who is this woman? You were just supposed to kidnap the one."

Pete was so startled by Jeff's sudden appearance he let go of Mary Alice and grabbed his gun from the ground where Jeff had knocked it.

"Sneaking up on me like that will get you killed," Pete said, obviously upset that Jeff had been able to take him by surprise. That wasn't exactly how he had planned their reunion to go. In his version, he would have the upper hand and Jeff wouldn't walk away with his life.

Mary Alice took the opportunity to run back inside to Nancy who was tied up against the far wall. She frantically tried to untie her friend's hands and feet. She was so tightly bound

Mary Alice couldn't loosen the knots. She fell down and wrapped her arms around her friend as if to protect her.

Jeff pushed by Pete and walked over to where Nancy and Mary Alice were huddled together.

"Do you want to explain what's going on?" Jeff stared at the other man, knowing he wasn't going to like his answer.

"I had no choice," Pete said, as he placed his gun again in his holster. "I couldn't take one without the other. When I caught her," he pointed to Nancy, "she," he pointed to Mary Alice, "would have alerted the cops before I could have got half a block. I had to bring them both. I was just fixing to correct that little mistake when you came up and knocked the gun out of my hand. She has outlived her usefulness now, and I'm going to take care of her."

With this, Pete grabbed Mary Alice again and started pushing her toward the door. The sound of an approaching boat made him hesitate.

Jeff intervened once again. "Are you crazy? Don't shoot her here. Wait till we get on board and out to sea, and then you can dump her overboard. That way her body will never be found."

Jeff walked over and pulled Nancy to her feet. It was time to get on board the boat and back to the compound. Pete was going to blow this entire assignment with his crazy desire to kill someone.

He noticed the way the women were tied and, for a moment, felt anger on their behalf. Pete hadn't needed to tie them that way. He could see that the circulation was cut off, and he was sure it had to be extremely painful. At the first opportunity, he would loosen the ropes. He was a criminal. He had killed, stolen and smuggled drugs, but he wasn't cruel by nature the way Pete was.

They waited at the dock for all the men to disembark and unload the cargo and the drugs that were to be taken to the island to be loaded.

No one looked in their direction. They knew who he and Pete were and who they worked for. They might have felt sorry for the two women, but not enough to cross Clint Montgomery and his cutthroats.

When the boat was ready to put back out to sea, Pete stepped aboard and motioned the others to follow him. When they were on board and had pulled away from the dock, he motioned them to the back of the boat.

They stood there for the next twenty minutes as they watched the land recede into the distance, then Pete grabbed Mary Alice and pushed her to the rail.

Jeff watched as Pete took out his gun. The man was smiling. He was enjoying this. Unlike Jeff, Pete loved to kill and would do so just for the pleasure of it.

Jeff slowly took out his gun as well. He didn't like Pete nor did he trust him. If Pete had a gun in his hand, Jeff wanted one also.

Nancy had begun to cry, but Mary Alice showed no emotion at all. She had promised when she left her abusive ex-husband, no man would make her grovel or beg again. If she had to die, she would do so without showing fear.

Pete raised the gun to Mary Alice's head but at the last minute turned it toward Jeff and fired.

Jeff had been ready and ducked to the side, pushing Nancy out of the way at the same time. Mary Alice dropped to the deck as well.

Jeff fired and hit Pete between the eyes, propelling him backwards over the side of the boat. He walked to the railing and watched as Pete's body floated on the waves and got smaller as the boat kept on its course.

He stooped down and helped Mary Alice to her feet and over to the other woman.

"Thank you," Mary Alice said as she sat down on the deck with her friend.

Jeff bent down and loosened the ropes on both women. "Don't thank me. I'm not much better than he was. I killed him to keep him from killing me."

And with that, Jeff walked to the rail and stared out over the water, leaving the women to themselves.

Chapter 15

Rebecca sat in the living room plotting her strategy. Hershel had been gone for less than 48 hours. She knew something wasn't right. Hershel had lied to her. In all the years they had been married, Hershel had never lied to her.

She had caught him stretching the truth once, and when she confronted him, he said it had been to keep her from worrying. He never repeated that mistake.

She took stock of the resources at her disposal. She had freshly-made chocolate chip cookies, and she knew which marshals were closest to her husband. If they couldn't be bribed with the cookies, she knew she scared them when she put on her tough social worker face. They had all seen her in action.

Her plan was coming together. She made three separate phone calls and began to set the stage. A warm homey atmosphere, fresh baked cookies and her scary face; yep that should just about do it. All she had to do now was wait.

At six o'clock sharp, one lone car pulled into her drive. Three men got out and hesitated before starting toward her front door. Evidently, they had a strategy as well. Safety in numbers. Well, that was fine. It just meant they were nervous.

"Hi guys," Rebecca said as she opened the front door. She put on her friendliest smile. No need scaring them if it wasn't necessary.

They came in one by one. These were her husband's most trusted marshals.

First, there was the youngest, Cliff Harrington. Like all the marshals, he was well-trained and good at his job. He was younger than the rest and hadn't been on the job very long. Hershel had been impressed with him from the start. He had told Nancy when Cliff gets a little older and loses that baby face and can control that blush that spreads across his face every time he gets nervous, he will make a formidable marshal.

Then there was Bill Everett. He was on the other end of the seniority line from Cliff. He had the most experience and had worked under her husband the longest. He and Hershel had formed a strong bond both inside and outside the office.

The last through the door was Andrew Long. He was the IT specialist for the Richmond office. Like with Bill, Andrew had worked with Hershel a long time. Another trusted friend. Hershel had worried for some time now that he might lose Andrew to a higher paying company. Andrew was the best; Hershel had numerous requests from others, both inside and outside the marshal's office, for Andrew's assistance. He also knew there had been more than one really tempting offer made to Andrew to leave the Marshals for a more lucrative job. So far, Andrew hadn't seemed inclined to make a career change. She was depending on his loyalty to help her now. In fact, she was depending on the loyalty of all three of these good men. Her husband was in trouble. She just knew it.

Rebecca led the three marshals into the living room where she had set out coffee, tea, water, and most importantly, chocolate chip cookies.

"Y'all have a seat. Since Hershel's been gone, I've had no reason to drop by the office and bring any goodies. I know homemade chocolate chip cookies are a favourite. Fix a plate and grab something to drink and tell me what's been going on in the office lately."

The three guys did as Rebecca directed. She grabbed water and had a seat facing them. She had given a lot of thought as to how to approach these agents. She didn't know how much Hershel had confided in them. It seemed he would have taken at least one of them with him. And yet, he was the only one missing. He may have confided something, but she was sure he hadn't told them everything.

They talked for an hour about what was happening in their lives and asked her how her job as a social worker had been going.

She could tell they were getting antsy and ready to leave. She knew they didn't believe her story about asking them over for cookies just because she hadn't been by the office lately.

Finally, Bill cleared his throat. "Well, Rebecca this has really been nice. Thanks for going to all this trouble."

When Bill stood so did the other two agents, Rebecca knew it was now or never. Her subtle approach hadn't worked. She had learnt exactly nothing about where her husband had gone.

It was time to change tactics. Rebecca put on her best scary face and held up one hand and pointed with the other.

"Sit." And all three men sat. They knew that look. They had seen it on her face when she was in court defending abused children. Each man was searching for his memory to figure out what he may have done to get on this little woman's bad side. Whatever it was, it couldn't be all that bad. She had made them chocolate chip cookies.

Rebecca paced back and forth in front of the three men. They watched and waited for her to reveal what this unexpected invitation had really been about.

Finally, Rebecca took a seat in front of them. "I need to know where Hershel went. And before you try to lie to me, remember who you're dealing with. I stand in court every day and chew up and spit out tough guys for a living. I'll know if you aren't telling me the truth." And then she waited.

After the stunned silence drug on for about a minute, Bill figured as a senior agent, it was up to him to speak for the group.

"We really don't know, Rebecca. He left the office and told us he had something he had to take care of. We offered to help, but he said he had to take care of it himself. Hershel's been acting a little strange for the past few weeks, but he hasn't confided in us. We really don't know where he is. I have to admit him leaving on his own like this is a little unusual, and I have been a little concerned. He hasn't been in touch with me since he left. He did say that if I ever had to step into his shoes and take over the reins of the office, he knew it would be in good hands. I didn't think anything of it at the time."

Bill took a deep breath and glanced at the other two men. They were nodding their heads in agreement.

Cliff spoke up, "I was in his office the day he left, and I noticed he was a little preoccupied. I thought it a little strange when he told me to let go of a case I've been working on. He said, cases like that didn't usually get solved, and I should shelf it and move on to something else." Cliff blushed a bright pink as he sat back on the couch and watched Rebecca. She had relaxed a little, but she still scared him.

Andrew guessed it was his turn, so he sat forward. "Hershel came down to the lab that same day. He was interested in what I had been able to find out about the Murphys' case. It was just a telephone scam. Come to think of it, I was a little stumped with the information I was able to retrieve from the tapes the couple had brought in with them. The scam had originated from a phone that was seemingly in the middle of the ocean. Not the usual for a scam devised to relieve an older couple of their savings. Hershel took a copy of everything I had on the case and said he wanted to review it if he had to work late for some reason."

Cliff sat forward. "Wait a minute! That was the same case Hershel told me to put aside. Now you say he wanted all the information you had been able to gather from those tapes? You think he didn't trust me to do my job? I know I'm the junior agent in the office, but I know what I'm doing." Now Cliff was a bright red and not from embarrassment but anger.

Rebecca didn't speak. She watched as the men put together the pieces. Now they were comparing notes and talking to each other. This was what she'd hoped for.

She let them put the pieces together. Hershel had been preoccupied ever since the Murphys had brought their tapes to the office. At the time it had only seemed like a simple scam. They felt sorry for the older couple and promised to do all they could. Unfortunately, these types of cases tended to go cold and never got solved.

So why hadn't Hershel confided in them? They looked at each other as the same thought occurred to each man. There was someone in the office he didn't trust. There was an informant in their office. Someone they worked with every day, someone they all had trusted. And because of this, their boss had gone off on his own and could be in grave danger.

Rebecca cleared her throat. The men had forgotten her presence, but at the look of fear on their faces, she had to speak up.

"Okay guys," Rebecca cut in. "I know you're the marshals and you're trained to deal with stuff like this, but we're talking about my husband. I knew if I got you all together and let you talk this out, you would come to the same conclusion I had: Hershel's in trouble. He needs our help."

"Rebecca, we're going back to the office and review those tapes and all Cliff's notes and see what we can piece together," Andrew said. "The office is closed. No one else will be there. We need to figure out who the informant is. We can't let him know we're on to him. That could put Hershel in more danger. We'll let you know what we come up with."

With this, the three men got up to leave. Rebecca knew they needed time to figure this out and make a plan, but if they thought they were going to Hershel's aid without her, they were very much mistaken.

Cliff, Bill and Andrew climbed back into the car and headed back to the office. Hershel had gone off on his own and was probably in danger. He needed them. They would figure this out. After all, that was what they did.

As they entered the building, everything was dark and quiet just the way you would expect in a building closed for the night. They made their way to the door of the marshal's offices, each lost in their own thoughts.

When Bill unlocked the door, he stopped and put his hand up to halt the others from going any further. Bill pushed them back and eased the door closed.

"Someone is in the office on the phone. I can see a light and hear him talking but not enough to be able to understand what he's saying."

"Do you think it's the informant?" Cliff said. "There's no reason for anyone to be here at this time of night unless he's making a call that he doesn't want anyone to overhear."

"I think you're right," Bill said. "Let's ease in and see if we can find out who this low life is. He's worse than an ordinary criminal. He's one of us. He's sold out not only the other men in this office but his oath to serve and protect this country. He needs to be stopped no matter who he is."

With this, the three men eased back in the door and made their way to the light at the far end of the room.

They listened to the one-sided conversation. They were shocked to see Jake Miller in Hershel's office rummaging through the draws in Hershel's desk. They were stunned. They hung back and listened. Maybe they would hear something that would lead them to their boss.

"He's been gone a couple of days now," Jake said to someone on the other end of the line. He wasn't talking on an office phone. It looked like a burner to the three men silently watching and listening to this traitor.

"No, I still don't know where he went. I don't think anyone else in the office does either. I'm going through his desk now to see if I can get any information that will help me figure it out." There was a pause. "You did what?" This time Jake's voice had risen. "You had that old guy killed and kidnapped his wife? What were you thinking? How do you know these goons of yours didn't leave behind some evidence pointing to you or even worse back to me?"

Jake stopped his search through Hershel's desk. "All right. I'll let you know if I find anything. In the meantime, stop doing stupid stuff before you get us both caught."

Jake slammed the phone down and turned just as the other three marshals stepped through the door.

For a minute, no one spoke. Jake went for his gun just as Cliff rounded the table and caught Jake with a fierce uppercut. He may have been young, but he knew what to do when someone drew a gun on him. And he didn't even blush a little bit.

"Man, you're fast," Andrew said as the other two agents reached Cliff. He reached down and pulled Jake to his feet and slammed him down in Hershel's desk chair.

"Well," Cliff said, "when you're the youngest guy in the office, you need an edge. Mine is speed."

For the next two hours, the three marshals interrogated their former friend. At first, Jake was belligerent and tried to bluff his way out of the corner he had put himself in.

"You can't get yourself out of this, Jake," Bill said. "If Hershel gets killed, you're going down for murder. The murder of a United States marshal is a serious thing. You won't get any leniency from a judge. You'll get the max. Death. If you help us get to Hershel before that happens, it'll go in your favour. You'll never be a marshal again and will serve some serious time, but at least, you'll avoid the death penalty."

"If I talk, I'm signing my own death warrant. These are ruthless men, and I wouldn't last a week in federal prison."

Bill just crossed his arms and stared at Jake. "You think you'll be any safer if you cross us? Hershel is not only our boss, but he's also our friend. These other guys you're so afraid of may try to kill you, but we'll make it our life's mission to make you wish you were dead."

With this, Bill stepped back and waited. Andrew found some rope and tied Jake to the chair and then handcuffed him to the heavy table. They weren't taking any chances with this guy. He was as well-trained as they were, and he was desperate.

While Bill took care of this, Cliff went to get all the information he had gathered on the Murphys' case, and Andrew went to his office to get his copy of the tape the couple had brought in.

If they couldn't get Jake to talk, they would have to figure this out on their own. Hershel had figured it out, so surely, the three of them could do the same.

When Cliff and Andrew came back, they joined Bill and waited for Jake to make up his mind who he had the better chance with.

"All right," he said. "I'll tell you everything you want to know. I know I've betrayed my oath and let this office down, but I never thought anyone would get killed. I've racked up some gambling debts with some bad guys, and I just didn't know how to get out of it. I have a gambling problem, but I've always been able to stay ahead of any trouble. This time, it got out of hand, and I was desperate. I'm not proud of what I've done."

With this confession, the other three marshals pulled up a chair to get all the information they could before trying to pick up Hershel's trail.

Jake explained about the drug smuggling ring and how he had passed the information along to Clint. "Honestly," he said, "I was just giving him a heads up if I heard anything that might be a threat to his operation. I didn't mean for it to go any further than that."

"Where is this smuggling ring located?" Andrew asked. "We know it's in the middle of the ocean, but where?"

"Man, I don't know. Honestly. They didn't trust me enough to give me their location. I only communicated by phone. If I knew I'd tell you. I have more to lose by not helping you find Hershel. If he gets killed, any chance for leniency is gone. Helping you now is all that will go in my favour. Besides, I don't want to see Hershel killed. Believe it or not, he was my friend too."

Andrew, Cliff and Bill left Jake and went to Andrews office where they went over and over the tape and checked again the location Andrew had pinned down where the call had originated from.

"See." Andrew pointed to a map. "This is where the call was made from. It makes no sense. It's in the middle of the ocean with only a few uninhabited islands close by."

"Well, it's a place to start," Bill said. "Let's take care of Jake and then see what we'll need to find this location. Even if Hershel went to see the Murphys first, this is where he would have ended up."

The three men now at least had a plan to help their friend and boss. They stood and turned toward the door and stopped in their tracks.

Rebecca was standing there, and she was dressed for action. No way were they getting by her.

Chapter 16

Hershel and his two new civilian agents stopped at Joe's house to gather everything they would need to track Joe's car. Time was important. Each minute took Nancy and Mary Alice further and further away.

They had already been by Albert's gym and picked up a few things they thought might come in handy. Between Joe's garage and Albert's gym, Hershel was amazed at what these two guys could put together. Maybe having a couple of civilians wouldn't be so bad after all. As long as he could keep them alive.

As they were packing the last of the supplies in Hershel's car, Joe's neighbour stopped in front of his house. "Joe, it's good to see you back. I see at least one of your friends found you. Sorry, you missed that other guy. He seemed really anxious to find out where you went."

The men looked at each other. Joe could still barely make a sound, so Albert spoke up, "When did the other guy come by? We must have just missed him." They were all wondering if it was the guy that had tried to kill Joe or the one that had taken Nancy and Mary Alice.

The helpful but somewhat noisy neighbour stopped as if to recall the correct day. "Well, let's see, that was the same day I bought Peanut his new collar, so it's been three days ago. Wait, it was just before your big friend there came by looking for Joe. I'm surprised the two of them didn't cross paths."

Hershel was thinking, *I wish I had crossed paths with that guy. I could have stopped some of this from happening to these good people.*

Joe wrote something on a piece of paper and handed it to Albert who passed it along to Joe's neighbour. "Here is mine and Joe's cell numbers. We are going to be out of town for a few more days, if anyone else you don't know stops by, please call and let us know."

The neighbour took the paper, promised to do that, then she and Peanut continued on their walk. She wondered what was going on. Joe hadn't said a word. And of course, she wondered about Nancy, but she had refrained from asking. After all, she wasn't one of those noisy neighbours who had to know everybody else's business.

"Come on, we're wasting time, and we still have to go back to Memorial General and pick up Beth." Hershel knew they were wasting precious time.

Albert threw the last of the equipment into the trunk of Hershel's car and climbed in. Joe followed suit and Hershel got behind the wheel.

As they pulled out onto the highway, Hershel noticed a storm brewing to the east. Just one more complication to slow them down. Storms this time of the year tended to be fierce. A tornado could form out of a thunderstorm in a heartbeat.

If they were able to track Joe's car, they would probably end up at some dock. That would make sense. The call, he had poured over, from the Murphys' tapes still buffaloed him. The only landmasses close to where the call originated were a few deserted islands. Well, he couldn't jump that fall ahead. They had to find the car first.

When they pulled up to the front of Memorial General, Beth was waiting. She was standing at the curb with a large bag, and then a small one strapped around her waist like the old fanny packs women used to wear when they didn't want to be bothered carrying a purse.

Joe watched as she stowed the larger of the two in the trunk but kept the small one around her waist. Couldn't women travel light anywhere? He wondered how many pairs of shoes were in that large bag and if Beth had her makeup in the smaller one.

He knew when Nancy, Mary Alice and Beth went anywhere together, they all had their makeup carefully applied and extra in their purses. He silently referred to it as their warpaint. The way they shopped for shoes, that description would fit. He wondered if there was any Native American heritage in their backgrounds.

Albert jumped out and opened the door for Beth to climb in the back seat with him. Joe sat in the front with his tracking equipment so he could give Hershel directions.

"Where have you guys been? What took you so long? You told me to hurry, but I've been waiting for thirty minutes."

Hershel mentally shook his head. This was going to be a long trip. At least she was on their side.

"Albert, I put my briefcase on the back seat. Open it and you'll see a map and a cassette tape. The map is marked with the location where the call to the Murphys was made from. See if you can determine anything about the islands closest to that location. Knowing the sizes and shapes and which are closest to where the call originated may help us later on. And pop that cassette into that player back there, and let's all listen to it carefully. Listen more for background noises than to what's being said. That might help as well."

Albert did as requested, and they rode in silence listening to the tape over and over for any helpful sounds. Anything that would help narrow down their search.

Albert and Beth studied the map and then passed it to the front seat so Joe could do the same.

Hershel waited as Albert and Beth poured over the map and then glanced over as Joe did the same thing. If he had to depend on civilians, these three weren't half bad. They were diligently doing everything he asked and weren't asking a lot of distracting questions. That was a good thing as he had very few answers.

"Wait. Rewind that last part again. I thought I heard something," Joe croaked from the front seat.

"Be quiet, Joe," Beth said as she rewound the tape. "If you don't let your voice rest, it'll never heal. Use your notebook and pen."

Joe wrote something on the paper, and when the tape reached the part he wanted to listen to again, he threw the notebook in the back seat.

"Not funny, Joe," Albert said as he picked it up off the floorboard. But he replayed the part Joe had requested and they all concentrated on the tape.

"Pause it, Albert," Hershel said as he steered the car to the side of the road and stopped so he could listen with no distractions. "What do you hear?" he said.

Beth had handed Joe back his notebook. He wrote one word, lighthouse, and handed it to Hershel.

"Seagulls," Beth spoke up from the backseat. "They would have to be fairly close to land for us to hear seagulls and a foghorn from a lighthouse."

Albert sat up on the edge of the seat. "I spent my summers with my grandmother who lived right on the coast. As a boy, I was fascinated by the ocean. I used to spend hours watching and listening to the waves. The sound of the tides ebb and flow are different from the sound the water usually makes as it hits the shore. What I hear is the tide coming in and going back out. Wherever this is, it's close to the shoreline."

"You're right, guys," Hershel said. "We now know the call was made on a boat but close enough to shore to hear seagulls, a foghorn from a lighthouse and the tide coming in and going out. We also know from the map that there are only three islands in that vicinity. It isn't that one." Hershel pointed to the map. "The lighthouse is on that one, and the sound we heard was too far away. It has to be one of those." He pointed to two islands on the map that looked to be about four miles apart.

As Hershel pulled back onto the highway, he watched the lightning off in the difference. They were headed right into the storm.

As they passed the city limits sign for the next small town, the sky opened and the thunder was deafening. Hershel flipped on his wipers, but they did very little to help.

"We just passed a truck stop. I'm going to turn around," Hershel said. "We need to wait out this storm. I can't even see the side of the road anymore. We've been driving for hours, and we need to stop and stretch our legs and get a bite to eat."

As Hershel pulled into the truck stop, the rain slackened enough for them to make a run from the car to the restaurant. No sooner had they got through the door than the lights flickered and went out.

A short bald man with an apron wrapped around his waist came out from the kitchen with candles and matches.

"Don't worry, folks. This is just a little southern thunderstorm. It'll pass in no time. Until then, we have plenty of candles." As he said this, he placed a candle on each table.

Hershel and his group weren't the only ones taking refuge from the storm. All the tables up front were full, so they made their way to the back of the restaurant. There were two tables left, so they took the very back one.

Hershel had been in law enforcement for a long time. It just came as second nature to guard his back.

As a young waitress made her way back to their table with candles and menus, the front door opened and two guys rushed in out of the rain. Hershel watched them as they surveyed the room and then made their way back to the only other table that was available.

Hershel couldn't say what it was about them that had caught his attention. They weren't really doing anything, but just the way they looked around the room made him uncomfortable.

"What can I get for you, folks?" the young waitress asked as she set the candle down on the table but didn't pass out the menus. "With the electricity out, all we can offer is what we already have cooked. The soup of the day is vegetable, and it's still hot. We have plenty of cornbread and the coffee is hot and the tea is still cold."

Everyone except Joe ordered the hot soup, cornbread and coffee. Joe didn't think he could swallow anything but the cold tea.

As the waitress wrote down their orders, Beth said, "Could you bring me a candle I can use to go to the restroom and wash my hands?"

The men didn't seem to mind eating without washing their hands, but she was a nurse and couldn't help thinking about germs. She would cut them some slack but she couldn't eat until she washed up.

The waitress was only gone a few minutes and she returned with their drinks and an extra candle for Beth. The two latecomers watched as Beth got up and made her way to the restroom, and Hershel watched them out of the corner of his eyes.

"Well," Albert said, "I guess it's a good thing we stopped when we did. It looks like the storm is getting stronger. Maybe by the time we eat, it will have passed."

As Hershel nodded his agreement, he looked over and noticed the two men were no longer sitting at their table. He scanned the room, trying to see where they had gone. No one had opened the door, so they were still inside somewhere.

Hershel didn't want to alarm anyone but he could feel in his bones something was wrong.

"I think I'll go check on Beth. She should be back by now," Hershel said as he got up and at the same time eased his gun out of his shoulder holster and held it at his side so no one would notice it.

He made it halfway across the room when two things happened at the same time. One of the men drew a gun and pointed it at the guy behind the counter, and the other grabbed Beth as she came back into the room and held a gun to her head.

"Don't anybody do anything stupid and no one will get hurt," the guy with the gun on the counterman said.

"We just want the money, and we'll be gone." He held out a sack to the man behind the counter and told him to empty the register.

The guy hurried to do as he was told. He didn't care about the money. He just didn't want anyone to get hurt.

Hershel was afraid to move. He hadn't taken his eyes off the man that was holding a gun to Beth's head. Hershel was an excellent shot and he felt sure he could take the man out, but he couldn't take the chance of Beth making a sudden move that would put her in the line of fire. She seemed to be fiddling with that dang fanny pack.

The next thing that happened would forever be impressed in Hershel's brain. Beth suddenly went completely still and the man holding the gun to her head got a really strange look on his face just before he dropped the gun and fell face-first to the floor. The distraction this provided gave Hershel the time he needed to raise and fire at the second man. He followed his friend to the floor and didn't move.

Hershel rushed over and kicked both guns out of the reach of either man should they make another move. The one he shot was trying to get to his knees, and Hershel pulled his hands behind his back and cuffed him.

He turned to Beth and the other man, but the guy was out cold on the floor.

"What did you do to him?" Hershel said as he checked to make sure Beth was unhurt.

She calmly held up a hypodermic needle. "He'll be all right; he's just taking a little nap." And with this, she stepped over his prone body and made her way back to their table.

The time it took for the local authorities to get there and haul off the two unlucky robbers held Hershel and the others up even longer than the rain.

When they were finally back on the road, Hershel looked in the rearview mirror and said to Beth, "You are even scarier than my wife."

Beth just smiled. "Never underestimate a woman, especially one that's a nurse on a mission to help her dear friends."

The rest of the trip was made in silence. Joe guided Hershel to a desolate parking lot beside a dock. It had stopped raining, but the lighting was dim and it was hard to see what was happening at the only boat docked there. It looked as if the boat was being loaded with packages that appeared to Hershel to be drugs.

He turned to Joe. "Do you see your car anywhere?"

They got out and kept to the shadows as Joe searched the parking lot. Finally, he stopped and pointed to the darkest part of the lot.

"There," Joe croaked.

They hurried over and searched the car for any indication of who had left it there and any sign of Nancy and Mary Alice.

"The engine's cold. It's been here a while," Hershel said. "The only way they could have left is another car or a boat. I saw no sign of tire tracks leaving this lot since that heavy rain. That means whoever left this car here left by boat."

"What do we do now?" Albert said as he nervously looked around them. He didn't like where they had ended up and was afraid of what Hershel would say next. He wasn't disappointed.

Hershel stood watching the men loading the boat at the dock. "We get on that boat and see where it goes. I have a feeling it's going to deliver a load of drugs to the very island we need to find."

"Won't we have trouble getting by those men?" Beth said. "They don't look like they will welcome us aboard."

"Let me handle it," Hershel said. "I have dealt with men like these. I don't think we'll have any trouble. Let's just wait for them to finish loading their contraband."

As the silent group watched, the men loaded the last of the packages and got ready to set sail from the dock.

"Come on," Hershel said. "Stay behind me and don't say a word."

The others followed close behind Hershel as he stepped on board. One of the seamen stopped in front of Hershel.

Not saying a word, Hershel pulled out his identification showing he was a United States marshal.

The man faded back into the shadows, and the others followed Hershel as he made his way to the back of the boat.

"These men don't want any trouble with the law," Hershel said. "They are just doing a job. They are afraid of whoever gets in their face at the time, and that happened to be me. I don't think we'll have to worry about them as long as we stay out of the way and leave them to do their job."

The boat had been moving steadily for about twenty minutes when Joe spotted something floating on the water. He touched Hershel's arm and pointed.

They all turned and looked out over the water in the direction Joe was pointing. A body was bobbing up and down with the heavy waves caused by the recent storm. It didn't appear to have been in the water for long.

Hershel turned to the others. "Looks like one of them didn't make it."

Chapter 17

Clint had prepared all day for the arrival of his drug supplier, Diego Garcia. He hoped they could conclude their business quickly and Diego would be gone by the following day.

He had prepared a meal from the limited supplies brought in by boat. He only allowed his men to build small, well-concealed fires. The island was supposed to be uninhabited.

Diego was bringing his five top lieutenants, so Clint had selected five of his own men to be concealed in the trees until Diego had come and gone. His other men would be visible and very well-armed. No honour among thieves. He had a nice thing going here and he didn't want Diego trying to take it over.

He had prepared one of the empty cabins for the outlaw and his banditos to use for the one night they planned to stay. It would be well-guarded as long as Garcia was on the island.

He briefly thought about Hershel Bing. His informant had told him Bing had left the office with no explanation as to where he was going or when he would be back.

The United States marshal was smart, and Clint knew better than to underestimate him. However, he could see no way Bing could have found out about his operation. If he had and was planning a raid on the island, he would have brought at least some of his men with him. According to his informant, no one but Bing was missing.

Clint walked around the compound one more time checking to be sure everything was in order for tonight.

When he entered his office, he decided to give his informant a call just to put his own mind at rest concerning Hershel Bing. He didn't know why he couldn't get the man out of his mind.

He took his private phone out of his pocket and punched in the number for Marshal Jake Miller, his informant. It was his good fortune to learn Miller had a gambling problem, and it hadn't been hard to exploit that weakness. Once he had Miller indebted to the right people, he had his informant.

He let the phone ring six times. No answer. He had instructed Miller to keep this secret phone on vibrate at all times and never let anyone in the marshal's office know he had it.

Clint disconnected after the sixth ring. The marshal's office should be closed now, and Miller should have answered after the first couple of rings. He always had on the few occasions Clint had initiated the call. The fact that Jake hadn't answered shouldn't have made Clint uneasy, but it did.

Before he could give this turn of events any more thought, there was a light knock on the door.

"Come on in," he said, as he took a seat behind his desk so it would look like he had been doing paperwork. He didn't want his uneasiness to telegraph to any of his men. He needed them sharp for the upcoming visit.

"Just thought you might want to know; there's a small boat in the channel," one of his men informed him.

Clint stood and walked around his desk. "Can you tell who's in it? Is it Garcia?"

"Sorry, boss. It's too far away, but I didn't see but three people. You want I should go down and wait for it?"

"No. Stay here. I'll check this out myself," Clint said as he pushed by his man and headed for the path that led to the bottom of the cliff.

Maybe it was Pete and Jeff with the woman. Clint was upset with both men. He had sent them on a simple job, and they should have been back long ago. How long does it take to kill one man and abduct his wife? They were an older couple. How much of a fight could they have put up?

When he reached the bottom of the cliff, he could only catch glimpses of the small boat as it made its way up the curvy channel. When, at last, he could get a clear view of the boat and the occupants, he cursed under his breath. What in the hell had they done? They certainly hadn't followed his orders.

Jeff could see his boss was in a rage way before the small boat reached the dock. The women hadn't given him any trouble since he had shot Pete on the boat over. They had only resisted a little when he had transferred them from the larger boat to the small one to make the trip up the channel that would give them access to the island.

He knew they were traumatised and probably exhausted. He didn't know how long they had been with Pete before he had joined them for the boat ride back to the island.

Knowing Pete, he was sure he had terrorised them if not physically abused them. He was certain Pete would have killed Mary Alice if he had not arrived when he had. If he had been five minutes later, it would have been too late.

Pete loved to kill and didn't need a reason. Pete had told him once he enjoyed seeing life go out of someone's eyes as they died.

Jeff, on the other hand, only killed when he had to. It wasn't something he enjoyed but didn't hesitate to do when necessary. He had found out early on in this line of work that killing was required to stay alive.

He had felt sure Pete was going to try to take him out before they got back to the island. So, he was ready when Pete had shoved the woman to the rail and had drawn his gun. Even at that, Pete had got off a shot that could have killed him if not for his fast reflexes.

One problem solved. The next one was waiting just up ahead, and he wasn't happy. Jeff had killed Clint's first lieutenant and was bringing back not just the woman Clint had sent them after but a second one as well. At least, he had the picture of the guy in the alley. That was the only part of this whole mission that had gone according to plan.

"Where the hell is Pete, and who is this other woman?" Clint bellowed as Jeff jumped out of the boat to secure it to the dock. "I sent you on a simple mission, and you couldn't even follow my orders."

Jeff turned to help the women out of the boat before he spoke. "If you wanted things handled right, you should have sent me alone. You couldn't trust me to handle it for you. You had to send Pete to watch over me, and he's the one who screwed things to hell and back. When we got there, the Murphys had both gone out of town, and they hadn't gone together. When I tried to talk Pete into taking the man out first and then grabbing the woman, he came unglued. He said as long as we weren't on the island, he was in charge. Then he sent me off to kill the guy while he grabbed the woman. Only he didn't take just the one. He took her friend as well. I wish he was here to explain all that to you, but unfortunately, I had to shoot him. He drew his gun on me after we were on the boat back and fired. If I hadn't ducked, I would have been floating face down in the ocean instead of him."

Jeff caught a movement out of the corner of his eye. He was just in time to catch Nancy before she hit the ground. The mention of her husband's death must have been too much for her. Evidently, Pete hadn't thought to torment her with that piece of news.

Before Clint could digest all that, he caught a glimpse of a boat making its way slowly up the channel. Damn, it was Garcia and five of his henchmen. He had let them catch him with his guard down.

"Take the women and lock them in one of the cabins. We'll discuss this later. At the moment, I have more important things to handle."

Jeff carried the unconscious Nancy up the hill while pushing her friend ahead of him. Halfway up, he stopped and looked back. He watched as the men below got out of the boat and greeted Clint. He couldn't hear what they were saying, but now he knew who Clint's supplier was. Diego Garcia.

Jeff locked the women in the last cabin on the compound. Before he left, he turned and stared at them a moment. "I'll try to get you some food and water but it might be awhile. We have more visitors, and it would be better if you stay out of sight. They won't help you. Just the opposite. These men make Pete look like a saint. They would kill you just for entertainment if they got bored." And with this, he was gone.

Mary Alice hurried over and knelt down beside Nancy who was slumped against the wall. She helped her friend up onto one of the cot-like beds in the cabin.

"Mary Alice, did you hear what he said? He said he killed Joe." Nancy was sobbing as her friend reached for her. What could she say? They had no way to know if that was true, but she couldn't stand to see her friend so broken.

"Listen, Nancy, these are cruel men. I don't know why they have kidnapped us, but I don't think we should take anything they say for the truth. Let's concentrate on getting out of here, and then we'll deal with everything else. Just hold on to the thought that Joe is a tough man. He wouldn't be easy to kill, and besides, he was with Albert."

With the thought of Albert, Mary Alice hesitated. The man had asked her out several times, and she had refused him. The thought that he too might be dead upset her more than she would have thought. Albert was a good man. If it hadn't been for the years of abuse she had endured at the hands of her ex-husband, she would have been attracted to Albert. He had many qualities she admired, and if they got out of this alive, she would have to rethink her response to him. If that is, he still wanted to pursue a relationship.

Mary Alice mentally shook her head. Why was she thinking about this now? Her friend needed some hope that her husband was fine, and they had to figure out how to get out of this place. Not that she even knew where this place was.

Nancy dried her eyes. The fear and heartbreak were replaced by a cold determination. "Mary Alice, you're exactly right. These are thugs. They would tell us anything to keep us subdued. Besides, I would know if Joe was dead. He's alive. I can feel him. We need a plan. We can't just sit here and do nothing."

Jeff had paused to listen outside the door after he had locked it behind him. He could hear the ladies talking, but he couldn't understand what they were saying. He hoped they would take what he had told them seriously. He might have killed, but he had never killed a woman, and he didn't want that on his conscious along with everything else he'd done.

Jeff turned away and hurried toward the path that led to the dock. He wanted to see what was happening with Clint and Diego Garcia. He had never met Garcia, but he was familiar with his reputation. He was ruthless. He wondered if Clint was up to dealing with a criminal of Garcia's calibre.

As Jeff approached the path leading down to the dock, Clint and the newcomers reached the top.

"Jeff, come on over here," Clint called to him. "I want you to meet our guests."

Jeff shored up his confidence and walked toward the group. He couldn't show weakness. Men like Garcia would pick up on that in a heartbeat, and then Jeff really would have a problem.

As Jeff reached the group, Clint said to Garcia, "This is Jeff Bloom. He's my first lieutenant." Jeff reached out and shook the bandito's hand. He wondered when he had become Clint's right-hand man. He guessed killing Pete had got him a promotion. He could work with that.

"Jeff, take our guests to the second cabin back. I have it ready for them. After getting them settled, come back to my office. I have another job for you."

As Jeff complied with Clint's orders, he wondered what would be required of him next.

Clint took a deep breath and retraced his steps back to his office. He wanted to try to call his informant again. He would feel better if he could touch base with him and be sure everything was still fine on that end.

As he reached his office door, he stopped one of his men and said, "We have two women in the last cabin. They are my hostages. Take them some food and water and then stand guard outside their door. They shouldn't cause any trouble, but I don't have time right now to worry about them. If they give you any trouble, kill one of them. I really only need one of them anyway."

As the man left to do Clint's bidding, Jeff was leaving the other guests to get settled. He noticed the other smuggler was getting some food and water and figured it was for the women. He thought he would stick around for a few minutes to see if Garcia and his men needed anything before he reported back to Clint.

Nancy was at the small window and watched as Jeff showed the other rough-looking men to their cabin. Something about his voice sounded familiar, but she couldn't place it. She was sure she had never met him before.

She watched as another man started their way with a tray and a couple of bottles of water. "Mary Alice," she called softly to the other woman. "A guy's coming with something for us to eat and some water. He has a gun, but it's in his belt. Are you up for a little action?"

"We've got nothing to lose, Nancy. We can't let any opportunity pass. We may not get many chances to get out of here. I'm going to hide behind the door and you stand there where he can see you. Try to keep his attention until he closes the door."

Mary Alice looked around for anything she could use for a weapon. All she could find was a chair that had been pulled up to a small table. She'd take what she could get.

She grabbed the chair and got in position behind the door. Nancy stood on the other side of the room facing the door as it opened.

When the man entered, Nancy ran to the window as if she was trying to escape. She was counting on him to just react and not realise she was much too short to actually climb out the window.

It worked. The man slammed the door behind him and set the tray on the table and came at Nancy. Mary Alice ran up behind him and swung the chair at his head. He went down and Nancy grabbed for the gun.

Just as she got it in her hands, the cabin door burst open and Jeff rushed in. Mary Alice jumped back, and Nancy did what she always did when she fired a gun at anything but a paper target. She closed her eyes and fired.

Jeff ducked and grabbed Nancy and knocked her back. Mary Alice ran forward to defend her friend. Just as Jeff wretched the gun from Nancy's hands, the door burst open again.

Clint ran in with his gun drawn. "What in the hell is going on? Who fired that gun?" He stopped short when he saw one of his men out cold on the floor and Jeff holding one of the women with one hand and a gun in the other.

"I thought you said they wouldn't give us any trouble," Jeff said as he let Nancy go and tucked the gun in his belt.

Clint stepped across the body of his unconscious man and grabbed Nancy by the arm and slapped her so hard she would have fallen if he had not been holding her.

Mary Alice ran forward and Clint turned and hit her in the face with his fist. She went down and didn't move. Clint reached in the back of his belt and pulled out his knife. He advanced on Nancy, and she backed up until her back was against the wall.

"Hold on, boss," Jeff said. "We might need them both for leverage. If you want to kill them, at least, wait till Garcia and his men are gone. We need to keep our attention on them right now. This can wait."

Clint hesitated. Jeff was right. They had more important things to deal with right now. He pulled out a set of keys Jeff had never seen before. "Follow me, and bring them with you."

With this, he turned and left the cabin. Jeff picked up Mary Alice and slung her over his shoulder and grabbed Nancy by the arm. He followed his boss down a path that wound away from the compound. Neither of them noticed one of Garcia's men watching from the cover of a small group of trees.

When Clint reached what looked to Jeff like a warehouse, he unlocked the door. Jeff had never been allowed to come back to this part of the island. The building was well-camouflaged and would be easy to miss unless you knew it was here. This must be where Clint stored his stockpile of drugs before he shipped them off the island. Good to know.

"Bring them in here," Clint said, as he swung the door open. "This should keep them out of trouble until Garcia leaves. I'll deal with them later."

Jeff pushed Nancy ahead of him into the building. He dropped Mary Alice on the floor and looked around.

Drugs were stacked against every wall. Jeff wondered how Clint got them off the island from here, but now wasn't the time to think about that. He followed Clint back out the door and waited as the other man relocked it. Neither man knew they were being watched.

Chapter 18

The three marshals standing in the middle of Andrew's lab looked guilty as hell. They had figured things out and had a plan of action. That plan, however, hadn't included Rebecca. The problem now was how to get around her. This tiny little woman was formidable, and it was her husband that was in serious trouble.

Each agent had witnessed her in court. They had seen her face off against defence attorneys, hostile parents, belligerent witnesses and even unsympathetic judges. She didn't give up, and she didn't back down. She was unstoppable.

The men backed up as Rebecca came in. "Well," she said, "it sounds like you figured everything out and have a plan. So, when where you going to call me?"

Bill had taken the lead the last time. This time, he kept his mouth shut. It wasn't his time to be the first to face off with Rebecca.

Andrew stood a little straighter. He was a good foot and a half taller than Rebecca. He had intimidated many a suspect this way.

Rebecca however, just smiled and walked closer to Andrew. "Where is my husband?"

She enunciated each word like firing bullets out of an automatic weapon.

Andrew froze, and Rebecca walked the rest of the way up to him until she was no more than six inches away.

She reached up and for emphasis poked Andrew in the chest as she repeated each word, "Where is my husband?" The fact that she had to stand on her toes to reach his chest, didn't make her action any less intense.

Andrew, having learnt the same lesson as Hershel about living to fight another day, decided to change tactics.

"Rebecca, come in and sit down. Let us tell you what we found when we got here."

The three men waited for Rebecca to take a seat and then joined her. They explained about catching Jake on the phone and his subsequent confession.

Andrew cleared his throat. "We were going back to arrest Jake and get him locked up. From what we heard from his side of the conversation, Joe Murphy may have already been killed and his wife kidnapped. We had planned to go to Hadbury to check that out, and depending on what we find there, we were going to use the coordinates from my map and the information we gathered from these tapes and track Hershel's location. We don't know what we'll run into, but we're going to be prepared to help Hershel whatever the situation is. I promise we'll bring Hershel home."

Rebecca had listened quietly without interrupting, but the stubborn look had never left her face. She was trying to digest what she had just learned. A man killed. A woman kidnapped. She knew these things were part of the job for a United States marshal. As a social worker, she had thought she had seen the very worse humanity could do to itself. But this was Hershel. Her beloved husband. The father of her children. Her marriage vows had said, *For better or for worse, till death do us part.*

"I'm going with you," she said, looking each man in the eyes. "This is your boss, but it's my husband. Besides, if that poor woman has been kidnapped and her husband murdered, she'll need someone to take care of her. She'll need another woman. I'm going."

For the first time, Cliff spoke up, "Rebecca, if we take you into a dangerous situation, Hershel will kill us. It's no secret in this office how important you are to him. How much he loves you. We kid him a lot about it, as men are prone to do. But when he's not here, we feel as if it's our job to take care of you in his place."

Cliff stopped and took a deep breath, his face and neck getting redder by the minute. From the look on Rebecca's face, he knew he had dug himself into a hole. He was a little young yet to have learned the old, live to fight another day rule, but his sense of self-preservation was as strong as any man's.

"Exactly," Rebecca said. "And how do you propose to take care of me if you leave and I'm here? I will tell you, and I will tell Hershel when we find him, if you leave me, I will follow you. How will you take care of me then, and what will you tell Hershel if I get myself killed and you could have prevented it?"

The men knew when they were beaten. They looked at each other and at Rebecca.

"How soon can you be ready to go?" Bill said. And just like that Rebecca was part of their group.

"I have everything I need. I came prepared. Let's go take care of that traitor you left in the other room and get on the road."

An hour later, they were on their way to Hadbury. The men talked amongst themselves, trying to come up with a strategy. They were going into an unknown situation, but they had done that before. The only difference: Hershel had been with them before, and this time he wasn't.

Rebecca was silent. She had crossed the first hurdle. In spite of her show of confidence, she hadn't been sure she would be able to persuade the men to take her along. She might very well not have been able to pull it off if it hadn't been for Cliff's little impassioned speech. He had given her the opening she needed. Later, he would probably get a lecture from the other men. But she hadn't been kidding when she had said she would follow them. She had come prepared to do just that.

It was around two in the morning when they pulled into Hadbury. The small town was still and quiet as most small towns tended to be in the middle of the night.

"We might as well get a room for the rest of the night," Bill said. "We can't talk to anyone until tomorrow. We'll get up early and find the Murphys' house. Maybe we can talk to some of the neighbours. I don't want to go to the local authorities unless we have to. If nothing has happened to the Murphys, I don't want to waste time with a lot of explanations that could tie us up for hours. If something has happened to them, it's too late to help them on this end. Our time would be better spent finding that island."

With that plan in mind, they found a small bed and breakfast and checked in. If the lady at the front desk thought it unusual for three men and a woman to be checking in at two in the morning, she was too polite to say so.

At seven, the next morning, the group met downstairs for breakfast. They needed to eat. It would be a long day. Breakfast was set out buffet style and offered a large selection from cereal to homemade blueberry pancakes with bacon and sausage. Coffee, orange juice and water were already on the table along with sugar and cream.

"Good morning," their hostess said as they filled their plates and took a seat at the table.

This time, Rebecca took the lead. "This looks delicious. Do you grow your own blueberries?"

"No. I wish I had the time. These came from the local market. I had twins last year, and now I'm doing good just to take care of them and this place."

"That sounds like more than a full-time job," Rebecca replied. She glanced at their hostess's ring finger, but it was bare.

"Surely, your husband helps when he can." Hershel had told her on more than one occasion not to meddle in other people's business. But heck, that was her job. She spent most of her days meddling in other people's business.

A sad expression came over her face. "Before my husband died, we ran this place together. It was our dream from the time we got married to have a place like this and a bunch of kids to raise in a small-town atmosphere. Well, I have the place and the kids and the small-town atmosphere, I just don't have Gary to share it with."

"I'm sorry," Rebecca said. "I was being noisy. That seems to be a habit of mine. I admire you for handling it so well. This place is just lovely, and you seem to have picked a perfect place to live and raise your kids."

"Thanks," the other lady said. She seemed anxious to change the subject.

"This afternoon is the one time each week I take for myself. I usually go to the gym and then have my nails done. It gives me something to look forward to. I'll miss out on that this time though. The owner and his friend Joe have gone to buy equipment, and Joe's wife, who is out of town too, usually watches the twins for me. It looks like the three of us will just hit the park."

Rebecca and the guys glanced at each other. Could she be talking about Joe and Nancy Murphy?

Andrew, who was on his second plate of pancakes, casually asked, "That wouldn't be Joe Murphy, would it?"

"Why, yes. Do you know Joe and his wife, Nancy?"

"I don't really know them, but I met them once. They seemed like really nice people. I thought we might stop by and say hello since we're passing through. How long have they been gone?"

"Well, they actually left on the same day; I guess that's been three days ago now. Nancy hasn't come back yet. She went with her friend Mary Alice to a conference for hospital volunteers that was going to last the whole week. Joe and Albert actually came back and left again. They had some guy I had never seen before with them. I guess it was someone selling gym equipment."

Andrew paused. "Was the man with them a large black guy? Maybe in his mid-fifties?"

"I only saw him from a distance, but yes, that would be about right. Do you know him too?"

"Actually, I do," Andrew said. "We were together the one time I met Joe. I would really have liked to have seen them both. You don't know where they were headed, do you?"

"Sorry, I don't. I just saw them from a distance standing in front of Joe's house, and then they got back into the car and

151

left. It must have been your other friend's car. It wasn't Joe's or Albert's."

Rebecca spoke up and described her husband's car. "Would that be the car they left in?"

"I believe, it was. I'm not good with car makes and models, but the size and colour are right."

The four travellers got up and thanked their hostess, collected their things and met back outside at the car.

They sat there for a minute, looking at each other. "Well, we know one thing," Andrew said. "Joe's not dead if he's with Hershel and his friend. Let's stop by the hospital and find out about Nancy and that conference."

It didn't take long to find out that Nancy and her friend were still at the conference, but that there had been a mix up of some kind. She and her friend had missed some classes, and Joe and Albert and another guy had stopped by looking for her. Joe had checked in at the emergency room with a problem with his neck.

"Do you know who Joe saw in the emergency room?" Cliff asked.

"Let me look." The helpful lady behind the information desk pecked on her computer. "Actually, he saw a nurse, Beth Thomas."

"Could we speak to her?" Cliff asked. "Joe is a friend of ours. We're just passing through and wanted to say hello. Now I'm a little concerned about him."

"I'm sorry, but Beth left that same day. She said she was taking a little vacation time and she wasn't sure when she'd be back."

Cliff thanked her, and they filed back out to the car. When they were settled, Bill had taken the wheel.

"Andrew, get out your map and your GPS on that fancy piece of equipment you brought along and find me the closest body of water and dock between here and that group of islands we think might be the headquarters for that smuggling ring. We have a lot more information than we started out with. Joe is alive. Hershel found him in time, but it seems like he was injured. And for some reason, Joe's friend Albert is with them. We also know that Nancy and her friend are missing. Hopefully, they are unharmed. It wasn't their intent to kill Nancy but to kidnap her. I would lay odds that the smugglers have Nancy and maybe her friend and that Hershel has enlisted the help of Joe and his friend to go after them."

Andrew did as Bill requested, and it wasn't long before they were on their way. Each was lost in their own thoughts.

Rebecca was thankful that at least thus far Hershel was safe. He also wasn't alone. She didn't know these other two men, but Hershel trusted them or he wouldn't have let them go with him. She felt a little better knowing he wasn't alone.

Bill was also thinking along the same lines as Rebecca. He too was glad his boss wasn't going into danger alone. But, damn it, he should have been with Hershel. If Hershel had trusted him and the other men enough, he wouldn't have had to rely on a couple of civilians. On one level, he understood Hershel's reasons. There had been an informant. Hershel had been hesitant to trust anyone with the lives of two innocent people at stake. But Hershel should have come to him. When this was over, he and Hershel were going to have a long talk.

Cliff sat back and let his mind wander. He had always wanted to be a marshal and couldn't understand how Jake could have sold out his badge the way he had. He knew he was young and a little naïve, but he couldn't imagine doing such a thing. He had faced a little danger since joining the marshals, but this time, he was glad to be with more experienced guys. He didn't know what they would run into, but he was determined to hold his own. He didn't have anything to prove to these other men, but he had something to prove to himself. He was worthy to be a United States marshal.

Andrew hovered over his equipment, giving Bill directions. He had found the spot where he was pretty sure the dock was located. It was just a matter of time before they found it. But then what? Where did they go from there? They'd need a boat to find the island. But that wasn't the only thing on Andrew's mind. He couldn't get the lady at the bed and breakfast off his mind. His heart went out to her. She had lost her husband and was raising their twins on her own and running a business. He admired her strength and courage. He also admired her looks. She was beautiful. Andrew had never thought much about marriage and children, choosing to put all his energy and time into his job. For the first time, he wondered what it would be like to come home to a wife and kids and a hot meal on the table. He had eaten takeout for so long he couldn't imagine doing that every day. The only home-cooked meal he ever got was when Hershel felt sorry for him and invited him over.

"Andrew, Andrew! Stop daydreaming. I've asked you three times where our next turn is." Bill wondered what was on Andrew's mind. They were all worried, but Andrew had been lost in a world all his own.

Andrew looked down at his equipment. "It's just about five miles down the road. Just before we get into the next town. I'll give you a heads up in plenty of time."

"Okay, then that's fine. Help me look for a place we can gas up and stretch our legs. We've still got several hours of daylight yet. There's no way we can reach our destination before dark, so it won't hurt to take a little break."

They drove on for several more miles. The scenery was mostly fields and forest. They passed a few houses that were set far back from the road. This was a rural country, as was a lot of this part of the state.

Andrew leaned forward. "Our turn is coming up in about a mile. Just before this next town, we'll take a left. I'll tell you when."

Cliff was looking out the window. "Bill, there's a truck stop up ahead. That might be a good place to gas up and maybe get some coffee."

Bill agreed and made the turn into the parking lot. He pulled up to the pumps, and everybody got out to stretch their legs. When the tank was full, they got back in and drove the rest of the way up to the diner.

They took a table just inside the door and ordered coffee when the young waitress came by with water and a menu.

She was only gone a few minutes. Lunch was long over, and the supper crowd hadn't started arriving yet.

"Can I get you anything else? We have some freshly-baked pecan pie that would go good with that coffee."

"That sounds good to me," Cliff said. He was young enough that his hollow leg hadn't got filled up yet. The others declined.

When the waitress came back and set the pie in front of Cliff, he looked up and just trying to be nice said, "This looks like a nice, quiet place to work."

"It is most of the time, but we had a little excitement earlier. We almost got robbed. If it hadn't been for a United States marshal and his friends, they would have pulled it off. It just so happened they were travelling with a nurse, and she stuck one of the robbers with a hypodermic needle and knocked him out. That was really gutsy because he had a gun to her head. Then the marshal shot the other robber but didn't kill him. The local police came and took the robbers away. It was the most excitement we've had since I've been here which will be a year next month."

By the time the waitress stopped to take a breath, Rebecca and the three marshals were on their feet.

"Can we get that coffee to go?" Cliff said. He wrapped his pie in a napkin while the bewildered young woman got their coffee in to-go cups.

In five minutes, they were back on the road. They now knew they were on the right track for sure. They knew Hershel had come this way. He had to be headed to the same place they were now.

It had been dark for a couple of hours when Bill turned into a dimly-lighted parking area beside a small dock. No one was around. No boat at the dock.

He pulled to the side away from the other cars parked there. They all got out and walked around. Besides the dock and cars in the parking lot, the only thing in sight was a small building at the edge of the woods. It looked like a storage building. They walked over to check it out.

Bill opened the door and walked in. He crossed the floor and picked something up and walked back to the others. It was a piece of cloth and it was bloody.

Chapter 19

Hershel, Joe, Albert and Beth had been standing at the back of the smuggler's boat for nearly an hour. After Hershel had flashed his badge, no one had bothered them. These men were the lowest on the chain of smugglers. They weren't suppliers or distributors. They simply transported the drugs between the two.

"I don't know much about boats," Beth said. "But it seems to me as if we're hardly moving."

Hershel nodded, "You're right, Beth. The high waves after that rain might be a reason. However, it's more likely these men are trying to figure out what to do with us when we get to the drop-off point. They're afraid of me and this badge, but they're also afraid of whoever is waiting at the other end."

Joe had found an old crate and upended it so he could sit down. He was still a little weak from being chocked and left for dead. Albert stood beside him watching his friend with a frown on this face.

They were both worried about Nancy and Mary Alice. What shape would they be in when they found them? Would they even still be alive?

Both men stood and walked over to Hershel and Beth when they felt the boat slowing. It was well past midnight, and the sky was still roiling with clouds. The moon only appeared occasionally and then not for very long.

Hershel walked to the front of the boat to see if they were approaching an island or maybe meeting another boat. He watched as a small vessel appeared as if out of nowhere. The men on board started to unload the cargo onto the smaller boat.

It was completely silent. No one from either boat spoke as they passed the packets of drugs from boat to boat.

Hershel carefully made his way back to the others. In a low voice, he said, "This must be the island. I can't see any way to access it. It's too overgrown with trees and bushes. I don't see any sort of beach. Let's slip over the side here in the back. Maybe we can follow that small boat with the drugs."

The three men went first. They caught hold of some low hanging branches and were able to find solid ground in the underbrush. Joe and Albert each reached out a hand to help Beth.

Beth had left her large bag in the trunk of Hershel's car, but she still had her fanny pack around her waist. She pulled the ends of her blouse out of her slacks and tied it under and around the fanny pack. She didn't want to take a chance of losing it in the water.

Beth then caught hold of each guy's hand and let them help her over. They then all eased back into the cover of the low hanging branches. They stood perfectly still hoping no one from either boat had noticed them.

They watched as the unloading was finished and the larger boat pulled back out into the deeper water.

"Come on, let's follow that smaller boat. It has to be going to a dock at the base of this island," Hershel said as he led the way.

Keeping up with the small boat wasn't easy. The terrain was marshy, and even though none were in sight, it was a good bet; alligators were around waiting for their next meal.

The channel was narrow and wound back and forth. One minute the boat would be close enough to see the two men aboard and the next it would be so far away Hershel was afraid they would lose it.

Finally, the boat reached a dock on a very small stretch of beach where other men were waiting with a cart of some sort.

Hershel held up his hand for the others to stop. They stayed hidden and watched the drugs being transferred from the small boat to the dock and into the waiting cart. The boat was left tied up at the dock alongside a slightly larger one, and the men with the drugs and cart started up a steep trail that seemed to go up the side of the mountain.

Hershel turned to the others. "Let's wait and let them go on ahead. We can't take a chance of them looking back and seeing us."

They had no way of knowing they were already being watched. Two of Clint's men flanked them on each side but stayed out of sight. Just watching for now.

When the coast was clear, Hershel took a deep breath and turned to the others.

"I don't see any way up the mountain except for that trail. There's no way of knowing what's waiting at the top. It would be my guess guards will be posted there."

He turned to Beth and said, "Maybe you should stay here and let us check it out, and if we find Nancy and Mary Alice, will come back for you."

"No way," Beth said. "I can help," and she patted her fanny pack. "I took out a robber, and I can take out a smuggler. If you guys go in with guns blazing, someone is going to get killed. If they're guards at the top, I can take care of them without a sound."

Hershel seemed to be thinking over what Beth was saying when Joe spoke up. His voice was hardly a whisper, but at least now he could be heard.

"I don't think we should leave her here alone. We don't know who else might come up that channel. Besides, she's right. She did great with the robber."

Beth rewarded Joe with a smile. She didn't even have the heart to tell him to stop talking so his voice could heal. She had no intention of being left behind.

Albert spoke up, "Why don't you go first, Hershel? We'll follow your lead. You're the marshal. We'll do whatever you do, and we'll put Beth in the middle so she'll be safe. If Nancy and Mary Alice are up there and are hurt, they'll need Beth to take care of them. Besides, if we leave her here, she might be in greater danger."

Hershel had no choice. He nodded. "Stay behind me and don't make a move unless I tell you to."

Working with civilians was, definitely, different from working with his men. What he wouldn't give to have Bill, Andrew and even Cliff here to back him up. When he got back to the office, he would charge a penalty on the informant, and when he did, he would strip him of his badge and personally see he got jail time. And if one of these civilians, who were so determined to find their friends, got hurt or God forbid killed, that jail time would be for life.

Hershel started forward, and the others followed in his footsteps. When Hershel slipped his gun out of his holster, Joe and Albert pulled theirs out as well.

Beth didn't have a gun, so she eased her hand under the front of her shirt and found her fanny pack. She took out another hypodermic needle. She wasn't sure she could shoot someone anyway. She was a nurse; she saved lives, not take them. But she sure as heck could stick someone with a needle. She did that every day and never flinched.

Clint's two henchmen followed at a distance. They were unsure of how to handle this situation. Clint had told them to stay out of sight. They were to stay hidden and watch Garcia's men until they left the island.

They didn't know who these people were, but they couldn't let them make it up to the compound. They had guns.

They signalled to each other and came out from each side of the path. One grabbed Beth around the neck using her as a shield. That didn't work any better for him than it had for the robber at the truck stop.

Beth stabbed him in the thigh with her hypodermic needle, and he went down. His friend was so shocked to see his friend hit the ground that he took his eyes off the men just long enough for Joe to act.

Joe caught him with an uppercut that knocked the hapless smuggler back against a tree, but Joe wasn't finished. He had been wanting to hit somebody ever since he came to in the hospital after being nearly choked to death. He grabbed the other man and pulled him away from the tree and hit him in the midsection. The smuggler doubled over and collapsed on the ground.

Hershel reached out and grabbed Joe before he could yank the man up and hit him again.

"Joe, wait. He's down. Let's pull them off the path and tie them up so they can't cause any more trouble."

Joe stopped and straightened up. He wasn't a violent man, but damn, he'd had enough. First, his wife had been scammed out of her money. Then he had nearly been killed. His wife and friend had been kidnapped, and now these goons had jumped them from out of nowhere.

"Sorry," he croaked. "Got a little carried away there."

Hershel slapped him on the back. "Understandable, man. You're allowed."

They pulled the two men to the side of the path, tied them up and covered them with a bush. They weren't going anywhere.

After making sure Beth was unharmed, they continued up the path. About twenty feet before they reached the top, Hershel motioned for the others to step off the path.

"We can't just walk into the middle of their camp. We need a plan. We need to see what we're up against and where the women are being held. Going in with guns blazing will only get us killed."

Albert spoke up, "You're in charge, but seems to me if we split up and work our way around the camp, we can get a good idea of how many we're dealing with and where everybody is."

"That's as good a plan as any, Albert," Hershel said. "Beth, you come with me. We'll go around to the right. Albert, you and Joe go around to the left, and we'll reconnect at the very back of the compound. Once we know how many we're dealing with and where they are, it will be easier to come up with a plan. And look for any sign of the women."

"Stay behind me, Beth, and don't make a sound." They eased off to the right, leaving Joe and Albert to ease behind the trees and go to the left.

Hershel counted men as they circled the compound. He saw a heavily-armed man in the midst of five armed banditos. They didn't seem to be part of the other men who were also heavily armed. It looked like a meeting of some kind was going on between the smugglers and these banditos. He would bet it was a meeting between the smugglers and their suppliers. Not a good situation for them to walk into. Their best bet was to find Nancy and her friend and ease back to the dock without being seen. If they were lucky, they could make it to the two boats he had noticed tied up at the dock.

They made it to the back of the compound without being seen. It was only a few minutes until Joe and Albert joined them.

"Boy, we could use some reinforcement about now," Albert said. "We saw a lot of heavily-armed men. Tell me you have a plan, Hershel."

Hershel explained his plan to find the women and make it back down to the boats.

"We don't have enough gun power to confront these guys head-on. And we have to find the women before we do anything else. Getting ourselves killed won't help them at all."

Beth had been looking around while the men were coming up with a plan.

"Look, guys, there's a path leading off down that way. Let's see where it goes. I didn't see any sign of Nancy and Mary Alice in the camp. Maybe they're being held away from the camp for some reason."

She eased off down the path and left the men to follow. The path led away from the camp and the armed men.

When they thought they couldn't go any further, they saw what looked like a warehouse camouflaged in the trees.

Hershel reached out and took Beth's arm to stop her from going any further.

He didn't speak but motioned to the building.

As they made their way around to the side, they saw a small window. It was the only one in the building. Unfortunately, the window was too high to see what was inside.

"Hershel, do you think you can lift me up that high?" Beth said.

Hershel just nodded. He could have lifted more than twice Beth's weight, but he knew better than to say so. Rebecca had taught him that one thing a man didn't talk about was a woman's weight.

Hershel lifted Beth, and she wiped at the dirty window so she could see inside. At first, she couldn't see anything except stacks of heavily-wrapped packages against each wall. Then a movement caught her eye in the far corner of the room.

She began knocking on the window and started wiggling so hard Hershel almost dropped her.

He sat her down. "What's wrong? What did you see? Is it where the smugglers stockpile their drugs?"

But Beth ignored Hershel and threw her arms around Joe's neck. She was crying so hard it was almost impossible to understand her.

"Nancy…" she said, holding on to Joe, and then she turned to Albert and said, "and Mary Alice."

Joe hugged Beth and then put her aside. His wife was inside that building. He couldn't get up to see in the window, and even though he didn't doubt Hershel could pick him up just as easily as he had Beth, he took off around to the front of the building.

He had come prepared. Not knowing what they would run into, he had stuffed anything he thought they might need into his pockets.

By the time the others had made it around, Joe had picked the lock and was opening the door.

Hershel grabbed his arm. "Wait a minute, Joe. We need to make sure they don't have guards on them before we rush in."

But Joe was tired of waiting. He had been sick with worry about Nancy for far too long. She was inside, and he was going in.

He stopped to let his eyes get used to the dark interior. And before he could move again, he was hit by a human torpedo, and Nancy was in his arms.

She was sobbing, and all she could say was, "Joe! Joe! You found us. They said you were dead, but I didn't believe it. I would have known, but I could still feel your spirit. I knew you were still alive."

Hershel looked around and then nudged them all inside and pulled the door to behind them. They had found Nancy and Mary Alice, but they still had to remain unseen and make it back to the boat.

Albert went further into the building. Mary Alice hadn't come forward with Nancy. Where was she?

He was halfway across the room when he saw her body crumpled in the far corner. He sprinted the rest of the way and bent over and gently took her into his arms.

"Mary Alice, can you hear me," he spoke softly as he brushed her hair back away from her bruised and bloody face.

The others gathered around them as Nancy explained how they had tried to escape and Mary Alice had come to her rescue and had taken a fist in the face for her effort to help her friend.

Beth gently pushed Albert aside and reached into her fanny pack. She had brought more than hypodermic needles. She broke a vial and held it under Mary Alice's nose.

They watched as Mary Alice slowly came around. She opened her eyes and looked directly into Albert's. She reached out, and he wrapped her in his arms.

"Listen, guys. I don't mean to be a wet blanket, but we need to get out of here. We could be discovered any minute," Hershel said.

They could all see the wisdom of this, and they filed toward the door. Joe was holding on to Nancy, and Albert was supporting Mary Alice.

When they got to the door, Hershel stopped them while he checked outside to make sure it was clear.

They slowly made their way around the perimeter of the camp and made it back to the start of the path down to the dock.

They had been lucky. They could have been discovered at any time. Hershel led the way down the path pausing when they came to the place where they had been jumped. He held up his hand for the others to stop.

He stepped over and checked on the men they had tied up and left in the bushes. They were still there and still unconscious. They were drug runners and probably killers, but he couldn't leave without making sure they were all right. They would be found when the women were discovered missing.

He stepped back on to the path and led the others to the dock. The boats were still there.

The others gathered behind Hershel while he untied the first boat. He turned around to help the ladies get in the boat first and froze when he saw the three heavily-armed men pointing rifles in their direction.

Chapter 20

Clint headed back to his office and motioned Jeff to follow him. He was upset with everything that had gone on lately. If he didn't have more important things on his mind, he would have finished the women off with his knife. He had wanted to. He never thought they would be any trouble. The cabin seemed secure enough to hold two old women. When he sent them food and water, he never suspected they would jump his man and take his gun. If Jeff hadn't intervened, things could have been worse. Who knew who the two old broads might have shot! He hoped that the roughing up would give them something to think about. Well, they wouldn't find it so easy to escape from the warehouse, and if they got hungry or thirsty, that was just too bad.

Clint considered his run of bad luck as he walked. First, he couldn't get in touch with his informant. If the idiot had got caught, he was all on his own. Clint wasn't just about to come to his aid. The man was expendable. He could buy or threaten another informant if he needed one.

Then Jeff had returned with two women when he had instructed them to bring just the one. And Jeff had killed Pete. Not that he cared that Pete was dead. The man had been stealing from him. It was just that he wanted to kill Pete himself in front of his men. Another example of what happened when someone stole from him.

Then Garcia had managed to slip up on him while he was confronting Jeff at the dock. At least, he had spotted Garcia before they reached the compound. He didn't want Garcia or his men wandering around unguarded.

Then the blasted women had tried to escape from the cabin. Well, he hoped the little roughing up he had given them would make them think twice before trying anything like that again. Blasted women. Where did they think they were going to go if they had managed to escape?

The two men entered the office, and Jeff closed the door behind them. Clint was furious and poured himself a drink.

It was a sign of Jeff's promotion that he turned and held the decanter up to see if Jeff wanted one too. Jeff shook his head. He needed to stay alert.

Jeff had to be cautious now. He had more to deal with than Clint's bad mood. Clint would have killed the two women if he hadn't stopped him.

And then, there was the matter of Garcia and his cutthroats. He had needed to know who Clint's supplier was before he made his move. He couldn't take over until he knew all the players and how the entire operation worked.

Clint took his drink and sat down behind his desk.

"Sit down," Clint said, as he motioned Jeff to a chair. He just sat studying Jeff for a minute. He had known after Pete was dead, he would have to appoint another lieutenant to help him. He had considered Jeff but hadn't been sure if he trusted him with this new responsibility.

Now, it seemed that he didn't have a choice. Jeff had completed his assignment. He had seen the picture of the dead man in the alley. He had returned with the women. He only had Jeff's word that it was Pete's fault he had ended up bringing back two women instead of one. And he only had Jeff's word that Pete had drawn a gun on him.

Hell, he wouldn't have any respect for a man who let another man draw down on him and lived to talk about it.

"Okay, Jeff. I've introduced you to Garcia and his men as my lieutenant. I've shown you the location of the warehouse where the drugs are stored waiting for shipment off the island. I've entrusted you with the knowledge that none of the other men that work for me have. Don't let me down. Men who let me down don't live very long."

"Fine, boss. You can depend on me. You depended on Pete, and he stole from you. I've never done that. You be square with me, and you can trust me to do my job."

"All right. Take your things and move them into Pete's cabin. As my lieutenant, you get your own place. Then get some rest. It's late, and tomorrow will be a long day. I expect to be working out details with Garcia for larger shipments of drugs. He should be gone by tomorrow night. Until then, I have men stationed out of sight in the woods. I have to deal with Garcia, but I don't trust him. I'm depending on your eyes and ears as well. I wouldn't put it past him to try a takeover. If that happens, none of them are to leave this island alive."

"I understand, boss. I'll get moved and see you in the morning." Jeff left Clint's office and headed over to gather his things and move them to Pete's cabin. Having the privacy of his own cabin would be a huge plus.

But now that he knew the identity of Clint's supplier, he had to plan carefully. Garcia was an animal, and his men were all just as bad. He couldn't afford to underestimate them. His life depended on it.

After Jeff left, Clint took out his private phone and made another call to his informant. The man was instructed to keep it with him at all times. There was no reason for him not to answer. Not unless he had been careless and got caught. But even if that had happened, that phone couldn't be traced to him. He had made sure of that.

He let the phone ring twice more, then hung up. He couldn't do anything about Jake tonight. After Garcia left, he would think of some way to find out what had happened to his informant.

The next morning, Garcia and his men joined Clint and Jeff at the outside tables under the camouflage nets for breakfast.

"Good morning. Have a seat and have something to eat before we go to my office and work out the details of our new business arrangements," Clint said.

Garcia motioned for his men to have a seat around the perimeter of the tables. A deliberate move to promote intimidation. The move wasn't lost on Clint. He gave a slight nod to Jeff who understood what his boss wanted. He eased out of his seat and walked to stand behind the five banditos.

He hoped the five men Clint had stationed in the trees were alert. If Diego made a move, he wouldn't be able to take all five of his men.

Garcia raised an eyebrow at the move but didn't comment. Instead, he said, "*Mi amigo*, your generosity overwhelms me. We will eat, yes, and then we'll get down to business."

One of Clint's men brought out fresh coffee and large platters of fruit and cheese. Another brought out scrambled eggs and sausage.

The two men made small talk while they ate. "This is a good setup you have here, my friend," Garcia said as he pushed his plate back and looked around the compound.

It looked to Jeff as if the outlaw was assessing Clint's security. It could mean Garcia was gearing up to make a move or it could just be he was making sure his investments would be safe here.

"We do very well. The authorities have never bothered us," Clint said. "As far as they are concerned, this island and the others nearby are deserted. We are very careful not to draw attention to ourselves."

"Yes, I saw how hard it is to find the entrance to the inlet leading to your beach," Garcia said. "A person would have to have the inside knowledge to find it. Then the inlet itself is so long and winding it would be hard for someone to get all the way to the dock without being seen. How many guards do you post to watch the inlet?"

Garcia paused. Not really expecting an answer to his question. When Clint didn't reply, he went on as if it didn't matter.

"Surely, you don't take the drugs out that way when you send them to your distributors. That much activity would soon attract the attention of the coastguard." Garcia paused again to see if Clint would reveal any details of his operation. He really hadn't expected it to be that easy.

Clint hedged. "Why don't we just leave our business for the office and enjoy another cup of coffee or maybe a shot of whiskey?"

Jeff watched this exchange between the two smugglers. It might be interesting to see how this played out if it weren't so serious. And if he was not sure to get caught in the middle of it. If the two men took each other out, it would make his plan easier to execute. But he didn't want Garcia dead. He needed him. He was the supplier. Clint, on the other hand, would outlive his usefulness as soon as he revealed to Jeff how the drugs were taken off the island.

The two men spent another hour with their back and forth game of evasion. Clint brought out a decanter of his best whiskey and Garcia and his men passed it around.

Jeff noticed Clint only poured enough in his glass so as not to seem rude to his guests. Jeff thought that a wise move on Clint's part.

Finally, Garcia got up and motioned to his men. "I need to walk around a few minutes before our meeting. All that food, you know, and then the whiskey can cloud a man's mind."

He stood for a minute, looking at Clint as if to let it sink in that he realised Clint had hardly touched his drink.

"We'll meet you in your office in about an hour." And with this, he turned and walked away. His men followed him.

Clint motioned to Jeff. "Follow him, but don't be too obvious. And don't allow him to venture down the path toward the warehouse under any circumstances. If they don't all stay together, get some of the other men to help you."

Jeff nodded and eased away to discreetly keep Garcia and his men in his line of sight.

Clint went to his office and locked the door. He placed another call to his informant but still didn't get an answer.

Damn, he thought. Something was definitely wrong on that end. If he lost this informant, he would have to figure out a way to replace him.

He put his phone back in his pocket and unlocked the door. Taking a seat at his desk, he took out the papers listing the general locations of his distributors. He wanted Garcia to see how much merchandise he could handle but not give him any specific information.

Jeff followed Garcia and his men as they wandered around the compound. It was obvious they were checking the layout.

When they approached the head of the trail leading to the warehouse, Garcia paused and looked around as if knowing he wouldn't be allowed to go any farther.

Jeff waited to see what the bandito would do. He had tried to stay out of sight, but he knew Garcia was aware he was being watched.

It was as if Garcia was gathering as much information by where he wasn't allowed to go as to where he was. He was smart.

Jeff faded back into the trees as Garcia turned and headed back toward Clint's office. Jeff didn't know if Clint would want him at the meeting, but he would show up anyway. He wanted to be in on the meeting. He needed the information.

When Garcia reached Clint's office, he knocked on the door and without waiting for an invitation opened the door, and he and his men filed in.

Jeff waited a minute and knocked on the office door. Unlike Garcia, he waited for his boss to acknowledge his knock.

When Jeff entered, Clint was behind his desk and Garcia had pulled up a chair so he could see the paper Clint was showing him. Garcia's men were leaning against the wall in different locations. It looked to Jeff as if he was again trying to give the impression that he had the upper hand.

Jeff nodded to his boss, leaned against the closed door and rearranged his shoulder holster. He could send a signal of his own, *I may be outmanned, but I'm armed, and you will have to go through me to get out this door again.*

Satisfied his message had been understood, Jeff settled back to listen to the details of the meeting.

The meeting lasted well into the afternoon. Evidently, a lot of details had to be agreed upon. Garcia wanted to introduce a new line of drugs. These were stronger and would bring in more money. He was concerned with Clint's ability to move them through his distributors.

Clint assured him he could handle whatever Garcia supplied. Once this last detail was agreed on, Garcia stood up and stretched.

"Well, *mi amigo*, I believe we've come to a satisfactory agreement. My next delivery will be double the regular supply with twenty kilos of the newest drug on the market in my country. If that goes well, we can increase the shipment of the latter as your market demands it."

Clint stood and moved across the room toward the door. Jeff moved aside and opened it so his boss and the other smugglers could exit. He fell in behind them.

"Well, I guess you'll be anxious to be on your way back to your headquarters," Clint said to Garcia as they all walked out into the compound.

Garcia slapped Clint on the back. "Oh, I thought I'd stay a few days and get to know a little more about your operation. I may even be able to pick up some pointers on how to run things more efficiently."

After dropping that bombshell, Garcia sauntered back to the cabin he and his men had been assigned.

Clint motioned for Jeff to join him. He was visibility upset. "I had planned for him to leave as soon as our meeting was over. I want you to stand guard outside their cabin tonight. I'll get someone to relieve you in the morning so you can get some sleep. But tonight, I want you on guard in case Garcia has something planned. I'm going to let the men I have posted in the woods know what's going on. They'll have to hold their posts a little longer as well."

In spite of his concern, everything remained quiet in the evening. Garcia and his men came back out and joined the others until late into the night.

Clint had resigned himself to the situation and settled in to keep an eye on his guests as long as they remained outside their cabin. Knowing Jeff would be on watch after the banditos retired.

It was long after midnight when Jeff saw one of Clint's men materialise out of the woods and make his way to his boss. He bent over and whispered something in Clint's ear.

Jeff could tell whatever the man said had made Clint furious. He watched to see what would happen next.

Clint caught Jeff's eye and motioned for him to follow as he and the other man walked out of the compound toward the head of the path leading down to the dock.

Jeff caught up with the other men just as Clint exploded.

"What the hell? Who are these people, and how in the hell did these two women get out of that warehouse?"

Clint was livid, and Jeff was afraid the man was going to pull his gun, and someone was going to die without further explanations.

Clint had reached his limit. He had to deal with Garcia and his cutthroats for longer than he had anticipated, and now his compound had been breached by these strangers. Not only that, but they had managed to find his warehouse and release his hostages.

Clint stepped up and got in the face of one of the largest men he had ever seen. "Who the hell are you?"

Hershel didn't flinch. They were in deep trouble. He started to keep his identity a secret but decided there was nothing to be gained by doing that. Maybe he could use his identity to bluff his way out of this. If this man thought he had brought backup with him, he might not kill them.

Without hesitation, Hershel straightened to his full height and said, "I am Deputy United States Marshal Hershel Bing, and you are under arrest. Put down your guns. You're surrounded."

Chapter 21

Rebecca stared at the bloody cloth in Bill's hand. It could be Hershel's blood. Dear God, were they too late? Had they come this far only to find Hershel's body in the woods behind this dilapidated shack? Rebecca swayed. She was a strong woman, but this was too much.

"Whoa," Andrew said as he grabbed Rebecca's arm, "hold on there, Rebecca. Take a deep breath. We don't know whose blood this is. Hershel was with three other people, and we know that Nancy and Mary Alice had to have come through here as well."

Rebecca's eyes filled with tears. "Yes, but Hershel's a marshal. If something went wrong, he would be the first to confront any threat. You know what kind of man Hershel is. If there was a threat, he would step between everybody else and whatever the threat was."

Bill came up to them. "We can find out right now if this is Hershel's blood. Andrew, go get your crime kit out of the car. We can get a blood type from that cloth. All of our blood types and DNA are in the system. It was a requirement when we joined the rangers."

Andrew hurried back to the car for his kit. He didn't want to think that Rebecca might be right. He had tried to think of anything he had done that could have caused Hershel not to trust him. He couldn't stand the thought that his friend was hurt or even worse, because of something he had done. If, no, when they all got back to the office, he and Hershel were going to have a heart-to-heart talk.

When Andrew got back to the group, he set his kit down on a nearby stump. "Hand me that cloth, Bill. I can tell you in two minutes if it's Hershel's blood or not."

Andrew took out a swab and rubbed it across the bloody rag and then put it in a test tube with a clear liquid and then punched in some information on his phone to access the database back at the marshal's office. He waited then looked up at Rebecca.

"It's not Hershel's blood. And if this is all the blood we find in the shed, it isn't enough to kill anyone. It's more likely someone got hit in the face and used this rag to wipe the blood away. A gunshot, even a flesh wound, would have caused more bleeding. Someone got hurt, but it wasn't Hershel and it wasn't fatal."

Cliff let out a big sigh. He didn't realise he'd been holding his breath. The thought that Hershel could be hurt had never occurred to him. Cliff was young and hadn't been a marshal as long as the others. Hershel was like a hero to him. The kind of marshal, and heck, the kind of man Cliff wanted to become.

Rebecca had closed her eyes for a moment in sheer relief. When she opened them again, she looked at each man in turn.

"Now what? Where do we go from here? It's obvious, even to me, the only way anyone left here is by boat, and we don't have one."

Bill spoke up; he too had been worried as to the outcome of Andrew's test. He waved his hand in the direction of the parking lot.

"All those cars belong to somebody. And all those people are on a boat that went somewhere. They have to come back eventually. We'll be waiting when they do, and one of them is going to tell us where that boat goes. Because wherever that boat goes is where Hershel and the others went and where we're going as well."

While they waited, the men unloaded the equipment and extra guns they had brought with them. Then they waited out of sight. They didn't want the men on the boat to see them and pass on by the dock.

They didn't have long to wait. A little after midnight, they heard a motor and watched as a boat came alongside the dock.

One man jumped from the boat and tied it securely to the dock. As all the men stepped off the boat with their gear, Cliff started moving forward.

Bill reached out and took his arm. "Not yet. Let them get all the way up here. We don't want to take a chance that one of them might get back to the boat and shove off again. Wrangling smugglers is like herding chickens. They tend to fly in all directions."

They waited in the shadows until the entire group was standing in the parking lot talking before getting in their cars and going their separate ways.

Bill said to Andrew, "Slip around and cut off anyone who tries to get back on that boat. Rebecca, stay here. Cliff, you're with me."

And with that, he stepped out of the shadows and said, "Nobody move and nobody will get hurt. Drop what you have and put your hands up. I'm a United States marshal, and you're all under arrest for drug smuggling."

All but one did as Bill had ordered. There was one in every group who thought he could outrun the law. This one had not counted on the speed of Marshal Cliff Harrington. The man only got a few yards before Cliff was on him. Cliff swung him around and up against the nearest car and handcuffed him.

When he took him back to the rest of the group, he said to Bill, "Add resisting arrest charges to this one."

The three marshals took the men into the shed and tied them up and leaned them against the wall. Rebecca followed at a distance.

Bill took the lead again. He walked in front of the men and stared at each in turn. He summed them up pretty quick. These weren't the top of a smuggling ring. They were only gofers. Someone told them where to go and what to do, and they did it. Either for money or out of fear.

"You're all under arrest. You're all going to jail. A friend of ours was on your boat not long ago. I want to know where you took him. The first one that talks might find he has a little leniency from a judge later on."

He stopped and let that sink in. The men were scared, but who were they more afraid of? The men they ran drugs for or the three marshals standing in front of them. If he had to guess, it would be their drug boss. Marshals didn't shoot people in cold blood, but drug cartels killed anyone who double-crossed them.

No one spoke.

Andrew stepped up beside Bill. "You guys are in a lot of trouble. We can protect you."

He waited, but still, no one spoke.

Andrew knew they could protect these men but not their families. The men knew it too. They had seen what could happen to the families of anyone crossing the cartel.

So, the men stayed silent.

Cliff joined the other two marshals standing in front of the group of obviously terrified men.

"Listen," he said, "I know you're all scared and wondering how you're going to get out of this. The answer is, you can't. Cooperating with us is all that's going to help you. Talk to us. Tell us what we want to know, and it'll go easier on you."

And again, no one spoke.

Bill turned around and said to the others, "Come on, let's give them a few minutes to think this over. We were on them pretty quick. They haven't had time to process how much trouble they're in."

Rebecca followed the men outside. She didn't want to give these guys time to process anything. She wanted to know where they had taken her husband. She wanted to do something, but the marshals were in charge. They knew best how to handle the situation. She would have to be patient.

Andrew said, "I'm going to put our gear on the boat and have a look around. Maybe I can find something that will tell us where the boat has been."

And with this, he walked back to unload the equipment from the car.

"Come on, let's help him," Bill said to Cliff. "Maybe by the time we get that done, one of our friends in there will decide it's in his best interest to talk to us."

Rebecca watched as the men transferred equipment from the car to the boat. They were marshals. They went by the book and some kind of code of honour. She was sure there were some marshal rules; they were required to memorise.

Well, she wasn't a marshal, and those rules didn't apply to her. She had her own rules. The first: no one hurt her husband. The second: If they did, they would suffer the consequences. The third: If someone knew where he was, they were going to tell her. The fourth: She wasn't going to wait around for someone else to do what she could do herself.

Rebecca looked around at what was at her disposal. Andrew had laid his gun down on the stump while doing the DNA test on the bloody rag.

Rebecca picked it up and looked at it. Hershel had one just like it. Unfortunately, Rebecca didn't know how to shoot it. Hershel had begged her to let him teach her, but Rebecca refused. She didn't really like guns. She didn't need one when she went into court, and when she visited unstable homes, a police officer always accompanied her. Now she wished she'd listened to Hershel. When this was over, she was going to a gun range and take lessons. For now, she'd have to fake it.

Rebecca glanced over to make sure the men were otherwise engaged. She took the gun and eased back inside the shack. She walked up and down in front of the smugglers with her scariest social worker face on. She held the gun like she knew how to use it.

Hershel had always told her, "If you find yourself in a threatening situation either in the home of an abused child or alone out on the street, size up your opponent first. Pick out the biggest. If you can intimidate him, the others will fall in line."

And so, that is what Rebecca did. She walked right up to the biggest man in the room and leant over and got in his face. She smiled her scary smile and slowly raised the gun to the man's head. She had no idea how to shoot it, but he didn't know that.

"Now let's get one thing straight. I'm not a marshal. I'm not in any law enforcement at all. I don't have to abide by their rules. They might not shoot you, but I will, and there's no one here to stop me. I want to know where you took my husband, and I want to know right now."

She had the man's attention. She had all the men's attention. They weren't sure of her. In their experience, a woman with a gun was a dangerous thing and to be avoided. There were women in the cartel that was as ruthless as any of the men.

The man had yet to speak. Rebecca reached out and bunched her fist into the front of the man's shirt and pulled him forward. As she did this, she slowly lowered the gun down the man's neck but didn't stop there. She lowered it again until it was pressed against the man's heart. She paused a moment and smiled and then lowered it even further. By the time she stopped, this time the man had broken out in a cold sweat and he was trembling.

"Now," she said, "where did you take my husband?" She pressed the gun a little harder. "For the last time. Where is my husband?"

Rebecca had been so engrossed in what she was doing, she hadn't heard Bill walk up behind her. Neither had any of the other men in the room. No one had taken their eyes off Rebecca and that gun and where she had it pointed.

"Rebecca," Bill said very softly, "let me have the gun, Rebecca. You don't want to do this."

Rebecca never wavered. "No, Bill, I don't want to shoot this man, but I'm going to if that's what it takes to make him tell me where Hershel is."

Bill laid a hand on Rebecca's shoulder. "Let me have the gun, Rebecca. I'll handle this."

Rebecca didn't make a move to hand the gun to Bill. In fact, she had it pointed at the same place as before. The place that had got the man's attention.

"We don't need him, Rebecca. We don't need any of them. The boat has a navigation system. Andrew has figured it out. We can trace where they've been, and we'll find Hershel and the others. Andrew and Cliff are waiting for us on board. Give me the gun, Rebecca, and let's go get your husband."

With this news, Rebecca stood up and handed the gun to Bill and walked out of the shed toward the boat. She hadn't looked back nor had she said another word.

The man she had held the gun on had passed out.

Bill faced the men. He handed out bottles of water. "We're leaving you for now. You'll be fine. We'll collect you on our way back. Don't even think about trying to leave." He gave them one last look and followed Rebecca.

When Bill reached the boat, Rebecca was seated on board with Andrew and Cliff. Andrew had figured out the navigation system and knew what direction they needed to head. What he didn't know was how to drive a boat.

He looked at the other guys. "Do either of you know how to drive this thing?" he said.

Bill walked over and looked at the controls. He shrugged. "Not a clue."

Cliff stood up. "Uh guys, I can drive it."

All three of the others turned and looked at Cliff questioningly.

"I'm a member of a yacht club," he said, then, at the looks he was getting from the other two men, blushed bright red. "It's a tradition in my family. My father's the president and my mother's secretary."

The other two marshals just shook their heads. "Get over here and get this thing started," Andrew said. "We're wasting time."

With Cliff at the controls and Andrew as navigator, they slowly pulled away from the dock and out into open water.

Bill stepped back to where Rebecca was sitting.

"Would you have shot him, Rebecca?" he said.

"I'm honestly not sure. Until now I would have said I would never be able to take a life. Now I'm not so sure. If you hadn't walked in and he had still refused to talk, I just don't know."

She stopped and looked up at Bill. "But I think I would have."

Chapter 22

Clint and the others were just out of sight of the compound. He looked behind him to make sure that neither Garcia nor any of his men had followed him.

"A United States marshal, huh? And where is this backup you're talking about? It looks to me like you're the one surrounded."

He walked around Hershel, who had to be restrained by two of Clint's henchmen. He looked at Joe and Albert who were trying to keeping Nancy, Mary Alice and Beth pushed behind them.

"And I guess the two of you are marshals as well," he said.

When neither man spoke, he reached around Albert and grabbed Beth's arm and dragged her forward.

"And you. You don't look like a marshal to me. I already had two women who have given me way too much trouble. I sure as hell don't need another one."

He took the knife out of the scabbard at the back of his belt and held it under Beth's chin. She didn't move, but Joe lunged forward only to be yanked back by one of Clint's men.

In spite of being held by two strong men, Hershel managed to turn and face Clint and the others.

"You don't want to do that. You're in enough trouble. I'm not kidding about the backup. They may not be here now, but they're not far behind us. We came on in ahead to get the women out. As soon as we had them safe, we were executing our raid with more gun power than you have here. We've had you under surveillance for months. You can't get off this island. We literally have it surrounded."

Hershel paused for a breath. He had never told so many lies in one breath in his life. There was no backup. He was the only marshal here. He looked at his fellow prisoners. Three women, two hospital volunteers and a nurse. Two men, one retired and the other the owner of a gym. All civilians. All his responsibility. What had he done?

Jeff stood to the side, watching this new drama play out. He recognised Joe from the alley. How had he and the others made it this far? The marshals might have figured it all out, but where did all these others come from. Things were getting more complicated, and he was getting more uncertain of the outcome.

Clint let go of Beth and turned on Hershel. The knife was now at Hershel's throat. He pressed it just hard enough to draw blood.

"Well, Mr United States Marshal. I don't see anybody but the six of you. And the only ones with guns are my men. I can assure you if you had men trying to access my island, I would've been notified by my lookouts."

Hershel swallowed, which was hard to do with a knife piercing his throat.

"We got on your island without your lookouts alerting you. Think about it. If we did, my other men will as well."

For the first time, Clint felt a moment of doubt. There was some truth in what this marshal was saying.

Jeff took this opportunity to glance back toward the compound. He could see Garcia stand up talking to his men. It looked like they might be headed their way. Jeff stepped forward and looked from Clint to Hershel. He and Hershel stared at each other for a moment before he said to Clint, "Garcia's headed this way. We may want to postpone this little meeting for a better time."

Clint looked over Jeff's shoulder, cursed and placed his knife back into its sheath at the back of his belt. For a moment, he had forgotten about Garcia and his men.

He motioned to his guards. "Take the men and lock them in one of the cabins as far away from Garcia and his men as possible. Go around that way and try not to be seen."

"Jeff, take these three women and lock them back in the warehouse, and this time, make sure they can't get out. We'll figure this out when Garcia's gone. He doesn't need to be part of our little drama. He might get the idea I can't control things on my end."

With one last look at Hershel, Jeff herded the three women off to the left, out of sight of Garcia and his men.

When everyone was gone, Clint started making his way back to the compound. He met Garcia and his men just as he topped the rise at the end of the path.

"Well, my friend, have you decided to leave us after all? I thought you might stay till morning and get an early start although leaving late at night in the dark has its advantages."

He waited for Garcia to speak. He wasn't sure how much the other man had seen. He thought they had been out of sight of the compound but couldn't be sure their voices hadn't carried on the slight breeze coming in off the water.

"Oh no, *mi amigo*. We're just stretching our legs. We're not used to the confinement of being on an island. We can't afford to sit around and get lazy. I thought we might walk down to the dock and check on our boat."

Clint couldn't think of a reason not to let his guests go down to the dock and check on their boat.

"You're right, a little walk would do us all good. I'll walk with you, and when we get back, maybe we should all call it a night and get some rest."

He needed Garcia, but he'd be glad when he and his men were gone. He had other guests that demanded his attention. He had to know how they had found his island and if he could expect any more surprises. He had to try again to reach his contact in the marshal's office. It was more important than ever. He knew who Hershel Bing was and knew his informant was in the same office. If Jake had sold him out, he would make it his business to make him pay with his life.

Hershel, Joe and Albert were taken to a cabin about twenty yards from the beginning of the trail that led back to the warehouse.

When they were locked in, Hershel turned to the other two men.

"Listen, guys, I'm sorry I got you involved in this mess. This is the kind of thing my office handles on a regular basis. I had no business bringing two civilians into such a dangerous situation. I wish I could tell you someone in my office would come looking for us, but the fact is no one knows where I am." He paused. "Not even my wife."

At the thought of Rebecca, a sadness overcame Hershel. Would she be all right if he didn't make it out of this? Would she understand why he had felt it necessary to lie to her about where he was going? Would the informant in his office keep causing trouble or would some of his men figure out what was going on? What he wouldn't give to see Bill or Andrew or Cliff pop up about now. But that wasn't going to happen. He hadn't trusted them enough to tell them where he was going.

Joe stepped forward and put his hand on Hershel's shoulder.

"You didn't get us involved, Hershel. We were involved from the time Nancy picked up that phone and was scammed out of her money. We were involved from the time someone chocked me and left me for dead in that alley. We were involved from the time they abducted my wife and Mary Alice."

Albert stepped up beside his friend and put his hand on Hershel's other shoulder.

"You risked your life for us and for those we love. If not for you, we wouldn't have found Nancy and Mary Alice. They would have been lost to us forever. Not knowing who you could trust in your office, you came alone. You put your life on the line for people you didn't even know."

Joe put his other hand on Albert's shoulder. "Albert and I have been like brothers for many years. Now I consider you the same. From here on out we stand together and we'll get out of this together. Now let's stop this blame game and try to come up with a plan to get our ladies and get out of here."

The three men sat on the edge of the cots that were lined up on three sides of the cabin. They went over the facts they knew, trying to come up with a plan.

Meanwhile, just down the path from where the men were being held, Jeff was locking the three women in the warehouse. He thought about tying them up. He wouldn't have thought they could have escaped but they had. Of course, they had some help. He thought it pretty gutsy the way the men had made it into Clint's compound and almost made off with his prisoners. Unfortunately, that gutsy move just might get them all killed.

Jeff stood at the door and looked back at the ladies. "I'm going to give you a little advice. I said this before, but you choose not to listen. These men are killers. They won't blink an eye to shoot you or put a knife in your heart. If you value your lives and the lives of the men who came to save you, stay put. The only reason you're alive now is that we have a pretty important guest on the island. My boss is more concerned with him than with you, but that will change the minute he leaves the island. Don't bring any more attention to yourselves, and you might live another day."

With this, Jeff walked out and locked the door behind him. Damn, these women, they were going to get themselves killed and him right along with them. He was skating on thin ice as it was. He knew who Hershel Bing was. The man had quite a reputation. He hadn't thought that he might end up here on the island. This changed Jeff's plans drastically. And seeing Joe Murphy had been another shock. The last time he had seen Joe, he was in a dark alley on the ground. He didn't know who the third man was, but if he had to guess, it was the friend Joe had been travelling with. He had no clue about the woman. Why they would have brought her with them was a mystery. All this certainly changed his plans.

Nancy, Mary Alice and Beth stood in the middle of the room and looked at each other. Nancy and Beth had been friends since school. When Mary Alice moved to Hadbury and opened her firing range, she had clicked right off with the other two women. She had just escaped from an abusive marriage and had been afraid to trust anyone. But Nancy and Beth had offered her support and acceptance. Now the three were fast friends and were also in deep trouble.

Beth took charge as she was app to do. As a nurse, it just was natural for her to tell others what to do.

"Nancy, I want you and Mary Alice to come over here and sit down. I want to check you over. Nancy, you have bruises all over your face. Some new and some look at least three days old. And Mary Alice, that black eye could only have been caused by a fist. We were in such a hurry to get away before, I didn't have time to properly treat your boo-boos."

Nancy laughed as she found a spot to sit on a stack of drugs that looked like they were waiting for distribution. Boo-boos were what the two girls had called the scrapes and scratches they acquired when they were children. The term had stuck.

"I don't want to know why you call my black eye a boo-boo," Mary Alice said. "Just tell me you have something to take some of the pain away."

Beth went from one woman to the next doing what she could to make them a little more comfortable. There had only been so much room in her fanny pack and her hypodermics had taken up part of it.

As she removed her supplies, she laid the hypodermic needles to the side.

Nancy was watching and said, "I hope those aren't for us because if they are, I think I'll pass."

Beth laughed and explained how they had come in handy at the restaurant with the robber and then again when the smuggler had attacked them on the path coming up to the compound.

Then as women do, especially ones who know each other well, they took turns telling what had happened to each of them and how they had ended up here.

Nancy had tears in her eyes when she looked at Beth. "Mary Alice and I were taken together. We've had very little say in what's happened to us since that time. But you didn't have to get involved. You could have stayed safe yet you chose to come with the guys to find us."

Now for the second time since this ordeal began, Nancy let the tears fall. Beth sat down between the other two women and put an arm around each.

"You are my two dearest friends. How could I not have come when I thought you were in trouble. The guys thought they were going to leave me behind, but I straightened them out at the start. Joe and Albert were harder to convince than the marshal. I heard him muttering something about being married to a woman just like me. I wonder what he meant by that?" Nancy and Mary Alice just laughed. They had a pretty good idea what the marshal meant.

When Beth had done all she could to treat her friends, she got up and walked around the warehouse.

"This must be where they keep the drugs waiting to be transported off the island and taken to the distributors who then pass them out for their flunkies to sell. As a nurse, I am highly offended by all of this. I've seen what this stuff does to the bodies of the young and old alike. Once it gets in their systems, it takes control, and then they'll do whatever it takes to get a fix. If I had a match, I'd set fire to every bundle of this."

"I know what you mean," Nancy said. "We have a programme at church for young adults who find themselves separated from their families because their families couldn't deal with them anymore. Most of them are gaunt and so skinny it hurts to look at them."

"They don't eat," Beth stated. "Food isn't important. Getting that next fix is. That's all that's important to them. Yea, I wish I could burn every bundle of this crap."

They walked around for a few more minutes, then Nancy turned and looked all around the warehouse.

"Where's Mary Alice?" she said. She walked around the entire room and then came back to where Beth was standing. "Where is she?"

"Well, she has to be here," Beth said. "There's nowhere to go. No way to get out."

"Okay, so, where is she?" Nancy said.

Beth frowned and circled the room again. She looked behind the stacks of drugs against the walls. There just wasn't anywhere for her to hide, and yet she was gone.

Beth walked back over to where they had been sitting and Nancy followed her.

"We were all three right here. We got up and started walking around, and I thought she got up with us."

Nancy called out in a soft voice, "Mary Alice, where are you? If you're trying to scare us, we're already scared. Come out right this minute, do you hear me?"

Nancy and Beth got completely quiet, listening. All they could hear was a muffled sound coming from the other side of this section of wall.

Beth put her ear up against the stone wall. "Mary Alice, are you in there?"

This time, she heard her friend's voice as if from far away.

Startled, Beth said, "Mary Alice, you come out of there this instant. You scared us."

A muffled sound came from behind the wall again. This time it sounded a little more agitated.

Beth pressed her ear against the wall again and listened. More muffled sounds came through.

Beth stood back and looked at the wall with a frown. "She said she doesn't know how to get out. She's in some kind of tunnel."

Nancy took her hands and started feeling all along the wall. It seemed solid enough. She even tried pushing against it but to no avail.

Nancy and Beth stood back and looked at the wall. It seemed to be solid. No sign of a door or opening of any kind.

"Beth, you start on that side, and I'll start over here," Nancy said. "Push and pull every inch of that wall. There has to be a way to open it if Mary Alice got back there."

The two women started on opposite sides and worked their way toward each other. Nancy pushed on a spot that stuck out just a fraction more than the rest. It would have been almost undetectable unless you knew what you were looking for.

She jumped back as a section of the wall soundlessly began to slide to the side, revealing a tunnel, a track, a railway cart and Mary Alice.

Beth rushed forward, put her hands on her hips and said, "What are you doing back there?"

Mary Alice just stood there staring at her two best friends.

Nancy came forward and pulled her friend out of the tunnel and sat her down on the nearest stack of drugs.

"Be quiet, Beth, can't you see she's had a shock? She's speechless."

"Oh pooh, Mary Alice is never speechless." But Beth took a seat on the other side of her friend and said, "You're fine now. Just tell us what happened. How did you end up behind that wall?"

Mary Alice hesitated, looking a little confused. "Well, I got up to follow the two of you, and I felt a little dizzy. I guess that hit I took affected me more than I thought. Anyway, I reached out to the wall to steady myself and the whole thing moved and I fell forward, and before I could get my balance and turn around again, the wall just moved back into place. I couldn't get out."

All three women got up and looked at the opening to the tunnel.

"I wonder where it goes," Beth said. "It might be our way out of here. Come on. Let's follow these tracks and see where it comes out."

They walked single file, following the track. It was light enough for them to see without any trouble. Evidently, when the door was opened, it also triggered a switch that turned on the lights all the way down to the end.

When they came to another blank wall, Nancy said, "Hold on. There must be something that triggers a door here too."

She felt along the wall, and since she knew what she was looking for, this time she was able to locate the switch. She pushed it just like she had the other one, and it slid open the same way.

The three women stepped through the door as it slid back and found themselves on a small beach.

The clearing was barely large enough for the three of them to stand side by side. There was a distance of about fifteen feet to the edge of the water. The undergrowth was so thick, the ladies could see no way to get to the water. And if they did, then what. There was no place to go from there.

Nancy walked as far as she could go and turned to face the others.

"Someone comes and goes from here. This is probably the way the smugglers get the drugs off the island. Let's go back up and close the doors so nobody will know we've discovered their little secret. The drugs are probably moved out at night. We'll slip back down here just after dark tomorrow and see if we can catch anybody coming up this way. Maybe if we hide over in those bushes, we can surprise them. If we can get to their boat, we can get off this island and go for help."

Chapter 23

Garcia and his men had finally retired to their cabin for the night, but instead of going to bed, they sat around the small table in the centre of the room, talking.

Garcia was watching one of his lieutenants very carefully as he described what he had seen and heard.

"The head gringo and his men had a group of three men and three women held at gunpoint," the man was telling Garcia.

"He was really upset. He took out his knife, and I thought he was going to kill one of the women. When the big one tried to stop him, he held the knife to his throat. But the man didn't seem to be afraid. He kept saying his men had the island surrounded, and he had better give up. I thought that kind of funny since they were all being held at gunpoint and the gringo had a knife to the big one's throat."

"Did you hear anyone say the name of the big guy that seemed to be in charge of the group?"

"*Si*, he said his name was Hershel Bing, and he was a United States marshal."

This got Garcia's attention. Hershel Bing wasn't someone he wanted to cross. The man had quite a reputation. He had shut down a rival cartel last year. The news had spread like wildfire. Now everyone paid attention when they heard that particular name.

"What did Clint do with them? They weren't there when we went down to the dock to check on our boat."

"Two of his men took the three men and locked them in one of the empty cabins. Another one, the guy that was in the meeting with us in Clint's office, took the three women down the path at the back of the compound."

"I see," Garcia said when his lieutenant paused.

"I know who this Hershel Bing is. I have known men who have gone up against him and didn't fare so well. He is the head of a group of United Stated marshals out of Richmond. It's impossible to know if he was lying about the backup and the island being surrounded. It may have been a bluff to buy some time for his men to get here. Whichever it was, I think our business here is completed for how. If this man is telling the truth, we don't have the men nor gun power to go up against a group of well-armed marshals. Let's get a few hours of sleep, and we'll leave at first light."

Clint had watched as Garcia and his men had retired to their cabin. He thought the tale about wanting to check on their boat had just been an excuse to see why he had left the compound with one of his men.

He didn't know how much Garcia had seen, but there was nothing he could do about it now. He might as well try and get some sleep. It wasn't long till dawn, and who knew what would happen then.

He had a marshal in his camp and if the man could be believed more on the way. He had two other men who had come with the marshal. They claimed they weren't marshals but had just come along to help rescue the women. The women that were not supposed to be here in the first place. He should have had only one woman, and Jeff had killed her husband. He had seen the picture of the man dead in the alley. He had wanted to kill the other two women, but maybe if any other marshals really were on the way, he could use them to his advantage.

He knew one thing for sure, after tomorrow, some of his unwanted guests were going to be gone, one way or another.

Clint walked by his office just to make sure it was locked up tight. He started to go in and try one more time to call his informant but changed his mind. What good would it do? The man had either bolted or got caught. That was a problem for another day.

As Clint entered his cabin, he noticed the lights were still on in the cabin he had assigned Garcia and his men. He wondered what they were planning. He was pretty sure he wouldn't like it. He had wanted them gone, but now with the potential threat of an invasion by the United States marshals, it might be a good idea if they stayed. It would be more gun power on his side.

While Clint was settling in for what remained of the night, Jeff was standing watch outside Garcia's cabin. He could see them through one of the windows. They were in a deep discussion over something. He wished he dared get a little closer so he could hear what they were saying.

He had wanted to know who Clint's supplier was. He had needed that information in order to carry out the rest of his plan. Now he wasn't so sure that this was the time to incorporate the bandito into what he had in mind. As long as he knew who he was, he could deal with him later.

His mind went back to Hershel Bing. He wished he knew what the marshal was up to. He didn't doubt that the man had come to get the women off the island. But he also figured that Bing had another agenda. Jeff knew how Bing had figured out this location as well.

What puzzled him was why he had come alone? He knew how the marshals worked. Bing should have had some of his men with him. Why would he take the chance of bringing civilians into a volatile situation like this? It just didn't make any sense.

Another loose end was Joe Murphy. He was pretty sure the man couldn't identify him. He had jumped him from behind, and the alley had been dark. If Clint found out who the man was, he would have a lot of explaining to do. Clint had bought his story about Pete messing up and then trying to kill him. If he found out not only Joe Murphy wasn't dead, he was here on the island, it might make Clint doubt the rest of his story.

Well, there wasn't anything he could do about any of it tonight. Maybe tomorrow he could take care of some of the loose ends. Before they got him so tangled up, his plan blew up in his face.

Nancy had climbed up on one of the piles of drugs so she could look out the window. Joe was out there somewhere. He was alive. She had to hold on to that thought. They would get out of here. She had no intention of letting their lives together end this way. She wasn't sure what she could do, but she had more to fight for now that Joe was here with her.

Mary Alice stood looking up at her friend. "Nancy, why don't you come down here and get some rest. We need to be fresh for tomorrow and whatever it brings."

"Mary Alice, my friend, I am ready for whatever we have to do to get off this island and get our lives back," Nancy said as she climbed down.

"Now that I know Joe's alive, I can face anything. When all this is over, someone is going to explain to me why we were caught up in this mess. Smugglers and drugs are not part of our everyday lives."

Beth called out from the corner where she had made a bed of sorts using some burlap sacks that had been wrapped around some of the contraband. "Girls, it's almost dawn. Come, lay down and get some rest. Tomorrow night is showtime. That is if the other players show up. If no one comes by then to start loading this garbage on a boat to wherever it's going, I'm going to start opening these packages one by one and emptying them into the water outside that secret passage. I bet I'll get some attention then."

Nancy and Mary Alice joined their friend on the makeshift bed. "All right, girls," Nancy said, "I'm ready for whatever tomorrow brings."

"So am I," Mary Alice replied. "I think Albert and I have a long-overdue date."

"About time," the other two women said in unison.

Mary Alice laughed. "Nothing like being kidnapped by a bunch of drug-running smugglers to change a person's attitude. Life's too short to be afraid of the future because of the past. I know now all men aren't like my good-for-nothing ex-husband. Besides, I have an edge now I didn't have then. I'm an excellent shot."

Beth was half asleep, but she managed to mutter, "Somebody better warn Albert about Annie Oakley over there."

The sun had barely risen when a knock on the door brought Clint out of troubled sleep. It had only been two hours since he dropped exhausted on top of his bed without even turning back the blanket.

"What is it?" Clint said, noticing more activity in his camp than was usual for this early in the morning.

"I think our guests are getting ready to leave," the man told his boss.

"Garcia?" Clint asked as he grabbed his knife and attached it to the back of his belt. His bed was one of the few places he didn't have the knife on him. He was more comfortable with it than the gun he also kept handy.

"I noticed activity in their cabin, so I got close enough to see what was going on. Jeff saw me and told me to get you while he kept watching."

As Clint came out, he saw Garcia and his men gathered at the tables under the camouflaged netting.

"Good morning, my friend," the bandito said to Clint. "I thought we'd get an early start. Our business is complete; no reason to stay any longer. I need to get back to my own camp. It's good of you to get up so early to see us off."

Clint searched around for something to say that would convince Garcia to postpone his departure. Yesterday, he had wanted the man off his island, but that was before he had discovered a United States marshal in his mist. He had wanted Garcia's gun power in case of a fight. If the marshal was telling the truth, more men were on their way.

"I thought you wanted to stick around a few more days. See how our operation runs. Any reason for this sudden departure?"

"No, *mi amigo*, it's just time for us to get back to our own business and leave you to yours. Our next shipment will be at its regular time. I look forward to our new arrangements. The addition of that new drug should make us both rich men."

And with no further delay, Garcia and his men started down the path to where their boat was waiting.

Clint stood watching them go. Well, maybe it was for the best, he thought. Garcia was an outlaw and always looked after his own interests first. He wasn't sure he could have trusted the man to have his back anyway.

Jeff walked up to his boss. "It seems our friends have decided to leave us."

"Yes, so it seems," Clint said. He turned to his lieutenant. "Follow him, and make sure he and his men get off the island. I wouldn't want them doubling back for any reason. Something doesn't ring true with his sudden decision to leave. Then check on our prisoners, the men and the women, then get some sleep."

Jeff nodded and went to do his boss's bidding. He was glad to see Garcia and his men go. He had a feeling that things were about to come to a head. Having Garcia out of the picture would be a plus. He still had plans for the man, but that was for a future time.

As Jeff entered the cabin where the men were being held, he found all three of them sound asleep. They looked like they didn't have a care in the world. He started to back out the door when Hershel sat up.

"I was hoping to have a word with you," Hershel said. He got up and sat on the side of the bed. Joe and Albert never moved. They were still fast asleep.

The one thing Jeff wanted to avoid at this time was having a conversation with Hershel Bing. He had a healthy respect for this marshal, but he couldn't afford any slip-ups at this crucial time. He still had to figure out how Clint was getting his contraband off the island. He had to have all the pieces to this puzzle. This one man could bring it all down around his head. He had done too much to get to this point. No one was getting in his way now.

"I don't think we have anything to discuss," Jeff said as he backed out and closed the door.

At the sound of the door closing, Joe and Albert sat up and faced Hershel.

"What was that all about?" Joe said as he swung his feet to the floor and got up.

"I think that man may be the key to some of this. Unless I'm mistaken, he's the same man who made that call to Nancy. His voice is the same as the one on the recording," Hershel said. "It was his voice and what he said during that conversation that first alerted me to the fact that more was going on than a simple scam."

Now Hershel had Joe's full attention. "So how do you think this guy fits in with all of this? He's obviously in this up to his eyeballs. Why would he make a call like that and take a chance on someone catching on to who he really is?"

"I don't know," Hershel said. "But we need to figure out how to get out of here so we can find out."

Jeff hurried down the path toward the warehouse. That had been close. He couldn't afford a conversation with Hershel Bing. The man was too sharp. He could foul up all of Jeff's plans. He had gone through too much to take a chance on that now.

When he entered the warehouse, the women were all curled up together on some burlap bags. They were probably exhausted. He didn't like to see women hurt, but there was nothing he could do about that now. He had more important business than these three unlucky women.

Since they didn't stir, he backed out and closed the door.

"Is he gone?" Nancy said as she raised her head and looked toward the door.

"I think so," Beth said as she got to her feet. She was stiff all over. She wasn't used to sleeping on burlap sacks on the floor of a warehouse.

Mary Alice turned over and looked at her two friends. "What now? Do you think they're going to feed us before they kill us? Or do we have to die on an empty stomach?"

"I don't know," Beth said, "But I need a shower. Let's look around and see if this place has any facility. If we have to die, I had just as soon die clean."

At the look of horror on her two friends' faces, she said, "I'm just kidding. Not about the shower but about dying. I have no intention of taking my last breath in a place like this. I plan to die at the age of ninety-eight, after a long and happy life, and even then, I'll probably go screaming and kicking."

They did a quick search and found a small bathroom at the very back. It only contained a toilet and sink with a small mirror hanging on the wall. It was so tiny; the women could only go in one at a time. It wasn't the shower Beth wanted but it would have to do. Just being able to wash the grim off her face was a plus.

"Well," Mary Alice said, "now what? We can sit here and wait for what comes next or we can come up with a plan to get out of here."

Beth looked at her two friends. "I say we go with our plan from last night. Let's go back down that tunnel to that small beach. Someone has to come and go from there. It's the only hope we have of catching anyone off guard. We can hide in those thick bushes and maybe take them by surprise and take their boat and go for help."

With this plan in mind, the three of them accessed the hidden spot in the wall that allowed the door to slide back and reveal the tunnel and track. They made their way to the other end and opened the last door that led to the outside. Finding a spot with a clear view of the water, they settled in to wait for dark.

Chapter 24

If the boat had not been moving slowly through the water, Bill would never have seen the bloated body floating on the surface. "Look," he said to the others as he pointed across the water.

"Do you recognise him?" Andrew asked as he squinted in the direction Bill was pointing.

"His own mother wouldn't recognise him," Bill stated. "But one thing for sure, he's been floating there for at least three days or better."

Rebecca strained to see what the men were talking about. The man floating on the water was so bloated his features were distorted. The only thing she knew for sure was that it wasn't Hershel. Even with the bloating, this man wasn't nearly as large as her husband.

"I can steer the boat close enough for you to check his prints if you want," Cliff said to Andrew. "I know you brought one of those fancy new portable fingerprint machines with you. No self-respecting tech guy would leave home without one."

From the looks he got from the other two men, Cliff knew his attempt at humour had fallen flat.

Rebecca turned her head. She had seen all she wanted to. She was strong. Her stomach just wasn't as strong as the rest of her.

As Cliff manoeuvred the boat closer to the body, Andrew said to Bill, "Hold on to me. I don't want to go into the water, and I'm not just about to bring that body on board unless he's one of ours."

At Andrew's last statement, Rebecca flinched. She had been so worried about her husband she hadn't given as much thought to the others as she should have.

She knew this wasn't one of the women, but there had been two other guys with Hershel. Rebecca closed her eyes and said a prayer that they all had remained safe.

Rebecca kept her eyes closed until she heard Andrew say, "According to this, the man is Pete Rollins and he has a rap sheet as long as my arm. He started off with petty theft and burglary when he was ten years old, got into dealing with drugs by the time he was fourteen and committed his first murder when he was sixteen. At least, the first we have a record of. I'd be willing to bet the killing started about the same time as the drug dealing. They usually go hand in hand. His record reads pretty much the same as he got older. Then about five years ago, he dropped off the radar. My guess is he didn't all of a sudden turn his life around, he just figured out how not to get caught."

As Cliff got the boat back on course, Rebecca stood up and walked over to the men. "I knew it wasn't Hershel," she said. "But I was afraid it might have been Joe or Albert. So, who do you think killed him? He had to have been tossed off a boat, and if the smugglers use this lane it was probably off this one."

"My guess," Bill said, "is that there was some kind of falling out with the smugglers, and this guy lost."

They continued, leaving the bloated body in the water. The elements and fish would finish him off. They needed to find Hershel and the others. It was beginning to look like things were getting a little unsettled with the bad guys.

Andrew was studying the navigation equipment as Cliff kept them on course.

"We're not too far away from our destination," he said. "Keep a sharp lookout toward the shoreline. The entrance to the channel leading to the base of that mountain is going to be hard to see. If it was readily visible, it would have been noticed by the coastguard before now. The navigation system will tell us where the smugglers stopped, but that would have been in the deeper water. A smaller boat would have been used to access the channel."

Cliff slowed the boat then brought it to a standstill. "What's up?" Andrew asked as he bent over Cliff's shoulder.

Cliff looked back at his fellow marshal and said, "Our destination seems to be just the other side of this mountain, but I swear I saw movement through those bushes. See if you can pick up anything with your binoculars. If we're passing a lookout, it would be good to know about it now instead of later. The element of surprise is one of the biggest things in our favour. We know we're going to be outmanned and outgunned. Let's try to keep a surprise on our side."

Andrew slapped his fellow marshal on the back. "We're going to make a marshal out of you yet," he said and went to retrieve his binoculars from the bag of supplies he had brought on board.

Bill and Rebecca moved up to join the other two.

"Have you spotted something, Cliff?" Bill asked. "It's so dark out there I don't see how you could see anything." He bent over to get a better view of where Cliff was pointing.

Without cracking a smile, Cliff said, "Being young has its advantages. I'm not only fast, but I have excellent eyesight too. And I saw a movement just over there in those bushes; that's not consistent with the slight breeze I've been feeling. Might just have been an animal, but Andrew's going to get his high-powered glasses and take a look."

Andrew came back and walked over to the side of the boat closest to the shore. He stood there looking for a few minutes then passed the glasses to Bill.

"I, definitely, caught a movement just to the far side of all those bushes and just before the sheer wall of rock. See what you think."

Bill stood, as his friend had done, studying the shoreline. He shook his head. "It's hard to tell, but I agree with Cliff. We can't go on until we know for sure. I saw a raft at the back of the boat. I'm going to check it out."

"I'll go with you," Andrew said. "You could be walking into a trap. You might need some help."

"No, if it's a trap, we'd both be caught in it and that would leave Cliff by himself to get Rebecca back to safety. We can't take a chance with her life. If the smugglers don't kill us, Hershel will."

With Andrew's help, Bill got the raft over the side of the boat and into the water. He used a paddle and as quietly as possible made his way to the edge of the bushes. For a few minutes, he paddled back and forth, trying to see a way through to dry land.

Finally, he noticed that some of the bushes had been strategically placed to hide a narrow path that led through them to what looked like a very small beach. He didn't see how anyone could be on that beach. There didn't seem to be any access to it except by water.

But just as he started to turn back to the boat, he caught a movement in the bushes closer to the beach toward the rock wall. He would have to go ashore and investigate. It couldn't be an animal. There was no way one could have got there. Not even a mountain goat could have climbed down that sheer wall of rock.

As quietly as possible, Bill tied the raft to one of the bushes and climbed out onto the narrow path. He nearly made it all the way to the wall when he was jumped from behind. He went down hard and the breath was knocked out of him. But that wasn't what kept him from moving until it was too late. What froze him in place was the sound of three women all talking at once.

"We've got him. I told you this would work," Beth said to the other women. "Wrap him up good so he can't get back up. We might not be able to bring him down again. He's pretty big."

Bill felt himself being rolled over and over until he was completely wrapped up in burlap. He tried to speak and identify himself. These certainly weren't smugglers. Unfortunately, the women had done such a good job his words were muffled and unintelligible even to his own ears.

"What's he saying?" Nancy said.

"I don't know, but if we can't understand what he's saying, he might not be able to breathe," Beth said as she fumbled with her fanny pack.

"What are you doing? Are you going to stick him?" Mary Alice asked, looking over Nancy's shoulder.

At this, Bill stopped struggling. Were they going to knife him? He had to think of a way to let the others know there were three lunatics on this small stretch of beach.

"No." Beth laid the hypodermic needles aside and pulled out a pair of scissors. "I'm going to cut a hole so he can breathe."

Beth felt around until she found a face and located the man's nose. He might be a drug-running smuggler, but she couldn't be responsible for killing him. She also didn't want to be responsible for poking his eyes out with the scissors.

Very carefully she cut a hole through the burlap to expose a nose.

With a little more freedom to talk, Bill said, "Let me go. I'm a United States marshal. If you don't want to be arrested, get this stuff off me and let me up." He was, obviously, angry.

Beth stood up and looked at Nancy and Mary Alice. "He said he's a United States marshal. Do you think he's the backup Hershel was talking about? I understood Hershel to say none of the other marshals knew where he was going."

Beth squatted back down and said, "Prove it."

Bill saw he wasn't going to be let loose unless he negotiated with these lunatics. Besides, they knew who Hershel was.

"My badge is clipped to the front of my belt. That'll show you I'm telling the truth."

"We'll see about that," Beth said. She took her scissors and started to make a hole where she figured the badge would be.

"Whoa, wait a minute," Bill yelled out. "That's not my belt. Move about ten inches up."

"Oh," Beth said as she yanked her hands and the scissors away from the burlap. She relocated her efforts and cut a small hole next to what she was sure this time was his belt buckle.

As she uncovered Bill's badge, she looked up at the others. "He's telling the truth. He's a marshal. Help me get him loose."

With the help of Nancy and Mary Alice, Beth struggled to free the marshal, but he was trussed up like a chicken and they couldn't untangle the burlap.

Finally, Beth stood up. "It's no use. I'm going to have to cut him out."

At these words, Bill let out a low moan and said, "Be careful with those damn scissors."

Beth bristled just a little and said, "Well, if you don't want to get cut, you'd better be very still." She'd dealt with difficult patients, and she wasn't going to cut this guy any slack even if he was a United States marshal and Hershel's backup and probably their only way out of this mess.

When Bill was finally free, he stood up and looked at the three women that had so effectively captured him. "Tell me you're Nancy, Mary Alice and Beth. And then tell me how you got here."

The three ladies all started talking at once, trying to explain how they had got kidnapped and brought to the island by smugglers.

Bill held up his hands for silence. "I know most of that. We've been following you for days. I mean how did you get here?" He motioned to where they were standing.

He pointed at Beth. "Speak," he said. He was still a little embarrassed at having been brought down by three women.

Beth put her scissors back into her fanny pack as she looked at the marshal. He looked to be about her age and not at all hard on the eyes. She wondered how long he was going to stay mad at her.

"It'll be easier to show you," she said as she walked back to the face of the rock wall. Bill followed her, and Nancy and Mary Alice fell into step behind him.

When Beth reached up and touched the wall, Bill's mouth dropped open. He stepped through and looked up the tunnel that, obviously, went all the way up the mountain.

He turned back to the three women and said, "Where does this go?"

This time, he listened as the ladies spoke one by one and told their stories.

He just shook his head, for the first time taking in the cuts and bruises that covered the three women.

"You two stay here. You," he pointed to Beth, "Come with me. I want you to show me how to get the door at the top open. I want to see this warehouse where y'all have been held. And I want you to point out to me as best as you can where Hershel and the others are being held." He stood back and motioned for Beth to go ahead of him.

Beth turned around and started walking up the tunnel, and if she swayed her hips a little more than usual so what. After what she had been through, she figured she was allowed.

The movement wasn't lost on Bill. He just grinned. He never thought he would find someone like Beth at the end of this mission. He'd pursue this a little further if they all got off this island alive.

At the top of the tunnel, Beth stopped and put her ear to the wall to make sure no one had entered the warehouse while they'd been gone. When she was sure the coast was clear, she stood aside and pointed to the spot that would open the door.

Bill reached up and touched the spot Beth was pointing to. This time he wasn't surprised when a section of the wall slid back revealing a room on the other side.

He stepped through, and Beth showed him how to close it once they were inside.

"Unbelievable," Bill muttered to himself. He walked around the room, looking at the packages of drugs stacked against each wall. He stopped and cut a hole in one of them and tasted a small amount from his index finger.

He looked up at Beth. "The street market value for this quality and quantity would be in the millions. We can't let this hit the streets. It would destroy too many lives."

Beth saw the honesty and conviction in his eyes and liked him on an even deeper level. "I told Nancy and Mary Alice that if we couldn't find a way to get out of here, I was going to start emptying this garbage in the water package by package. I'm a nurse, and I have seen what this stuff does not only to the people that get addicted to it but to their families as well."

Bill looked at Beth with new respect. "If it wasn't for those scissors you carry around with you, we might end up being friends."

Beth blushed and looked away. She had spoken from the heart, not intending to try and impress him. However, she couldn't say she didn't like the way he was looking at her. Maybe when this was over, who knew.

Bill stood up. "Now tell me all you remember about the layout of the compound and the other entrance from the water."

Beth tried to remember all she had seen before being locked in the warehouse.

"When we found Nancy and Mary Alice, they were in here, but I know they had been locked in a cabin first. Joe picked the lock, and we got them out, but before we could make it to the boat and get away, we were caught and brought back here. I don't know where they took Hershel, Albert and Joe. We were taken one way and the guys another. There was someone else on the island, and the guy who seemed to be in charge didn't want him to see us. He had a knife to my throat, and if he hadn't been in such a hurry to get us out of sight, I think he would have killed me."

Beth had to stop and swallow hard to keep her composure. She hadn't let herself think of that terrifying moment when she thought she was going to die. Telling Bill about it now brought it all back.

"I know it's not much, but I hope it helps. Nancy or Mary Alice may be able to tell you more." Beth paused and looked worried that she might not have been much help.

Bill couldn't help himself. He reached out and drew Beth into a brief embrace. This brave woman had put herself in danger to try and save her friends and almost paid with her life.

"Come on," he said. "Let's go back, and I'll talk to Nancy and Mary Alice and see what they can add. Then I'm getting you off this island."

Bill and Beth retraced their steps back down to the beach, locking the doors behind them.

When Bill had got all the information he could from the women, he started to lead them back toward where he had left the boat tied up.

About three feet from the edge of the water, what appeared to be a river monster surfaced. He had seaweed hanging from his head and just appeared to pop up out of nowhere.

Nancy would have screamed if Bill hadn't put his hand over her mouth.

"Andrew, what are you doing? You nearly scared these ladies to death?" He didn't add that for a minute he had been stunned as well.

Andrew came the rest of the way out of the water. "Well, hell Bill, we were worried about you. You've been gone a long time. Cliff and I flipped a coin to see who would come and check on you and I lost."

He nodded at the ladies hiding behind Bill. "Is that who I think it is?" he said.

"Yes. I don't have time to explain it all now. Follow this short path back up to the beach and stay out of sight. I'm going to get these ladies to the boat then Cliff and I will be back." With that, he helped Beth, Nancy and Mary Alice into the raft.

When they reached the boat, Cliff was there to help them aboard. Bill introduced him to the ladies. Cliff remembered Nancy from her visit to the marshal's office but now wasn't the time to reminisce. He never dreamt that the scamming case he had been assigned would lead to this. He guessed no assignment with the marshals would ever be just routine.

Rebecca came up and took charge of the ladies. "I'm Hershel's wife. I came with these guys to find my husband. You can trust the three of them to bring our men back safe. It's what they do."

"Can any of you drive a boat?" Bill asked the ladies. "The GPS is set, and it will take you back to the landing where we all started out from."

"I can," Mary Alice stepped up. She didn't add that her ex had chased her to the waters' edge with the threat of yet another beating. Desperate to get away, she had stolen a boat. She had no idea how to operate it, but the keys were in the ignition and fear made her a quick learner. When she finally got up the nerve to leave her abusive husband and moved to Hadbury to open her gun range, she had taken lessons at the local boating club.

"Good. Go back and wait for us at the landing. If we're not back by daylight, take our car and go for help." He handed the keys to Rebecca, and then he and Cliff were over the side and out of sight.

The four ladies stood for a moment just looking at each other. Rebecca's husband was on that island. Nancy's husband was on that island. Mary Alice's soon-to-be beau was on that island. Beth's friends and now a certain marshal she hoped to get to know better were on that island.

They all nodded at the same time as if they could read each other's minds. Go back to the landing and wait? Who did Bill think he was kidding?

Chapter 25

As Bill and Cliff loaded their gear into the small raft and climbed overboard, Cliff said, "I sure hope you have a plan, Bill. Did you get enough information from the ladies to be of any help?"

"Some," Bill replied, as he manoeuvred the raft back toward the thick bushes and hidden path that led to the secret entrance to the smugglers' warehouse.

"I have a pretty good idea of the layout of the camp and the number of men we'll be dealing with. Beth thinks there's someone else on the island. Could be a supplier of some kind. His distributors wouldn't have any reason to be involved with this end of the operation, and different smuggling rings don't usually socialise with each other. Too much competition between them."

Bill paused long enough to move the bushes aside and reveal the start of the path leading to the shore.

"What I don't know is where Hershel, Joe and Albert are being held. According to Nancy, she and Mary Alice were held in one of what seemed to be a group of cabins, when they were first brought to the island. They tried to escape and were caught and roughed up pretty bad, then locked in the warehouse. When Hershel and the guys and Beth found the island, they were able to get the women out of the warehouse and almost to the dock when they were caught. Nancy said after that she and the other women were taken back to the warehouse and the men were taken off in a different direction."

Bill tied the raft to a bush, and he and Cliff started up the path. "Do you think they're still alive?" Cliff asked.

"I think more likely than not." Bill paused and looked at Cliff. "It seems Hershel kept saying the island was surrounded and his backup would appear at any minute."

"What backup?" Cliff looked puzzled.

"Us, I guess." Bill shrugged. "You know the ones that weren't even supposed to know where he was going. The ones he didn't trust enough to confide in. The ones that had to figure it all out without any help from him. The ones that have been following, always close enough to follow his trail but not close enough to catch up. The ones he's going to kill for bring his wife into this dangerous situation."

"Let's just hope he's really glad to see us," Cliff said as they reached the spot where Andrew was waiting.

Andrew stood up when he saw the other two marshals approaching. He had taken off his clothes and wrung them out as best as he could and spread them on a boulder to dry. Even though it was night, the heat from the day still lingered enough to help them dry.

"Now that is a sight I wish I could erase from my memory," Bill said as he and Cliff reached their friend.

Andrew was a tech guru and spent a lot of time in his lab back in Richmond. Therefore, most of his body was ghostly white with only his arms and the lower portion of his legs a somewhat darker colour.

"You just wish you had this physique," Andrew muttered as he reached for his still-damp clothes.

"Maybe, but not that colour," Cliff replied. Then he turned a bright red. He wasn't used to seeing one of his fellow marshals naked.

"All right, guys, come on. I'm going to show you something that is going to blow your socks off." Bill paused and looked back at Andrew who was still struggling to get dressed. "Well, maybe not you since you don't have yours on yet."

"Ha, Ha," Andrew shot back as he stood to stomp on his wet boats.

Ignoring the sarcasm, Bill walked up to the rock wall and touched the spot he knew would open the door and at the same time turned so he could watch the expression on Andrew and Cliff's faces.

He wasn't disappointed. For a minute, the other two were speechless. They looked at Bill then stepped through to the other side.

"Where does it go?" Cliff said as he followed the track a few feet up the tunnel.

Bill explained about the door at the other end of the tunnel and the warehouse on the other side.

"That's our way in. According to the ladies, the warehouse sits at the end of a trail that leads back to the smuggler's camp. There are a group of cabins between the head of the trail and the compound itself. It would be my guess, one of those cabins is where Hershel and the others are being held. Figuring out which one is our second problem. The first problem is getting out of the warehouse. Except for food and water once a day, the ladies were left alone, but the warehouse was kept locked up tight. When Beth brought me up here, I looked around, but other than the tunnel, all I saw was a small window and the door leading out toward the camp."

"Let's go up and check it out." Cliff started up with Andrew and Bill following. At the top of the tunnel, the others stood aside so Bill could find the spot on the wall that would give them access to the warehouse.

After they entered, Bill closed the door behind him. He had to wonder if all the smugglers knew about the passage or just the leader and a few of his more trusted men.

Andrew and Cliff walked around studying the stacks of drugs much the same way Bill had done when he had first seen them.

"This is not just a small-time operation," Andrew said to the others. "It would take a large distribution network to distribute this amount. If Jake is to be believed, Clint Montgomery is the leader. I didn't much believe Jake at the time. When we caught him on the phone, he had been so afraid to give up the name of the guy he'd been talking to, I thought he might be lying. I thought Clint Montgomery had been killed in a raid several years ago. But then again, his body was never identified."

"As I recall, we lost several agents in that raid," Bill added.

"I remember hearing about that. I was still in training," Cliff said. "To us, those guys were heroes. They had died in the line of fire while serving their country. We all wanted to be like them." He paused. "Except alive."

"Well, we all want to stay that way so let's see if we can find a way to get out of here and locate where the others are being held." Without waiting for a reply, Bill walked off to examine the window on the far wall.

He climbed up on the stack of drugs much the same way Nancy had and looked out the window. All he could see was the forest. He couldn't see any sign of a path, so the window must not be facing the path leading to the compound. That would be a plus if they could figure out how to get out the window. Even if they broke the glass, it was too small for any of them to crawl through.

He climbed back down and faced the other two men. "No way out through that window. It's too small. Let's check the door. Maybe we can Jimmie the lock from this side."

When they reached the door, Andrew knelt down to take a look. "Let me see what I can do. I'm pretty good with locks." He took a small kit out of his pocket and went to work.

Twenty minutes later, he sat back on his heels. "I can't make any headway. Whatever kind of lock this is, it's a good one. I get through one set of tumblers just to find another. We're not getting out this way without a key."

"Then we'd better come up with a plan. It's almost daybreak, and someone may be coming to check on the women," Bill said as he crossed the room and sat down on the burlap bed the women had slept on.

The other men joined him, and for a few minutes, no one spoke. Finally, Cliff said, "I have an idea. They're probably used to seeing the women asleep on these burlap sacks when they come in to check on them in the morning. There were three of them, and there are three of us. We can pull the burlap

213

over us and cover up our faces so they can't be seen, and when they get close enough, we can jump up."

"We're a lot bigger than the ladies. Don't you think they will wonder how they grew so big overnight?" Bill said.

As Cliff was trying to come up with an answer to that, they heard a noise at the door and all dove under the burlap.

Bill watched as the door slowly opened and a man came through carrying three bottles of water. Didn't look as if he had thought to bring any food. Bill clenched his teeth. They probably weren't planning to keep the ladies around long enough to worry about feeding them. He positioned himself to strike if the opportunity presented itself.

The smuggler set the water down just inside the door and started to leave again without coming any further into the room. He stopped and looked back. Something had caught his attention.

Bill held his breath as the man approached. He was armed but hadn't drawn his weapon. When the man leant down to pull the burlap back, Bill lunged and caught the man around the legs and brought him down.

Cliff grabbed him in a chokehold until he was unconscious. "They taught me that at the academy," he said.

The other two marshals just rolled their eyes. "We know we went there too," Andrew said.

They stood up and watched to make sure the guy wasn't going to get back up.

Bill reached down and relieved the smuggler of this gun. He also found a small knife in his boot. "Let's use this burlap to tie him up." He knew first-hand how well a man could be restrained with burlap.

When the man was tied up enough that he couldn't give them any trouble, they stood and waited for him to regain consciousness.

"If we can get him to talk, we can find out where Hershel and the others are being kept." Bill looked at the other two marshals. They nodded, and so they sat down to wait.

Twenty minutes passed, and when the man still hadn't come to, Bill said, "Are you sure you didn't kill him, Cliff?"

As Cliff was fixing to explain how he had been taught the right amount of pressure to apply to put a man down without killing him, the man groaned and tried to sit up.

The marshals stood and Bill yanked the smuggler to his feet. "We want to know where our friends are," he said.

The man looked around as if confused. Who were these men and where were the women? He seemed to be thinking.

Bill shook the man until he focused on Bill's face. "I said, where are our friends," he enunciated each word carefully, giving the man time to focus.

It only took the men a few minutes to get the information they needed. They left him in the cart on the track behind the secret door where he couldn't cause any more trouble. The look on his face when the door slid back answered Bill's question about how many of Clint's men knew about this exit. This one, obviously, didn't.

Bill, Andrew and Cliff made their way up the path toward the compound. They went slowly, watching for any sign of Clint or his men. It had been light for an hour. Everyone in camp should be awake by now.

Andrew reached out and touch the other two marshals on the shoulder. He nodded to a cabin just ahead of them. According to the man, they had left tied up in the cart, that was the cabin Hershel and the others were being held in.

Andrew whispered, "Stay here. I'm going to move around and see if I can get a look through the window on the other side. This side is too exposed. If anyone walked out of the camp and came this way, they could see me. The other side faces the tree line and has more cover."

Bill and Cliff eased back into the cover of the underbrush and watched as Andrew made his way to the other side of the cabin.

When Andrew reached the side of the cabin facing the woods, he silently crept forward and peered through the window. He silently let out the breath he hadn't realised he'd been holding. He had been afraid Hershel and the others wouldn't be there. It was a great relief to see Hershel, Joe and Albert sitting around a small table in the middle of the room talking. He wasn't sure what to do now. If he went around to the door, he would be exposed to anyone who happened to walk by.

He knocked softly at the window. He didn't want to attract any unwanted attention by making too much noise.

Hershel glanced around. He thought he had heard something. He scanned the inside of the cabin but decided it must have been an animal of some sort outside in the nearby woods.

Just as he turned back to the others to finish what he had been saying, he caught a movement out of the corner of his eye. He knew stress could do strange things to a person, and heaven knows he had had plenty of that lately but still.

Hershel rubbed his eyes and looked back toward the window. Now the apparition had stopped knocking and was waving at him.

Joe, noticing something seemed to be wrong with Hershel, stood up. "What is it, Hershel?"

Hershel just raised his hand and pointed toward the window.

Andrew afraid of being seen had dropped down to the ground and was listening for any movement coming from the smugglers' camp.

Joe looked in the direction Hershel was pointing. Not seeing anything out of the ordinary, he looked back at Hershel.

"What?" Joe said.

"The window," Hershel said. He slowly got out of his chair and walked toward the window.

Just as Hershel got to the window, Andrew deciding the coast was clear, jumped back up.

Hershel was so startled he stumbled backwards. Andrew, knowing he had got his boss's attention, grinned and waved again and then was gone.

By this time, Joe and Albert had joined Hershel at the window.

Joe took Hershel's arm. "I think you need to sit down, Hershel. You're a little pale, and for a black man that's alarming." Joe tried to lead Hershel back to the table, but Hershel wouldn't budge.

"I think our backup has arrived."

Joe, knowing there was no backup, turned to Albert for help. "Let's get him back to his chair."

Before the two men could get Hershel to move, a sound at the door of the cabin caught their attention. They watched as it slowly opened and three men came in and hurriedly shut it behind them.

"Lord, am I glad to see the three of you," Hershel said, hurrying across the room.

Joe, remembering the three marshals from the office in Richmond, followed Hershel to greet the new arrivals.

Albert, knowing only his two friends knew who these men were and seemed glad to see them, followed.

After Hershel introduced his three marshals to Albert, they gathered to the side of the room away from the window in case any of Clint's men happened by and glanced their way.

Before Bill could explain how they had got on the island, Joe grabbed his hand. "My wife and two other women are being held in a warehouse outside the compound. We have to get them out."

"They are fine. We've already got them off the island. They've taken our boat and gone back to wait for us at the dock."

Now wasn't the time for Bill to tell Hershel that Rebecca was also on that boat. He wanted to be away from this island and the gang of smugglers before that explosion. Just because Hershel was glad to see them didn't mean they were going to get by unscathed when he found out they had allowed Rebecca to come along.

Andrew, knowing his friend needed some help, said, "Listen, we can talk all this over later, but right now we need to get out of here. We can't go back the way we came and get off the island. Nancy told us there is a channel the smugglers use to get the drugs on the island from their supplier. Is there any kind of boat there we can use?"

"Yes," Hershel said. "But we will have to get around to the other side of the camp to get to it. Let's go before they send someone to check on us."

The three marshals passed out the extra guns they had brought with them and then they eased out the door single file.

Not saying a word, the men followed Hershel who stayed in the trees and as far away from the camp as possible.

When they were almost to the head of the path leading down to the dock, Bill reached over and touched Hershel on the arm. Hershel stopped and Bill nodded to their right about thirty feet away.

They watched as a guard stopped to light a cigarette. His back was to them and he was intent on what he was doing.

Bill motioned Cliff forward. Hershel didn't know why his senior agent would send his junior agent to dispatch this man, but he trusted him enough that he just waited to see what would happen.

Cliff silently made his way up close to the guard's back. He had him around the neck and on the ground before the man could make a sound. Cliff didn't bother to find something to tie him up with. They would be gone before the man regained consciousness. He made his way back to the others.

Hershel started to ask a question when Bill whispered, "He'll tell you later. Let's just get out of here."

Hershel nodded, not sure what Bill meant, but now wasn't the time to worry about it. They checked to make sure no one else was posted at the head of the path and slowly started down.

They made it less than halfway down when a bullet pinged a rock close to where Joe was walking. They all took cover and waited to see if another shot would give away the shooter's location.

They didn't have long to wait. Another shot rang out, and Andrew returned fire. He had the satisfaction of seeing the man fall forward and tumble down the incline.

"Let's go," Hershel said. "Those shots had to be heard back at the camp."

They hurried down the path but didn't get far before more shots were heard coming from the top of the path. They took cover again. The rest of the way down was too exposed to try to make a run for it.

Cliff jerked back suddenly and then hit the ground. Andrew got to him first and motioned for the others to stay down and keep him and Cliff covered. He dragged Cliff further off the path as more shots rang out.

Cliff had been hit in the shoulder and blood was running down the front of his shirt. Andrew tore off a piece of his shirt to try and stop the bleeding.

Cliff was pale and Andrew was afraid he was going into shock. "Don't you die on me," Andrew said. "I'm not through making a real marshal out of you yet."

At this, Cliff opened his eyes. He was obviously in pain but managed a small smile. "I already am a real marshal. Didn't you see me take down two men with a chokehold and that's besides taking down Jake back at the office."

Cliff coughed and Andrew saw fresh blood oozing from the side of Cliff's mouth.

Oh God, Andrew thought, *had the bullet hit something internal? Was Cliff going to bleed to death before they could get him out of here?*

Cliff raised his head and spit and then gave Andrew a weak grin, minus one of his front teeth.

Andrew felt a rush of relief. A tooth could be replaced. He checked the shoulder wound and found that it had almost stopped bleeding.

He could see the others where they had taken cover and were still returning fire at the group of men making their way slowly down the path. He didn't have a good feeling about the outcome. They were outnumbered and now they had one man down, and Andrew couldn't leave him. He was afraid if he took the pressure off Cliff's shoulder wound, it would start bleeding again.

He watched as Albert went down. He held his breath until he saw him getting up again holding his arm. He was shot, but it didn't look to be serious.

And then it was over. They were surrounded with no choice but to put their weapons down and their hands up.

Andrew helped Cliff to his feet to join the others. He watched as the rest of the smugglers came down the path to join them. One man pushed ahead of the others. He recognised him. Clint Montgomery. For the first time, Andrew was afraid they weren't going to make it out of this alive.

Clint stood facing Hershel. "Well, I see your backup arrived. A lot of good they did you." He then reared back and hit Hershel on his head with the end of his rifle.

Hershel staggered but didn't go down. Cliff hit him again, and this time Hershel went to his knees.

Clint turned to Jeff who was silently watching this exchange. "Lock them back in their cabin and stand guard. I'm going to my office for a minute and then we are going to have ourselves an old-fashioned firing squad. I have no more patience for this. They're all going to die."

He turned and started back up the path toward the compound, leaving his men to deal with the prisoners.

Nobody noticed the group of women huddled in the bushes by the water. They hadn't moved since the shooting had started. Their faces showed shock, horror and fear. But above all, determination.

Chapter 26

Rebecca gasped as she saw Hershel go to his knees. She had never seen anyone hit her husband before. She knew the danger he faced every time he went out on an assignment. She'd seen bruises at times when he'd come home, but never, never had she seen anyone hit her husband must less knock him to his knees.

She hadn't realised she had started forward until she felt Nancy and Beth holding her back.

Nancy's heart went out to her new friend. "Wait. Not yet. If we make a move now, we don't have a chance. They're bigger than us, and there are more of them and they have more guns. We, on the other hand, are smarter. We'll take them down even if we have to do it one by one."

Rebecca nodded. She knew her friend was right. Still, when they took down the one that had hit her husband, he was going to pay.

Mary Alice had watched as Albert had been hit but had jumped up again. She hoped the bullet had gone through and not lodged in his arm. She was glad Beth was with them. When they got to Albert, she would know what to do.

"Which one of the marshals got shot?" Beth asked. "I couldn't see." She didn't add that it was because she hadn't taken her eyes off Bill. She knew he hadn't got hit during the gunfire, but she had seen one of the others go down.

"It was Cliff. One of my husband's marshals. The youngest one. I couldn't tell how bad he was hurt, but I saw Andrew helping him up the hill," Rebecca told the others. "Thank God, no one was killed."

"All right," Beth said. Taking charge came naturally to her. "Before we go any farther, let's take a quick inventory of what we have at our disposal. We each have a gun. Bill made sure we were armed before he left us on the boat. Mary Alice is an excellent shot. So is Nancy if she keeps her eyes open. I have six hypodermics left. I also have scissors and a roll of white medical tape. Does anyone have anything else?"

"I have this." Rebecca held up a hammer she had brought with her off the boat. "I'm saving it for the guy that knocked my husband down. That doesn't mean I might not practice on somebody else until then."

The others laughed, knowing exactly how Rebecca felt. Also knowing she was serious.

Rebecca took a deep breath. "Hershel always told me if I have to go up against a gang, to confront the biggest one first. If I could intimidate that one, the others would leave me alone. As a social worker, I was usually accompanied by a police officer when I had to go into a home to remove an abused child. But this one time, I had to go alone. There were three large men in the home. The father of the child and his two brothers. The mother was there also, but she was too cowed by her husband to be of any help. Anyway, the child was in the back bedroom, and I had to get him out. I couldn't wait for the police to get there. The men were drunk, and I was afraid for the child's safety. I thought about what Hershel had told me about picking out the largest first. The trouble was they were all large and all about the same size. I had two things going for me. They were drunk and not thinking clearly and they thought because I'm so small, I was no danger to them. In other words, they underestimated me. Since they were all about the same size, I decided to divide and conquer. The father was in one of the front bedrooms. When I walked by, I closed the door and wedged a chair under the doorknob. One of his brothers was in the kitchen with the child's mother. He was eating breakfast and had a glass of tomato juice. While he was looking the other way, I emptied a whole bottle of hot sauce into his glass. He turned it up and drank the whole glass without taking a breath. When he set the glass down, he took a deep breath and couldn't get another. He was no more trouble. The last guy was standing on the back deck. I locked the back door. Then I grabbed the child and ran."

Rebecca stopped and looked at the other women. "I just thought since we're outsized and outnumbered, we might try the divide and conquer trick in this situation."

"Everybody for divide and conquer, raise their hand," Beth said to the group.

Four hands shot into the air in unison.

The four women worked their way up the hill from the dock. They had put some distance between each other, giving them a better chance of locating any guards that might be posted between the dock and the top of the path.

They had gone about halfway up when Nancy held her hand up for the others to stop. She pointed about thirty feet in front of them. Beth started to open her fanny pack and remove a hypodermic, but Rebecca motioned for her to wait. She held up her hammer. The others nodded, and Rebecca silently advanced on the man. His attention was focused on reloading his gun, and he never heard Rebecca's footsteps until it was too late. One hit with the hammer was all it took.

Beth hurried to her side and with the medical tape and scissors soon had him bound and pushed under a bush.

The women continued on up the hill without saying a word. At the top of the path, they came across another guard.

This time Mary Alice took the lead. She picked up a hand full of rocks and threw them to the left, drawing the man's attention in that direction. While he was scanning the bushes in that direction, Mary Alice used the butt of her gun to put him out of commission. He went down, and since he was at the top of the path, he took a header down the side of the mountain. The women watched; and when they didn't see any movement, decided it was safe to move on.

When they came to the edge of the camp, they hesitated. Nancy whispered to the others, "Should we split up or stay together?"

Beth looked around and not seeing anyone in the camp said, "I think we're doing pretty good as a group. Let's stay together."

As they advanced a little farther, Mary Alice motioned for the others to stop and group up.

They all formed a circle around Mary Alice so they could hear her whisper. "We haven't seen anyone in the camp. I wonder where everyone has gone? We need to check the cabins so we can eliminate them. The cabins are fairly close together, let's each take one. Look through the window, and if the cabin is empty, hold up your right hand. If someone is inside hold up your left hand, and the rest of us will come to you. We'll do this until we've cleared all the cabins."

The first four cabins were empty, but when they moved on to the last four, Rebecca and Nancy both held up their left hands.

Beth and Mary Alice hurried over to Rebecca and motioned for Nancy to join them.

"There's one man inside. It looks like he's fixing to come out," Rebecca said.

"Hold on; I've got this," Beth said. "Just be ready to pounce when I bring him down."

Beth took a strip of her medical tape and wrapped it around one post at the front door and then across in front of the door and attached it to the other post. It was just high enough to trip the man if he wasn't paying attention to his feet. She then positioned herself so he would see her when he opened the door.

It was only a couple of minutes until the cabin door opened, and the first thing the man saw was Beth. He never noticed the tape in his haste to get out the door and catch Beth before she could escape.

Beth stood her ground until she saw the tape catch his back foot as he hurried the rest of the way out the door. Then she ran forward to where the other women were holding him down. Rebecca had taken off her blouse to wrap around his mouth to keep him from calling out an alert to anyone who might be nearby.

Beth took more of her tape and bound his feet and hands. She then tore off a section of Rebecca's blouse and fashioned a gag for his mouth. She handed Rebecca back what was left of the blouse and Rebecca put it back on.

"What about the other one?" Nancy asked when they had rolled the man back into the cabin and shut the door.

"I have an idea." Mary Alice motioned for the others to follow her. "Beth, how fast are you with those needles you're carrying around?"

Beth smiled. "I've never had a patient get away from me yet."

"Good. I'm going around to the window at the back of the cabin and get his attention. When he comes out of the cabin and around the corner, stab him anywhere you can when he goes by. Rebecca, you and Nancy be ready in case she misses."

At her friend's last statement, Beth bristled a little. "I never miss."

Mary Alice just smiled at Beth and gave the others time to get in place then made her way to the window at the back of the cabin.

She waited for the man to notice her at the window. When she decided he was too occupied with what he was doing to look her way, she tapped on the window and waved and then ducked down out of sight.

As expected, the man bolted out the door and around the side of the cabin.

Beth was waiting as he rounded the corner. He never felt the stick nor did he make it to the back of the cabin.

When Mary Alice re-joined the others, they were already taping him up. Beth turned to Mary Alice and held up her needle and blew on the end like a gunslinger would after a showdown.

"Show off," Mary Alice poked her friend in the arm and then put her arms around her for a hug. "I never doubted you for a minute."

The four women leaned against the side of the cabin for a moment to catch their breath.

"I wonder where the rest of them are and where they've taken the guys." Nancy looked around as if expecting them to appear any minute. "Since we've eliminated the cabins, the warehouse is the only other place I know they could be. Let's check it out."

As silently as possible, the women made their way out of the compound and to the head of the path that led to the smugglers' warehouse and what had been a prison for Nancy, Mary Alice and Beth for a while.

The warehouse looked the same as the last time they'd seen it. But still, no one was around.

"Listen. I hear voices that sound like they're coming from farther down the path. What's down that way?" Rebecca asked.

The others just shrugged. None of them had been farther down the path than the warehouse.

Rebecca stared forward. "That has to be where they all are. Let's see how close we can get without being seen."

They followed the path as it wound on past the warehouse. They stayed in the trees. Rebecca and Beth on one side of the path, Nancy and Mary Alice on the other.

When they made it to the clearing, they weren't sure what was happening. The four marshals Hershel, Bill, Andrew and Cliff were standing in front of what looked like a two-hundred-feet drop off the side of the mountain. Cliff was leaning against Andrew for support. He looked like he'd lost a lot of blood. Their hands were bound behind them.

Joe and Albert were in the process of being similarly tied. They were then led to the others so that all the men were standing shoulder to shoulder in a line.

The smugglers were all armed with rifles and seemed to be waiting for something or someone.

Jeff stood off to the side, watching. This was getting out of hand. He thought Clint had gone a little crazy. Why would the man want to kill all his hostages? He knew Clint didn't tolerate being crossed, and these men had pushed his patience to the limit, but still, this was too much. He checked his gun and waited for whatever came next.

Nancy turned pale. She whispered to her friends, "This looks like a firing squad. They're going to shoot them all at the same time and let them fall off the side of the mountain. If the bullets don't kill them, the fall will. We can't divide and conquer any longer. We have to attack."

The women backed a little way into the forest to prepare. Mary Alice, Nancy and Beth took out their guns, checked to be sure they were loaded and waited for Rebecca to do the same.

Rebecca held her gun and just stared at the other women. "I don't know how to shoot a gun."

"Don't worry, there's nothing to it," Mary Alice told her. She took Rebecca's gun and checked to make sure it was loaded and handed it back to her. "All you have to do is to point at what you want to shoot, pull the hammer back like this and pull the trigger like that." Mary Alice simulated the motions a few times for Rebecca. "When we get out of this, I'll make an expert markswoman out of you, but for now just aim and fire."

"And don't close your eyes," Nancy added.

"Why would I close my eyes? Then I couldn't see what to shoot at."

Mary Alice just smiled. "I'll explain that one later."

The four women slipped into place. They stood three feet apart with their guns drawn and waited to see what would happen next. They hadn't seen Jeff or Clint who had just joined him. They were back about fifteen feet from the firing squad and off to the side.

At some signal the women didn't see, the smugglers came to attention with their guns all pointed in the same direction. All pointed at the men with their hands bound behind their backs waiting for their fate.

Knowing it was now or never, the four women stepped forward with their guns raised.

Knowing she could never shoot someone in the back, Rebecca said, "Drop your guns, you are surrounded. This is the United States marshals'…wives," she added just to clarify the matter.

It was hard to decide who was the most shocked, the smugglers or the marshals. It didn't matter. The smugglers dropped their guns.

What happened next took the women by surprise. Clint and Jeff both stepped forward. They were the only two smugglers still armed.

Clint aimed at Rebecca's head. There was nothing Hershel or the others could do. Their hands were still tied behind their backs.

Clint paused a moment as if he were enjoying himself. He pulled the hammer back and had his finger on the trigger when he felt cold steel pressed against his temple.

"Drop that gun," Jeff said. "I'm United States marshal Jeff Bloom...undercover." Jeff kept the smugglers covered while the women cut Hershel and the others loose with Beth's scissors.

When all the guns had been collected and the prisoners were tied up in one of the cabins, Jeff walked over to Hershel and handed him his phone. "You might want to call in some help getting these guys and all those drugs off this island. My contacts are dead. I had to play this to the very end. I had to be sure you guys were on the up and up. I've been undercover too long on this case to take a chance on you guys not being who you said you were. When you walked into the compound, I almost confided in you, but I knew you were from the Richmond office, and that was the same office Clint's informant was in. I just couldn't take the chance you might be dirty too."

"I wished you'd trusted me," Hershel said. "Things might not have gone this far."

By this time, Andrew, Cliff and Bill were flanking Hershel. They all cleared their throats at the same time.

Hershel got the message. "Let's get this cleaned up. We can discuss all this back at the office. But one thing I want to know right now. Who's responsible for bringing Rebecca into this danger!"

The other three marshals suddenly found pressing business elsewhere.

Chapter 27

Hershel looked around the room. He had called them all into a meeting at the Federal Court House in Richmond. They all sat together in the conference room. The same conference room Joe and Nancy Murphy had sat in the day they had come in to report a telephone scam that had relieved Nancy of $1500.00 of her savings.

Hershel just watched and listened for a few minutes. This group of individuals had been brought together in the most unusual of circumstances.

First, he studied his wife, Rebecca. He had always been sure of her love for him. But to put herself in danger to come to his rescue was still hard for him to wrap his head around. If he lived to be a hundred, he would never forget the sight of her facing off against a group of ruthless drug smugglers. She and her new three best friends, Nancy, Mary Alice and Beth sat at the end of the table.

These three amazing women had entered that camp alongside his wife. They should have been heading for safety. Instead, they had walked straight into the teeth of danger. None of them had been trained to deal with such a dangerous situation.

Nancy was retired. She should have been living the good life. Instead, she had got caught up in more danger than any retired lady should ever have to face.

Her friend Mary Alice had the misfortune of being at a conference with Nancy when they both had been kidnapped. The two friends had stuck together through the entire nightmare. They hadn't sat passively, accepting whatever came their way. They had tried to escape at every opportunity that presented itself.

Beth had insisted on coming along when he, Joe and Albert had been tracking the smugglers in an effort to get the other two ladies back. Beth was a nurse and had insisted when they found Nancy and Mary Alice, her friends would need her help. And they had.

He went on to study his three marshals. Bill, his senior marshal. Cliff, his junior marshal. And Andrew, his IT specialist. He could think of no three individuals he'd rather have as a backup. Even though he had not trusted them with his mission to warn the Murphys of potential danger, they had managed to figure it out. They had trailed him all the way into the mist of a smuggling ring that had almost got them killed. They had made it out alive but not before Cliff had taken a bullet in the shoulder and lost one of his front teeth as a resultant fall. The shoulder was healing and the tooth had been replaced, but Cliff had yet to stop talking about his adventure.

His mistrust had emerged when he had realised there was an informant in his office. He had not known whom to trust. While he had not suspected any three of these men, he was equally surprised to find out the informant was Jake Miller. Jake was now sitting in jail, awaiting trial. The charges were many. He had not only betrayed his oath of office but he had put his fellow marshals in danger. Hershel would try to get him help for his gambling problem, but the man would never be a marshal again and needed to pay for his crimes.

Across the table from the ladies were two men he had come to trust and respect, Joe Murphy and Albert Smith. They had refused to stand by and do nothing when Joe's wife, Nancy, and her friend Mary Alice had been kidnapped.

Even though Joe had been attacked and seriously injured, he had refused to be left behind in Hershel's quest to rescue the ladies and bring them home.

He glanced back to where Jeff Bloom stood with his back against the closed door. He had listened to the man's story and wanted to share it with the others but wanted it to come from Jeff himself.

Hershel took a seat. "Thank you all for being here. It's been ten days since the end of our little adventure. I've had a lot of loose ends to tie up. I know you have a lot of unanswered questions that you want answers to. You deserve those answers. Even my marshals," he nodded to Bill, Cliff and Andrew, "haven't been completely briefed. I wanted you all together. It's quite a story."

He turned to Jeff and motioned him to step forward. "Before I try to answer your questions, I want you to meet Jeff Bloom. Y'all know him as a smuggler and a pretty scary guy. Well, he is a pretty scary guy, but he's on our side. Jeff is a United States marshal out of the New Orleans office. He's been undercover for the past three years. That's a long time to stay under, but he'd been determined to bust this ring of smugglers and find out not only who their supplier was, but how the drugs were being distributed. We have plans to go after the supplier and we are trying to track down all the distributors. This operation was massive and stretched all the way across the country. I'm going to let Jeff tell you his story, and then we'll try to answer any questions you have left."

He motioned Jeff to take over.

"First, I want to apologise to all of you for getting you caught up in my undercover work. I never intended for any of you to get involved, and I certainly didn't want any of you to get hurt." At this, he paused and looked at Joe. He had, after all, choked Joe and left him in a dark alley.

"Let me start at the beginning. I'm out of the New Orleans office as Hershel has already told you. We had been investigating a smuggling operation that had been spreading across the country. We were getting nowhere. If we managed to shut down one group, another popped up before we could process the ones we had taken into custody. It was finally decided someone was going to have to go undercover. I volunteered. The other men had wives. I'm single. I was assigned a handler. This was the person I was supposed to report back to. Any information I was able to glean, I passed on to him. He would pass that information back to the office and the only other person who knew what I was doing and where I was. He was also my way out if things got too hot."

Jeff stopped and took a breath. This next part was hard for him.

"These other two marshals weren't just my backup; they were my friends. I wasn't hooked up with Clint Montgomery at the time. I didn't even know who he was. The gang I had infiltrated was a rival gang. They had a large operation, and I was trying to find out if they were the ones we were looking for. Things seemed to be promising. I passed the information along to my handler, and he passed it along to our contact back in the New Orleans office. The two of them decided they both needed to be there for the takedown. The plans were for them to wait close by for my signal."

Here Jeff paused again. He could still see his two friends where they had bled out in the dirt. He would see them that way for the rest of his life. He glanced at Hershel, who seemed to understand.

"That's when things went south. Before we could make a move, Clint and his men moved in, and I was the only survivor. My two friends were killed along with the band of smugglers. I was knocked unconscious and had fallen into a thicket of bushes. They thought I was dead. When I came to, there was nothing I could do for any of them. I buried my friends so I could come back and retrieve their bodies and return them to their families. All the others were dead. After that, I knew who my mark should have been. Clint Montgomery. I had no way to let anyone back at the bureau know any of this. Both my contacts were dead. Now I was more determined than ever to bring these thugs down."

He stopped and took a drink of water then continued with his story.

"My cover was still intact. I knew it would hold up to any scrutiny that was brought to bear. I infiltrated Clint's operation. I could tell he didn't trust me. I knew he had checked me out, and since he hadn't killed me, I knew my cover had held. I needed to find out who Clint's supplier and distributor was. I also knew I had to let someone know where I was. I couldn't take this gang down without some help. The problem was how to do this. I came up with a plan. It wasn't a very good plan, but it was all I could come up with. I decided to use my phone to perpetrate a scam. I pulled it on several unsuspecting folks. I hoped that someone would record our conversation and take it to the marshals to file a complaint. I had used several words and phrases that I hoped a really smart marshal would pick up on. If that happened, maybe he would take the time to trace where the phone call came from and realise a normal scammer wouldn't be calling from the middle of the ocean very close to where smugglers were known to operate. That plan had some flaws. First, I couldn't count on anyone reporting my scam. A lot of people are embarrassed by something like that and don't want their friends to know about it. They just suck up their loss and keep quiet. I also had no way of knowing what office it would be reported to. I didn't know which of the other offices were following what was going on in the smuggling arena."

He paused again and looked straight at the Murphys. "I'm sorry you guys were dragged into this. I never dreamt that Clint would catch on and come after you. From that point, all I could do was keep my cover intact and at the same time try to keep anyone from getting killed. I have to say y'all didn't make it easy. That's some friendship you all have going there. Each one trying to rush in to save the other."

He nodded at Hershel. "Hershel figured part of it out when you guys brought in that tape and your story about being scammed. He also figured out he had an informant among his men. Not being sure who he could trust, he took off to handle things on his own. He thought he could just warn the Murphys, and then he could figure out who the informant was and get to the bottom of the rest of it.

It didn't turn out that way. When he got to Hadbury, he found Nancy gone and Joe injured. He had to get Nancy back, so he had no option but to take on two civilians to help him. Not that he could have kept Joe and Albert out of it. Then he had taken Joe by the hospital to get him checked out and had run into Beth. I'll have to let him explain how Beth convinced him to let her come along."

Beth and Rebecca turned and smiled at each. They had already figured that part out.

Jeff then turned to the other three rangers in the room. "I have to commend these three guys. They not only figured out where I was, but they were also able to track Hershel and the others to the smugglers' compound. But like with Beth, I have no idea how Rebecca convinced them to take her with them."

Again, Rebecca and Beth smiled at each other. Strong women recognised the tactics of other strong women.

"I guess you know the rest. I just want to make sure you know," and here he turned to look at the other men, "I would never have let those men gun you down. I was ready to take them out when the ladies showed up. When Clint stepped up and had Rebecca in his sights, I knew I had to act fast. You already know everything that came after that."

Jeff hesitated until Hershel nodded for him to have a seat.

Hershel looked around at everyone else in the room. "If any of you have any questions that Jeff didn't answer, now's the time to ask."

Beth raised her hand. At Hershel's nod, she spoke up, "What happened to the bodies of your friends? Did someone recover them and return them to their families?"

Jeff nodded. "Yes. That was the first thing I took care of. I personally went with a recovery detail and accompanied them back home. They were buried as heroes.

I'll stay in touch with their families and help them adjust in any way I can. Like I said these men were my friends."

Beth sat back satisfied those families had been able to bury their loved ones.

Nancy sat on the edge of her seat and raised her hand. "I still don't understand why they came after me and Joe. What possible threat could we have been to them?"

She sat back and took Joe's hand. She was still a little shaky at how close she had come to losing Joe. Her heart wanted to go into overdrive every time she closed her eyes and saw him in front of that firing squad.

Jeff was touched by the obvious affection between Nancy and her husband. "Clint Montgomery is a ruthless man. He's not the type to leave loose ends that could come back and tangle him up. To him, you and Joe were loose ends. When Jake informed him of your visit to the marshal's office and that you had agreed to testify, he had to do something to prevent that possibility. He dispatched me and Pete to kill Joe and kidnap you. Thankfully, he'll have the rest of his life behind bars to regret that action."

Joe couldn't hold his question back any longer. He stood up so he could face Jeff on an eye level. "But you choked me and left me for dead in that dark alley. Wasn't that taking things a little too far?" Joe hadn't quite been able to put his anger at that behind him.

Jeff, realising Joe's frustration and residual anger, came around the table to where Joe was standing. "I truly am sorry. I had to make it look real. Pete had already taken Nancy. If I had failed that assignment, Clint would have killed me. Then who would have been there to look after Nancy? He would have eventually killed her too. I was trained to know how far to take a chokehold. I'm sorry I had to go that far." And with this, he held out his hand to Joe.

Joe didn't hesitate. He took Jeff's offered hand and shook it. "I didn't look at it that way. I guess I should be thanking you for looking after my life and my wife. One wouldn't be much good without the other."

After the handshake, Jeff went back to the head of the table to stand by Hershel. "Any more questions?" he asked.

Mary Alice raised her hand. She had been sitting beside Albert listening while the others had talked.

"Why take me? He only wanted Nancy and yet he forced me in the car as well. I know having two of us was more trouble for him. Why didn't he just leave me behind? How was I a threat?"

Albert reached over and took Mary Alice's hand. "I can answer that one. You would have screamed your head off as soon as he had driven away with Nancy and shooting you would have caused just as much commotion. He didn't have any choice but to take you." He squeezed her hand. Something good had come out of this ordeal for him and Mary Alice. They had reached an agreement concerning their future.

"He's right," Hershel said. "You became a loose end just by your proximity to Nancy. What I haven't been able to figure out is why he wanted to take you all the way to the compound. He had ample time to dispose of you along the way. Maybe he thought Clint would reward him for bringing two hostages back instead of one. We'll never know. He never made it back to the compound himself."

Mary Alice glanced at Nancy. She still could feel the fear when she thought Pete was going to shoot her on the boat headed back to the compound. She knew if it had not been for Jeff, she would never have made it to the compound with Nancy.

When no one else spoke, Hershel stood up. "Before you all go, I have an announcement to make. I usually only make this type of announcement in the privacy of my office with only my men present. This is something civilians wouldn't normally be privy to."

He walked up to Jeff. "Because of our deep involvement in your case and the deaths of the other agents you were working with, your New Orleans office has agreed to turn this case over to us. We will track down each and every one of Clint's distributors and shut them down. We will also find his supplier and bring him back to the States to stand trial. They have also agreed to transfer you here to work under my command if that's agreeable to you."

Jeff had not seen this coming. He had dreaded going back to his office in New Orleans knowing his friends would no longer be there. He looked at the other marshals in the room. They had already become his friends. Then he looked at the civilians and somehow knew this would not be the last time their paths would cross.

He held out his hand to Hershel. "Looks like you have a new marshal."

Ingram Content Group UK Ltd.
Milton Keynes UK
UKHW010722070423
419773UK00013B/1032